THE SNIPER

CHANG KUO-LI

TRANSLATED BY RODDY FLAGG

SPIDERLINE

First published in English in Canada in 2021
and the USA in 2021 by House of Anansi Press Inc.
www.houseofanansi.com

House of Anansi Press is committed to protecting our natural environment. This book is made of material from well-managed FSC®-certified forests, recycled materials, and other controlled sources.

House of Anansi Press is a Global Certified Accessible™ (GCA by Benetech) publisher. The ebook version of this book meets stringent accessibility standards and is available to students and readers with print disabilities.

25 24 23 22 21   1 2 3 4 5

Library and Archives Canada Cataloguing in Publication

Title: The sniper / Chang Kuo-Li ; translated by Roddy Flagg.
Other titles: Chao fan ju ji shou. English
Names: Zhang, Guoli, 1955– author. | Flagg, Roddy, translator.
Description: Translation of: Chao fan ju ji shou.
Identifiers: Canadiana (print) 20200370944 | Canadiana (ebook) 20200371401 | ISBN 9781487008574 (softcover) | ISBN 9781487008581 (EPUB) | ISBN 9781487008598 (Kindle)
Classification: LCC PL2929.5.N5 C5313 2021 | DDC 895.13⅗—dc23

Cover design: Alysia Shewchuk
Text design and typesetting: Jennifer Lum

House of Anansi Press respectfully acknowledges that the land on which we operate is the Traditional Territory of many Nations, including the Anishinabeg, the Wendat, and the Haudenosaunee. It is also the Treaty Lands of the Mississaugas of the Credit.

 Canada Council   Conseil des Arts
for the Arts   du Canada

 ONTARIO ARTS COUNCIL
CONSEIL DES ARTS DE L'ONTARIO
an Ontario government agency
un organisme du gouvernement de l'Ontario

We acknowledge for their financial support of our publishing program the Canada Council for the Arts, the Ontario Arts Council, and the Government of Canada.

Printed and bound in Canada

MIX
Paper from
responsible sources
FSC® C103567

With thanks to Hou Er-ge,
the mischievous old man by the sea,
for the inspiration and expertise

THE SNIPER

PART ONE

"There are three types of sniper. Combat snipers work within a platoon or company to create fear and confusion during a battle by taking out individual soldiers, officers, and vehicles. Tactical snipers are assigned to units at the brigade or division level, and take out enemy snipers, senior officers, and other valuable targets. And then . . ."

He paused a moment, the end of his cigar hissing as he dropped it into a coffee cup before it singed his fingers.

"Then you have snipers who rarely take a shot. Snipers embedded behind enemy lines who wait to be told to eliminate some particular target. These, I call strategic snipers . . ."

1

Rome, Italy

5:12 A.M. LA SPEZIA, ITALY. He boarded the train and napped, rocked to sleep by the swaying car, his hood pulled low over his face.

6:22 a.m. Pisa Centrale. He would not take the shuttle bus to the Piazza dei Miracoli. He would not gaze at the Leaning Tower and imagine Galileo dropping spheres to discover his law of falling bodies. He would not demonstrate his creativity by taking a photo of himself propping up the tower.

Before disembarking the train he visited the toilet, stuffing his bright yellow hooded sweatshirt into the garbage bin and replacing it with a red tracksuit top. He switched platforms and boarded the 6:29 a.m. to Florence. He found a seat and slept again.

The earliest trains are rarely late. At 7:29 a.m. he arrived at Florence Santa Maria Novella. The train had filled up on the way; most passengers headed southeast as they exited the station, in search of the grand dome Brunelleschi had designed for the Cathedral of Santa Maria del Fiore, where they would puff and pant up 461 narrow steps to gaze proudly down upon the wind-blown ancient city below.

The plan was to change platforms and take the 8:08 a.m. train to Rome. He changed the plan, entering the station toilet to change into a short black coat. He was about to conceal the tracksuit top in the space above the toilet, but then recalled the old man he'd seen slumped outside, curled up in a corner by the toilet entrance, face buried in his arms. He carefully draped the red jacket around the man's shoulders.

He left the station and walked to the bus terminus. There was an 8:02 a.m. to Perugia. It stopped at all the small towns, but there was plenty of time yet. One mistake, though: he should have kept the hooded top. The coat was too formal for a tourist. Nothing to be done now. He retrieved a backpack from his suitcase and left the suitcase tucked behind a newspaper kiosk.

The bus left on time. At a stop in Arezzo he purchased a coffee and a chocolate croissant. The Italians did love their sweet foods. They were like ants.

10:54 a.m. Perugia. He hurried to the station for the 11:05 a.m. to Rome — no time to reminisce about the local braised rabbit. No change of clothes at this stop, just the addition of a Yankees cap. Three more hours to catch up on sleep.

The train was quiet: four backpackers with Scottish accents; three businesspeople eager to get to their laptops; a single female traveller from Taiwan, maybe Hong Kong. He chose a seat at the back of the carriage and went to sleep. It wasn't just that he hadn't slept the previous night; it was that he didn't know when he would have another chance.

The train pulled into Roma Termini at 2:01 p.m., five minutes late. He descended from the carriage into a fractious crowd. Leaving the station, he turned south, away from the mob bound for Piazza della Repubblica, towards a row of luggage lockers adjacent to a coffee stall. He used a key to open one of the lockers. Good: as expected, two plastic bags taped shut. He took the bags and walked to an alleyway opposite, where he turned into an Algerian-run store. He emerged clad in a dark brown safari jacket with leather patches on the elbows and pulling a wheeled suitcase.

The alleys surrounding the station were populated by refugees and immigrants. He checked an address and soon came to a tall building covered with a yellow-grey layer of dirt. He pressed the button for the fifth floor. The glass door buzzed open.

The building was home to three hotels: Hotel Hong Kong, Hotel Shanghai, and, on the fifth floor, Hotel Tokyo. The beer-bellied middle-aged man at the Hotel Tokyo asked no questions, handing over a key in exchange for 30 euros.

The room was plain. A bed, a chair, and a television too small to watch without your nose pressed to the screen. The phone, so old it might have been vintage, rang at 2:40 exactly. He answered.

A woman's voice, which unsettled him. Was it her? "Hotel Relais Fontana di Trevi," she said.

"Where's Ironhead?"

His interlocutor lowered her voice, betraying no emotion. "The room's booked. Second passport."

The line went dead before he could ask again.

He opened his new suitcase, which contained a long Adidas holdall and more clothes. He removed the safari jacket and his jeans, tossed them in the suitcase, and pushed it under the bed. Then he dressed in black trousers and coat, adding a black woollen hat and earphones. He left with the holdall slung over one shoulder.

There was nobody at the front desk, the beer-bellied man now in the back office watching football. He pushed through the hotel door and picked his way down the cluttered stairway.

Back on the street, he slipped a multitool from his sleeve and freed the chain securing one of several bikes to the railings. He pushed the bike forward a few steps before swinging onto the seat.

Heading west through back alleys, he reached the Barberini metro station, where he abandoned the bike and trotted to catch up with a group of flag-following Japanese tourists. At the Fontana di Trevi he veered away from the silver-haired travellers and weaved through the bustling crowd to a hotel on the south side of the square.

He handed over a passport to the beaming clerk, who checked his details and returned it with a key card. "Just one night?"

He smiled and nodded.

"From Korea? My girlfriend can speak a little Korean."

He smiled and nodded again. The man at Hotel Tokyo had seen a nondescript Asian man. The clerk here saw a shy Korean man with poor English.

He walked calmly to the elevator and made it safely to Room 313. A hundred and fifty euros for a basic room with a window that failed to block the noise of the crowds outside.

He tore open the first of the plastic bags from the luggage locker and a large manila envelope fell out. It contained two photographs: one of a middle-aged Asian man in semi-profile; the other, what looked to be an outdoor table at a café, marked with an X. In the second bag was a very non-smart mobile phone, a silver candy-bar Nokia 7610. He put it in his pocket.

From the holdall he retrieved a telescopic sight from its protective layer of underwear. He surveyed the Fontana di Trevi and its square from the window. Despite the seasonal cold there were still too many people, blurry figures passing back and forth across his field of vision. Did they have to choose the world's most popular tourist spot for the job? Three thousand euros' worth of coins tossed into the fountain in the centre of the square every day, tens of thousands of photos posted online of the sea god Oceanus with grinning tourists.

He changed into a turtleneck sweater, put his sunglasses back on, and hung a camera around his neck. Just like Ironhead said, if you can't change the environment, be a part of it.

Immersing himself in the tourist flow, he browsed a few souvenir stores before taking a seat in a café. He ordered a macchiato, to which he added two small spoonfuls of sugar as the Italians did, and bit into, of course, a Sicilian cannoli.

He flipped through the Donato Carrisi novel he was carrying and glanced at the photo lodged within its pages. The round table just outside the window was the one marked with the X. He would have a view of that table from the hotel room, a distance of about 125 metres. The buildings surrounding the plaza would block most of the wind and there would be nothing in the way. Except people.

But there's an answer to every problem. On average it takes four seconds to react to a scare, say three seconds to be safe. That meant he would have three seconds after taking care of any pedestrians in his line of sight. Three seconds from the moment that pedestrian hit the ground in which to take his second shot.

It would mean one more bullet, but that was no cause for concern. He snapped a quick shot of the fountain, keen to make sure the café staff remembered nothing more distinctive than a monochromatic blend of all the Asian faces they saw every day.

The trouble with cannoli was the crumbs, crumbs that left oily marks on the pages of his novel. He'd just read about the death of the orphan Billy, the child who had once calmly cut down the corpses of his parents from their nooses, the happiest of the orphanage's sixteen charges. A boy with a smile always on his lips. According to the death certificate, Billy had died of meningitis. Yet when the police exhumed the corpse two decades later, they found that every bone in Billy's body had been broken. He had been beaten to death.

Was Billy still smiling as he died? He reluctantly put the novel away. There might be time to finish it on the return journey. He had to know who had killed Billy. The question bothered him; it stuck, phlegm-like, in his throat.

And no more cannoli until it was finished.

2

Taipei, Taiwan

WU PUT DOWN his chopsticks and paid his bill. Reluctant to return to the bureau just yet, he hailed a taxi and took the expressway across Shenkeng to the station in Shiding, where Chen Li-chang had said he would wait.

Chen must have been seventy and was short several teeth. His ten-minute explanation left Wu spattered with spittle. As far as Wu could make out, village resident Wang Lu-sheng was missing. Every time Chen went to visit, Wang's two sons said he was in hospital. Which hospital? Family matter, they said, no need for you to know. So old Mr. Chen had checked the lists at Veterans General, then asked at Tri-Service General. No sign of a Wang Lu-sheng. Worried, he had filed a missing person report.

Perhaps Mr. Wang had lost his memory and couldn't find his way home. Or been hit by a car and left lying in some nameless alley. Well, neither of his sons was going to report him missing. It was up to Mr. Chen.

Let's take a look, then. Wu requested a car from the station. It came staffed by two greenhorn training-school grads, each bearing the single-bar, three-star insignia that betrayed them as brand new. Then, off to Wutuku. They turned off the provincial road onto a county road, then onto a village road, and finally onto an access road that petered out after a few kilometres.

On a hillside in the rain stood a sheet-metal shack of dubious legality, appended to an older structure that lay in a heap of its own fallen bricks and tiles like some underfunded historical ruin. Saplings sprouting from cracked corners grew slowly towards the roof they would eventually pierce. No chance of keeping wind and water out, except perhaps with a tent pitched inside. It looked as if the owners had decided the cost of repairs was too high and instead opted to erect a metal shack against one wall, in the process acquiring a bit of the surrounding state forest land.

The car pulled up at the end of the muddy track and three black dogs rushed up, barking. His two escorts seemed unsure of themselves, so Wu got out and threw the remainder of a takeaway meal someone had left on the back seat towards a dog bowl by the wall. After they finished the food, they lay down quietly.

"Are his sons here?"

"They were here two days ago," Mr. Chen replied, anxious.

"What are their names?"

"They call the older one Waster, the younger one Rake."

Wu nodded and walked up to the metal door, sniffing. A strong smell of glue. He unclipped the safety strap on his holster, brushed the drizzle off his grey flat-top, rolled up the sleeves of his jacket, and kicked in the door.

"Waster! Rake! Get out here, you fuckers!"

A clatter from inside, but no reply. Wu stepped inside and soon came out again, dragging a gaunt man of about fifty with each hand. He slammed them down onto the hood of the car.

"Cuff 'em. There are drugs inside. Have a look around for Dad."

The site backed onto a cliff and was otherwise surrounded by forest. The nearest neighbour was at the bottom of the hill.

There was no sign of the old man. Traces of heroin on the plastic bags and needles in the shack, though. Class A — up to three years, but previous convictions and two rehab failures would mean more. There was also a large container of glue on a table, two-thirds empty, and piles of yellowing plastic bags. No money for heroin, so they'd turned to glue. A junkie's fate.

But never mind the drugs. Where was the father?

Big brother Waster looked confused, the crust around his eyes well matured. He squatted by the car, drooling. The younger, Rake, could at least stand, one foot bare and muddy, the other — equally muddy — in a cheap plastic sandal.

"You're not going to dodge this one by going into rehab, Rake. This is jail time, and you'll be sixty before you're out. So tell me, where's your dad?"

Rake looked down at the mud on his feet.

"Your father," Wu continued, checking the notes on his phone. "Wang Lu-sheng, eighty-seven, retired army sergeant. Ring any bells?"

Still no response.

"One more time." Wu glowered, voice now booming. "Where did you two bastards bury your father?"

He took Rake by the neck. "How long has he been dead? How many years have you been stealing his pension?"

Going by Mr. Chen's report, it was what Wu thought most likely. And it wouldn't be that unusual. The two men had been doing drugs and stealing since their late teens — no big crimes, but all the small ones. Neither had ever had a proper job and the whole family relied on Wang Lu-sheng's state and army pensions. But it had been years since anyone had seen him. Wu's guess was that he was dead and his sons had quietly buried him to keep the money coming.

Backup arrived, from the Criminal Investigation Bureau and the Xindian sub-bureau.

Wu continued to let fly at the two junkies, then pushed the sobbing, sniffling Rake into the forest. "He looked after you two failures your whole lives. Then when he's dead, it's a shallow grave in the forest? Aren't you ashamed? Animals do more for their dead. Where is he?"

Rake collapsed into the mud. It was his brother, supported on each side, who led them deeper into the trees and pointed out a pile of five stones in a clearing. "We . . . we . . . we always come and tidy the grave on Tomb-Sweeping Day." The wail of a mourning son.

"Oh, fuck you." The snarl of an angry cop. Wu couldn't help but take a swing that sent the man sprawling to join his younger brother in the mud.

Everyone donned masks. After the first few shovelfuls of earth were shifted, the remains of a body became visible. It was a rainy place and the body had been laid directly in the mud— no coffin or even a mat. Wang's reward for continuing to look after unfilial sons.

He'd died of an illness four or five years before, not that his two sons could remember exactly when. They weren't even sure what had killed him. One day Rake had come home to find his father on the bed, not breathing. How long had he been lying there on that scavenged mattress? Again they didn't know. Waster said he'd been working construction in Yilan and Rake had been on the fishing boats. They hadn't been back for months.

Their father had died alone in a remote hillside shack. Rake didn't call the police or an ambulance. He slept in the room with the corpse for two weeks, waiting for Waster to come home. They decided to conceal the body and, using their father's seal and passbook, continue to draw his pension.

If Mr. Chen hadn't taken an interest, on paper Wang Lu-sheng could have lived to be a hundred years old. Immortal, in fact, Wu thought.

He watched the prosecutor flee the forest with nostrils clamped shut and drive off after he had signed arrest warrants for the two men. The CIB team refused to transport them for fear of stinking up their car. Then someone from Xindian was clever enough to find a hose, so they both got a dousing. Spraying two criminals with icy water in that weather . . . was it torture? a breach of human rights? Maybe. Not Wu's business, though.

He wandered around the shack a few more times. A gas cylinder outside was rusting away. There was no power. The fridge, used as a cupboard, lay empty. Wu saw no sign of anything to eat, apart from empty instant noodle containers crawling with cockroaches. How had they not starved? He found a pile of electricity bills. They'd stopped paying fifteen months before and had been cut off half a year back.

There was an old barrel they'd used to cook in, a pot hung over the ashes. The remains of whatever they had last made sat at the bottom of the pot under a layer of green mould. The pair of them were ruined, shrunken by their glue habit. Not much chance of them taking care with their diet.

Wu explored the forest, taking a narrow path so overgrown he had to crouch till his face was in the grass. A foul smell alerted him to another, smaller shack, formed of three iron sheets and a rickety wooden door. A toilet, by the look of it. There was no need to open the door. Below it a pair of feet — female, still in sandals — protruded.

There was no mobile signal, so he went back towards the cars and yelled to one of the Xindian lads. "Back here! There's a woman's body!"

They checked records on one of the in-car computers. Rake had been divorced twice, both times from the same woman, a cleaner at a hot springs resort. It looked as if they'd gotten back together one last time.

The CIB car was summoned back to the scene before it had even got off the hill.

She'd been beaten to death, the bruises still visible amid the rot. An aluminum baseball bat turned up in the nearby grass, bashed and bloody. Hand and fingerprints were clear in the blood. Wu could almost smell Rake's stench on it.

A few phone calls revealed that Rake and his sometime wife had a son who was currently serving ten years in a Guangdong prison for telecom fraud. At least his room and board were coming at the expense of mainland taxpayers.

Wang Lu-sheng had joined the Nationalist Army in Shandong even before he was fully grown. He'd served all over, first fighting the Japanese, then fighting the Communists. He'd been on Kinmen during the artillery barrages and had won medals for his bravery. He had finally made it back to Taiwan proper to settle down, only to have three generations of his family come to ignominious ends.

Wu grabbed the hose and turned it on Rake for a second time. Naked, the man hopped from foot to foot in the mud, cupping his hands over his genitals. "Your dad would have been better off raising dogs!" Wu yelled at him.

Wu's boss, Egghead, saved Rake from pneumonia by choosing that moment to call. Egghead seemed in good temper, though his words were cryptic. "Wu, how would you like to go to Keelung for one of those delicious sandwiches they have at the night market?"

"How would you like me to tell you how long it is till I retire?"

"Twelve days — it's written on my board. I take a day off for you every morning."

"And rather than let me have some peace, you're sending me to Keelung?"

"It's always busy at the end of the year. And then there's the new chief — you know what he's like. Anyway, it's a straightforward suicide. Take a poke about, give the body and weapon a look, write up a report, and leave the rest to the medical examiner."

"Ah, so you do have a conscience. You've carefully selected the dullest job you can find to make sure these last few days really drag."

Egghead's strangled-chicken laugh. "And bring me a couple of those sandwiches — with ketchup, not mayo. Doesn't look like I'm getting home for dinner, again."

Wu waved down one of the Xindian cars as it was trying to drive off. "We're going to Keelung."

The uniform at the wheel dared a question. "Keelung, sir?"

"Yes," said Wu as he climbed into the back seat. "And be happy about it. You're getting lunch at the expense of the organized crime squad."

To no applause, the car drove off into the rain. The temperature was down to eight degrees, the coldest yet that winter, and the rain never-ending.

3

Keelung, Taiwan

NEVER-ENDING RAIN, and now even heavier. Keelung was a port town, but Wu was starting to think there was as much water in the air as in the harbour.

The car pulled into the driveway of the Laurel Hotel, on the southern side of the port, just as Wu was draining the last of a large 7-Eleven coffee he'd picked up to revive himself. On the way up, the glass-walled elevator looked out over the port and two Cheng Kung–class frigates rocking at anchor at the naval base.

As he left the elevator Wu saw uniformed officers clustered at the door to Room 917. A sweet stench clawed at the back of his throat as he approached, and he stopped to borrow a face mask.

So, Kuo Wei-chung, Petty Officer First Class on a Kee Lung–class destroyer, had shot himself that morning. The hotel had called the local police, who rushed to the scene and then alerted the CIB.

The deceased was dressed neatly in a blue-grey uniform and was sitting with a view of the ocean. He had shot himself in the right temple. The bullet had exited the left side of his skull, accompanied by blood and various brain chunks and bone fragments that had proceeded to splatter the previously pure white and still creaseless bedsheets. The gun was a T75 semi-automatic pistol, a version of the Beretta M92F made by the 205th Armory — 9 mm, effective range of fifty metres, fifteen-round magazine, known primarily for being out of date and inaccurate. But it was hard to be inaccurate when shooting at your right temple with your right hand.

The local police had sealed off the entire floor and, thirty minutes earlier, informed the Navy, which had sent seven uniformed sailors to stand to attention at the door of the room. But it was still Wu's crime scene; the Navy could wait.

Wu glanced over the available info: Kuo Wei-chung, thirty-eight, time-served Petty Officer First Class, married, two sons, lived in Taipei. Kuo's wife was on her way to identify the corpse, courtesy of a navy car.

At a full-throated cry of "Attention!" Wu turned to see three naval officers enter the room. The man in front, a captain, wrinkled his nose in disgust as he surveyed the scene.

"Who's in charge here?" the captain asked.

Wu was not pleased. Who had let them into his crime scene? "The name's Wu, Criminal Investigation."

"Let's find somewhere we can talk," the captain said.

They made their way to a window by the bank of elevators. Wu was almost six feet, tall for the police, but this captain was a head above him. Well-muscled too, perhaps a bodybuilder in the past.

"We're shocked that this has happened. There's an ambulance on the way from Tri-Service General to take the body back to Taipei."

Tri-Service General? Wu pulled off his mask. "We haven't finished examining the scene yet, and we're still waiting for the medical examiner."

"Wasn't it a suicide?"

Like hell it was, Wu thought. What he said was: "Maybe not."

"If it wasn't a suicide, then what was it?"

Murder, Wu thought. But what he said was: "We just need to clear up a few things."

The captain scowled. "What things?"

Tamping down his temper, Wu forced himself to explain. "The handle of the mug on the table in front of the deceased is pointing left. There are two boxes of takeaway food and two sets of chopsticks. A six-pack of beer, one opened and half-drunk . . ."

"So?"

"He must have arranged to meet someone, and . . ."

"Keep going," the captain told him, glaring.

"The position of the mug, with the handle to the left. He was left-handed."

"Fine, so he was left-handed. What else?"

There were limits to Wu's patience. "So he's there by himself, drinks some beer, eats a mouthful or two of takeaway. His friend doesn't turn up, or turns up but doesn't eat, and in a moment of madness Kuo decides to try shooting himself with his right hand, just to see if he's as good a shot as with his left."

"Your name, Detective?"

"For the second time, Wu. That's spelt W-U . . ."

"Show a bit more respect."

Ignoring the attempted provocation, Wu continued.

"The chopsticks. The deceased's were on the left side, on a plate, and had been used. The other pair were still wrapped and placed on the other side of the table. He was waiting for a friend."

"A friend?" The captain frowned.

"The takeaway packaging in the garbage was from a branch of Nanjing Roast Duck on Xinyi Road in Taipei. So he picked up food in Taipei, took the train or bus to Keelung, bought the beer on his way to the hotel, then set the table. Food, beer, chopsticks, hotel mugs . . . he's waiting for someone. But he's from Taipei, so why is he doing this all the way over here in Keelung and paying for a hotel room? If it was a lover and he was worried about his wife finding out, why's he still in uniform? A towel would have sufficed."

"So, Detective, you think it's murder?"

"Suspected murder, to be precise."

The elevator doors opened and Yang, the medical examiner, stepped out in his white coat, trailed by two assistants. He nodded to Wu and headed to Room 917.

"Are you doing an autopsy? He's Navy. Dead or alive, we should be in charge."

"You'll need to talk to my superiors. I'm a mere detective, with rules to follow. Whether or not there's an autopsy depends on the examiner."

Without even a farewell nod, the captain waved over the other two officers and entered the elevator. Wu joined them, getting a raised eyebrow in return. "Just popping down for a smoke." The captain's eyebrow stayed up. Not a smoker, perhaps.

Wu stood outside the hotel, lighting a cigarette as he watched the military-green Toyota jeep drive off.

His mobile rang. Egghead again, no longer laughing. "Ministry of Defence has been on the phone, saying the deceased is a petty officer who killed himself, and you're insisting it's murder —"

"Suspected murder."

"Okay, suspected murder. The boss wants a report before you knock off."

"Shouldn't I wait for Yang's people to finish?"

"Come back now."

"Then I won't have time to buy you that delicious sandwich."

"Pick up whatever you can. A not-very-delicious sandwich, an entirely unremarkable sandwich. Okay?"

Normally a case like that would involve reports submitted by both the investigating officers and forensics before the boss decided whether or not a meeting to discuss further action was needed. And everyone knew the boss was a busy man, his days occupied with hand-pressing and backslapping. But today was different. Did the Navy get better treatment than the public? How many stars had been on the epaulettes of whichever general had made that call, and what bureaucratic strings had been pulled?

Wu didn't like how it felt.

Like when his son slammed down his chopsticks and left his dinner half finished.

Like when his son, late for school, left shoes scattered at the door.

Like when his wife came back from an early hill walk and complained about him festering in the bed, when he was just trying to recover from an all-nighter.

Like when the Chief answered his mobile in a meeting.

Like squeezing off a packed airport bus only to find his passport missing.

Like now, his driver just realizing the car was out of gas.

Like an empty-tanked police car joining a long gas station queue.

Like filling up between two garbage trucks, a hot stench flowing from open hatches.

Like the gas station poster announcing a fifty-cent price increase.

Like getting only the "mother" out before the Chief walks in and forces him to swallow the hard, undigestible "fucker."

It felt like being twelve days from retirement and landing a murder that would never be solved that quickly.

4

Rome, Italy

UP AT SIX-THIRTY A.M., martial arts exercises, a hundred push-ups. Downstairs to the café for a ham salad panini and a latte, eyes patrolling the fountain and its surroundings. A chilly, damp day. The forecast said a long, hot summer was coming, hence the cold winter. Snow would be good. Snow would send the tourists scurrying inside and make for a cleaner shot.

But it never snows in Rome. Was that a song? No. It never rains in southern California, that was it.

He scanned the square again, checking his egress route. Fewer tourists would mean less cover, but also less risk. Thousands upon thousands of photos being snapped with cameras and phones. All that was needed was one whiz to do the programming and it'd be a matter of just tapping in the right search terms: *male, alone, holdall, concealing face, rushing, hiding in crowd, Asian.* And a few seconds later there he'd be, in front, profile, and rear views.

Camouflage. Ironhead, the Foreign Legion, they'd all hammered it home. A sniper's first job isn't shooting, it's

23

disappearing. No room for anything noticeable. He looked at his unshaven reflection in the window. His most distinctive features? Asian, male.

After breakfast he goes back upstairs to transform himself. Western, still male. He's downloaded an image of an American man from the Internet to model himself on. Let's call him Tom.

Tom has a gut: a forty-eight-inch waist. He is clad in shorts and sandals, despite the near-zero temperatures, his naked calves and goosebumps a sure sign of a holidaymaker. A Sony SLR hangs around his neck, a bulging backpack from his shoulders, with a sleeping bag strapped below. It might come in useful, even if he is staying in hotels. And below the sleeping bag, a pair of hiking boots. A Yankees, Redskins, or Dodgers baseball cap — the Yankees one comes in handy — with curly ginger hair poking out from underneath. And a finishing touch: a temporary tattoo of a Chinese character, *zen*, on his calf. An eye-catching but easily discarded feature makes for good camouflage.

In a café on the square, Tom drinks a macchiato, the milk making the drink easier on his just-awakened stomach, and eats two rolls with honey. Wiping his mouth contentedly, he lets his belt out a notch, puts on his bulky jacket, and walks back to the fountain.

Screams. Tom is as stunned as everyone else, looking for the source of the noise. Hearing shouts of "Gun!" he ducks and yells along with the middle-aged Swiss, the young Japanese, and the camera-wielding Korean tourists. And on the shout of "He's dead!" Tom flees backwards, alongside the Swiss, shoving the Japanese to the ground, knocking the Koreans' cameras from their straps. Tom runs for his life, losing one sandal. But never mind; he wears socks, as all American men do with sandals.

Several minutes later Tom pushes his way into the metro station at the Spanish Steps, where he waits two minutes for a train. At Termini he disembarks, and in the station toilet he removes his shorts, sandals, wig, baseball cap, and bulky jacket, plus the cushion shoved inside his shirt. He dons a Boss coat and trousers from his backpack, puts on a pair of walking shoes, covers the backpack with a bright green rain cover, pulls on a woollen cap, and then strolls out, backpack slung over one shoulder, visiting the platform coffee stall before boarding a train to Florence.

When the Italian police check the cameras around the scene and identify Tom as a suspect, the shooter will be in an alley off Florence's main square, enjoying a hot *lampredotto* — tripe, the stomach of a cow — sandwich.

But he'd just finished a croissant, and the sandwich would have to wait. He returned to the hotel to check on the gun.

It was a type generally referred to as the Springfield M21. There were also improved MK15 and M25 versions. He thought of it as the M14. When he first joined up, they'd used the Taiwanese-made T65 assault rifle, modelled on the U.S. M16. Then, during sniper training, he was given an elderly M14.

The U.S. Army had made the switch from the M1 to the M14 in 1969 and created the M21 sniper rifle by adding a 9x scope to the new M14. But it was still a semi-automatic, with

3.5 stars for range and accuracy. In 1988 it was replaced by the bolt-action M24, which earned an extra star in each category.

Gramps had used the M14 back in his day and spoke of it fondly and at length. Easier to clean than the old M1, lighter, more accurate. But old age comes to us all: compared with a Vietnam-era M16, the M14 was a clumsy weapon, nowhere near a match for the more portable SRS or the futuristic Barrett M107 heavy sniper rifle.

—

On his first day of training, Ironhead had stood in silence at the lectern as he assembled an M14 from its component parts, lightly stroking the wooden stock between action and butt before speaking.

"From today, your beloved is no longer your girl, or your wife, or the cock in your trousers. It's this weapon. It is ugly. Uglier than your girl, even. It has a ten-round magazine and weighs four and a half kilograms empty. Sounds too light? Worried that a breeze might push you off target? Let's bulk it up."

Ironhead pushed a rectangular magazine into the stock and fixed an ART tactical scope to the mount. "Now it weighs 5.6 kilograms. Starting to see how lethal it is?"

Nobody was going to risk denying it.

"I'm afraid we had to borrow these from the marines, but it's the best we could do. Now, you won't find any indoctrination nonsense on our timetables. You'll get up at six a.m. — half an hour later than bootcamp, at least. You'll sort yourselves out, you'll have a lovely long piss, and at six-fifteen you'll form up, carrying this beauty. And then you'll take it on a five-kilometre run. If you can't finish the run in the morning, you'll run it at noon. If you can't finish the run at noon, you'll run it in the evening. I don't care if I keep you fuckers up the whole night, you will finish that run."

The squad shifted in their seats. A five-kilometre run wasn't much, but carrying that old gun? Your arms would fall off.

"Oh, you will. You'll run with it every day, in wind or rain, holding it as gently as you hold your girl. Then you'll clean it, until the inside of the barrel is spotless and the stock is as smooth and soft as her ass. Understand?"

Everyone: "Yes, sir!"

"Like hell you do. Do the run, then tell me you understand."

Ironhead continued, stroking the M14 as he spoke. "After your run, it's breakfast time. Now, for a little morale-booster, here's the breakfast menu: steamed buns as soft as your girl's tits, soy milk as foamy as her saliva . . . Then there's jam, butter, meat, pickles, boiled eggs. Anyone fancy a burger? I'll get the kitchen to make them Chinese-style: fried chicken in a steamed bun."

On the training ground, Ironhead issued a rifle to each of the trainees. "These were used in Korea and Vietnam; they made 1.38 million of them. Much rarer than the AK-47. About a hundred million of those were made. This is an improved version of the M14 — the M21 — and even rarer, so be careful with it. Both hands: left hand behind the forward strap mount, right hand at the wrist — that's the narrow part of the stock. On my mark . . . Run!"

And from then on it was a five-kilometre run with an M21 rifle. Even on a day off the run had to be completed before you went off base. Three months and a day of those runs and the rifle became a part of you. It didn't matter what stance you were shooting from; your arms were a steel frame, a solid support for your weapon.

And during the live-fire practice he became fond of the feel of the wooden stock pressed up against his cheek. He'd used all types of sniper rifles since then, all better than the M21, but none he had felt so at one with.

—

He sat in the hotel room near the Fontana di Trevi and broke down the M21 into its dozens of components before wiping each gently with an oiled cloth. Just as Ironhead had stroked the curves of the stock all those years ago.

Accuracy needs a solid base. Get three points of support and anyone can be a sniper. Back in training he'd been taught to check for those three points: the butt of the rifle firm in the hollow of the shoulder was one; the right hand curled around the wrist of the stock — just holding it, not too tight — with a finger on the trigger was another; the left hand, supporting the barrel in its palm, was the third.

—

"Lightly, like you're cupping your balls, not wanking off. Hold too tight and the gun can't breathe."

—

Oiled and reassembled, his M21 had a range of eight hundred metres. One of his squad mates had once tried shooting a target a full kilometre away, to good effect. But Ironhead had taken offence.

—

"What do you think you're going to be shooting at that distance, airplanes? Are you an anti-aircraft battery? We've got missiles for that. There's no point waving that old thing up at the sky. Stick to two to four hundred metres. I don't care how far you can shoot; I care about you making every fucking bullet count."

Rain slammed into the mud, splattering his legs with dirt. Three hundred metres away a silhouette target hung.

"One bullet, one life. Will it be your target or you? Clear your head, focus, carry out your mission!"

Ironhead stood in front of a row of rifles, each rising and falling with the steady breath of the trainees. "You live to carry out your orders. Whose orders?"

Ten voices, in unison: "Yours, sir!"

"You are soldiers. You do not have lives; you do not have feelings. You have orders."

Ironhead walked out to the hundred-metre mark, rain bouncing off the green of his uniform and the black of his boots. His hands folded behind his back, he looked towards the targets and shouted: "Open fire!" Then he walked between the shooters and their targets, blocking their line of sight as he went.

Shots cracked down the range. Ironhead paused a moment here, as if a thought had occurred to him, or quickened his pace a bit there. Bullets whistled between the two hills bordering the range, each an airborne object in great haste to reach its destination.

—

On past jobs he'd had a ten-round magazine and one more in the chamber. Only that first round was for the target; the remainder were for defending himself once the target was dead. But there was nothing to defend himself from here. He'd use five rounds. One to eliminate obstacles, one for the target, three in reserve.

He selected five rounds from the dozens on the bed. Sometimes, he found, some rounds had a certain glow that demanded to be chosen.

The M21 had come to him in Iraq, left behind by the Kurds. Spoils of war, in a way. Paulie had made the silencer. Shooting without a silencer, Paulie liked to say, was like fucking without a condom — something was bound to go wrong. Everyone expected Paulie to work for an arms firm after leaving the Foreign Legion, or at least a garage. But those deft hands had turned instead to prayer, and Paulie now wore the hessian robes of a monk. No more gunsmithing for Paulie.

He checked the action and was rewarded with a crisp, clean sound. Seated on the bed with legs apart, he used only two points of contact: the butt of the rifle in the hollow of his shoulder, his right hand on the wrist of the stock. With his left hand he slid the scope into its mount and rotated the weapon towards the window. He fixed the crosshairs on Oceanus.

He imagined a bullet flying from the barrel and arcing over the selfie-snapping tourists and the coin-filled water, penetrating the statue's forehead and splattering stone brains all over the Grecian columns, the Roman capitals, and the Baroque dome behind.

His checks over, he put the rifle away. It had been more than half a year since he'd held one, but nothing had changed.

At 10:05 a.m. he put on his ginger wig and Yankees cap, stuffed a pair of jeans under his vest for the expectant-mother look, and became Tom, clad in shorts, sandals, and socks. He picked up the M21 and chambered a round. The magazine containing the remaining four slotted into place with a reassuring click.

The forecast had been unusual but correct: it was sleeting in Rome, tiny chunks of ice clattering off the window. But tourists still thronged around the fountain with the expected selfie sticks and garish hats. And umbrellas! How had he forgotten Asian women and their umbrellas? The fountain was half-hidden from view. Why always the umbrellas? Sunny days, rainy days, every day . . .

There were too many of them. He'd need to move. He ascended the hotel stairs to the roof, where he hid behind a chimney, only the barrel of his rifle jutting out. The wind was blowing harder than desired; the sleet hampered his view.

He couldn't rely on luck. He removed his belt, threaded one end through the strap mount at the front of the barrel and twisted the other end around the biceps of his left arm. His left hand reached past the tensioned belt to take some of the weight of the barrel, while his right repositioned the butt against his shoulder. Three points of support, and his left hand as good as nailed in place.

He referred to the photo before taking aim. Sure enough, there were three men sitting outside the café, a grey-haired Asian man on the left, a European in a fur-lined coat in the middle, and to the right an Asian man with hair combed shiny smooth — and memorable ears. Snipers might not remember what a target looked like, but they did remember ears.

—

Everyone's ears are different, Ironhead informed them.

"Isn't that fingerprints, sir? Not ears?" You weren't meant to question Ironhead, just shout, "Yes, sir!" But he'd asked.

"And who's got the time to check fucking fingerprints before taking a shot?"

—

Safety off. Breathing off. And as soon as a red umbrella moved clear, he centred the scope on the glistening hair of the target, shifted the crosshair to an ear — a curved ear, a question mark missing its dot.

—

"What if the target has long hair?"

"Then bad luck for you, idiot."

He'd had to frog-jump across the training ground for asking that question.

—

The dot-missing question mark grew as he zoomed in, an elephant in the scope. Aiming at the root of the ear, where it grew from the skull, he pulled the trigger.

A puff of white smoke emerged from the barrel, immediately invisible in the sleet. But he could see the bullet, spinning as it dived through the air, arcing slightly as it fell to enter the target's skull. A spray of blood from the entry wound, one drop blemishing a waiter's white apron, another landing on the damp stone below.

One, two, three.

One. The European in the middle blinked.

Two. The European opened his mouth.

Three. The European fell backwards.

He didn't bother watching to see if he would hide under the table or at the feet of the other Asian man. He broke down the rifle and placed it in his backpack, straightened his Yankees cap, and padded downstairs in Tom's sandals.

He shivered as he exited the hotel, the chill wind raising every hair on his legs. Why did American tourists always have to wear shorts?

Tom, the Yankees cap–wearing American, turned right, heading north through an alley. Nobody noted his shorts or sandals; everyone was staring towards the fountain.

Police sirens. Tom knocked into a Prada bag–carrying Korean woman, then nodded in apology to the French-speaking man helping her up. He knew every alley in this part of Rome. Ten minutes and several turns later, he arrived at the Spanish Steps.

Tourists of all nations sat gazing at the Baroque fountain. "The Fountain of the Old Boat," he remembered it was called, and it did look past its prime. He found his own spot to sit and admire the fountain, removing his cap and ruffling his ginger curls before smoking a Marlboro Red. Then, satisfied, he trotted down the steps to the metro station.

The Rome subway is always packed on a holiday. He crammed into a carriage corner until Termini, where he entered a toilet. Five minutes later, Tom the ginger-American had disappeared, and a dashing Asian man dropped a bag into a garbage bin, downed a coffee-stall espresso, and headed for a train about to depart south to Naples. It was a local train, the trip taking two and a half hours. With one last glance around, he boarded.

He dialled a number, the Nokia's call quality clear. "Fried the rice, one egg. Just washing up now."

"Lose the phone. I'll be in touch." Again, no chance to ask the woman on the other end any questions.

He'd forgotten something. In the train toilet he peeled the *zen* Chinese-character tattoo from his calf and stuck it to the wall. A little something to help the Italian police, if they did decide to take an interest in Tom the red-haired American.

Tom's collision with the Prada bag–carrying Korean woman had been observed from an open window in a nearby hotel. A window from which protruded the mouth of an AE sniper rifle.

The AE was a reliable weapon, and the bipod stand on the dressing table in front of the window put it at the perfect height. It was accurate to within half a centimetre up to 550 metres, and with the addition of a silencer it made virtually no noise.

Through a Schmidt & Bender scope the observer scoured the surrounding windows and the square before looking towards the three men outside the café. With a .44 magnum cartridge in the chamber, the AE could destroy its target, leaving only a gory mess.

First, a slim, grey-haired Asian man, one side of his mouth curled upwards in a smile. Add the actor's trademark toothpick and you'd have an older version of Chow Yun-fat. Next, the European, face pale against his fur collar. Then the side of a head, its hair perfectly combed. The gun held steady, the thumb turned the safety, and . . . Before he could pull the trigger, the head in the sights crashed to the table.

He watched the tableware shake and the blood flow, then scanned the umbrella-studded square once more. His phone rang.

"Status?"

"Target is down."

"Clear out."

"My love to the family."

The phone call ended; the AE receded.

5

Jinshan District, New Taipei City

WHY DID BODIES turn up only when he was asleep?

North-East Point's northeasterly wind howled demonically as it rounded Lion's Head Mountain. The winds were said to be so vicious they had carved the two pillars of the Twin Candlestick Islets from solid rock. A particularly evil blast set the chains hanging from the arms of the two deities guarding the temple gate clanking ominously. The Ghosts of Impermanence, charged with escorting the spirits of the deceased to the underworld. At least he wasn't the only one working today.

Wu walked through the eerie spray whipped up from the sea until the corpse came into view, Popsicle-stiff in the cold air. He suppressed a wave of nausea.

11:27 p.m., December 30. Wu and four duty officers, spread across two cars, had arrived at Midpoint Bay, where the Shimen and Jinshan Districts of New Taipei met, to see this body, naked, torn, battered by the rocks.

Four searchlights mounted on the coast guard pickup truck illuminated the scene, the red and blue of the police cars caught against the white of the breakers. Wu pulled his coat collar tighter against the bitter sea wind and used its shelter to light a cigarette.

A single gunshot. This was a triad execution. There was little need for forensics. The corpse told the story: a dark hole in the centre of the forehead. The organized crime squad was called in.

Amidst the wailing wind and battering rain, Wu stood smoking in the beam cast by one of the searchlights. It seemed warmer there somehow.

Every late November the bitter northeasterlies came howling down from the Mongolian plateau, rushing mercilessly into the ports and deltas of northern Taiwan. A dry cold when it set out, it absorbed moisture as it crossed the sea, to better penetrate shivering bones.

Lan Pao from forensics had arrived ahead of Wu. He'd been playing mah-jong when he got the call and was now rubbing his hands together for warmth. He looked up as Wu approached. "Going to take a dip, Wu? They say a cold bath is good for your health."

Wu was about to repay the suggestion with abuse but was mollified by a uniformed officer handing him a bottle of kaoliang liquor.

Lan spoke again once he'd had his own turn with the bottle. "One shot to the forehead. No sand or seaweed in the mouth, so most likely shot dead, then dumped in the water. Less than a day ago, judging by the bloating. Clothes could have been removed before or after death, presumably to avoid leaving clues. Left him all nice and clean. Like a chef preparing an eel: the eyes, the skin, the bones — take it all away and leave beautiful white flesh."

A local surfing teacher had found the body while out collecting wood to build a fence. Wu cast an eye over the driftwood, drink bottles, plastic bags, and fragments of polystyrene, and sighed. According to the regs, he was meant to search the surrounding area for clues. But where in this garbage dump of a beach was he meant to start?

There was no indication of the deceased's identity. Notable features: three false teeth, thinning hair, two scars from hernia operations.

Wu's height and bulk had allowed him to dominate the karate and wrestling mats at training college. He'd almost made it to the Olympics, but a back injury had ended that dream and led him to focus instead on a career with the police. He'd always been able to rely on his body to do what was needed, though — until now, overwhelmed by exhaustion, reaching out to take the bottle from Lan for one more warming pull to keep him going. Drinking on duty was, under special circumstances, permitted.

The continental cold roared past at gale strength, stripping the coast of any warmth. Wu felt his testicles flee upwards, seeking warmth.

"How many days to retirement?" Lan asked.

Wu looked at his watch. "Eleven."

"Keep earning the karma, Wu. Got to get ready for the next life. Thirty years of prayer and meditation and you might get to come back as an immortal." The forensics lads loved to talk bullshit, and Lan was the worst of them.

Eleven days in which to bring his police career to a successful end, and he'd ended up with two murders. Wu rubbed his hands together and stamped his frozen feet.

Okay. First, who was he? He sent the fingerprints obtained from the corpse back to the office and asked Control to take a look through recent missing person reports from across Taiwan. The lack of tattoos or scars from earlier stabbings or shootings bothered him; that didn't make sense for a triad member. Possibly someone who'd failed to repay a debt to a loan shark, shot as a warning to anyone else considering a similar path? He put it out of his mind until he had more to work with.

At seven-thirty, just as he was walking into the Neihu branch of Lailai Soy Milk, Wu's mobile rang. The switchboard, passing on orders from the Chief. Wu hung up without replying.

He ordered a salty soy-milk porridge, a beef pastry, and a piece of turnip cake, then turned back to the counter to order an extra porridge and pastry and a fried dough stick. The four uniforms enjoying their own breakfast opted not to comment on the extent of Wu's appetite.

The foliage-green Toyota jeep pulled up outside just as he was swallowing a last gulp of porridge. Three uniformed military officers made their way inside, their heads bowed to avoid the rain. Two army lieutenants and a naval captain. Wu looked up before returning his gaze to a pastry.

The captain ignored the lack of red-carpet welcome and sat without ceremony opposite Wu. He freed a meaty hand from one glove and patted Wu on the shoulder.

"Detective Wu, we meet again! Hsiung Ping-cheng, Ministry of National Defence."

Wu picked up a toothpick and tried to remove a strand of beef from between his teeth. "So, tell me about it," he said.

"About what?"

"Captain Hsiung, tell me the deceased's name, rank and role, date and time of birth, and star sign. He's military, you're military; you have the access. Then my boss won't need to phone your boss, your boss won't need to phone you, you won't need to come and find me, and we won't need to send all those memos back and forth. It's bad for the environment, wasting that much paper."

Hsiung raised the corners of his mouth. "Very funny, Detective Wu." A pause. "But you'll know within a day anyway, even if I don't tell you. The fingerprints that your esteemed bureau ran through the system belong to one Chiu Ching-chih, a colonel in the army procurement office. So there was a very quick phone call to the Ministry and, twenty-seven minutes and eight seconds ago, I was called in."

"And battled through wind and rain to have breakfast with me."

"Before we'd even properly woken up. That pasty looking lieutenant there didn't even manage to clean his teeth."

"Ah, no wonder he's not eating. Wouldn't be hygienic."

"You don't seem in too good a mood yourself, Detective Wu. Not sleeping well?"

"Hold on. Procurement?"

Hsiung stared at Wu, unblinking, until the other two officers arrived with his soy-milk porridge. He raised the bowl to his lips and took a large gulp. "Are the police cuts so bad they've cancelled your newspapers? The Weapons Procurement Office. He'd just been promoted to colonel and made head of weapons procurement for the army."

"So that's the office buying the M1A1 tanks from the U.S.?"

Hsiung did not look up from his breakfast. "Military secret."

"I've got this funny feeling that anything to do with that office is also a military secret."

Hsiung finished his porridge, pulled on his gloves, and pointed two fingers, gun-style, at Wu. "You're a clever man, Detective Wu. But I'm not here just for the porridge. Once your esteemed bureau is done with the body, send it on to Tri-Service. We like to look after our own."

This was a big one. The biggest case of his thirty-five-year career, if he wasn't wrong. And eleven days left in it. "If only I had a month. A cooked duck —"

Hsiung pushed his face up against Wu's, finishing the saying. "— can still fly away."

"It's not flown yet. I still have eleven days."

Hsiung grinned widely, exposing the silver fillings in his molars.

6

Taipei, Taiwan

GIVEN THE USUAL winter northeasterlies, Chiu must have been dumped somewhere north of where his body was found. A car with military plates was soon spotted parked on a stony beach not far from Midpoint. Unfortunately there were no cameras nearby.

Wu gave the scene a look-over. It was Chiu's car, but the heavy overnight rain had wiped away even the tire tracks, never mind footprints. The Chief had been clear, though: get it solved, quick.

There had to be some link between Chiu and Kuo. Did they know each other? One Army, one Navy; one a colonel, one a petty officer.

He took the Danshui line to Zhongshan and sat by the window on the second floor of a muffin shop beloved of Taipei's trendy youngsters. Kuo had lived on the fourth floor of an old apartment building across the park. It all looked perfectly ordinary.

He was about to leave when one of the apartment windows opened and a woman's face appeared — thirties, short hair, slim figure, angular features. She rested her left elbow on the window frame and held a cigarette in her right hand. She ignored the bustle of the Japanese and Hong Kong tourists on the street below, her empty eyes seeing nothing, betraying nothing. She blew quick puffs of smoke through thin lips, disappeared for a moment, then returned with an ashtray and another cigarette.

Grey walls, a window frame, gloomy skies, a woman in half-profile.

Wu recalled the speculation in the press. Had Kuo been shot by a cuckolded husband during a lovers' tryst? The papers were just making it up. There wasn't a single crease in the bedsheets, and only the intended ones in Kuo's uniform. No lovers' tryst.

The woman stubbed out her cigarette and continued to gaze up into the dreary skies.

His text message alert sounded and Wu put down an almost untouched muffin. He made it onto the next metro train just as the doors closed, changing trains twice before reaching his destination.

Yang, the coroner, was a known jester. Once, during a television interview, he had dragged a finger through the liquid seeping from a corpse, tasted it, and claimed that in that manner he could discern the time of death. The reporter, an attractive young woman, was unable to speak and then vomited all over her microphone. Yang, delighted with his trick, later explained to Wu that he had run his index finger through the liquid but placed his middle finger in his mouth. Which, Wu thought, made it no less revolting.

Yang was just emerging from the autopsy suite and removing his gown as he spoke. "The fingerprints on the gun are Kuo's, but it's not his gun."

"How so?"

"It's one of the new T75 semi-automatics. Even after being fired there's a layer of oil on it you could stir-fry in. But naval officers do regular target shooting, and Kuo was no recent recruit. There's no way he'd have a new gun."

"Maybe they just issued him one?"

"The Navy's still using the old T51s, not T75s."

"Anything else?"

"Well, whoever shot him isn't short of money. Brand-new gun, used once and left behind like disposable chopsticks. Or maybe he's a bit OCD and likes to have a clean weapon."

"And?"

"You were right; he was left-handed. Left arm was stronger than the right, and there were traces of food grease on the left thumb and index finger. And, most importantly" — Yang pointed a glistening finger at Wu's nose — "our great Detective Wu had already determined the deceased was left-handed before the coroner even arrived."

"So it's not suicide."

"In the words of the bureau spokesperson, we are unable to confirm that it was not suicide."

"Any clues as to the culprit?"

"Not one. If — and I mean *if*, Wu — there is a murderer, it's someone Kuo knew, maybe a friend. Someone who could come in, get Kuo sitting down nice and quiet, fire a point-blank shot into his temple, get Kuo's prints on the gun, and then head home for a nap."

"Did you use your brain for that? I had it figured out using my ass."

"Well, what your ass doesn't know is that Kuo's prints are on the gun but the killer made a mistake — no prints on the trigger."

"Okay, keep going."

"Killer's star sign was Virgo."

"Yang, a minute ago he was OCD, now he's a Virgo. Are you the coroner or a psychic?"

"Wait. He probably knew Kuo was left-handed, but he still shot him in the right temple. Guess why."

Wu cocked his head to consider. "No idea."

"Well, if you're not going to play along . . ."

"Fine, I'll guess. He noticed the white bedsheets to Kuo's left. Shoot him from the right, splatter blood everywhere in a nice abstract pattern. He's an Impressionist?"

"You're getting abstraction and Impressionism mixed up. No, he likes to keep things clean. If he'd shot from the other side, the blood would have splattered the whole room. Messy."

"For fuck's sake, Yang, is that all you've got? The killer's a neat freak?"

"That's what I think, anyway. All the brains, the blood, the bone — all blown out onto the sheet. All the hotel needs to do is swap the bedding; they don't even need to repaint."

"Well, thank you for your limited contribution."

"Okay, here's another bit of intel. Kuo had a tattoo, upper left arm, about the size of an old dollar coin. Hard to make out, probably done a long time ago. Guess what of?"

"An anchor, since he was a sailor?"

"Would I be making this much fuss about an anchor?"

"A fish?"

"It's all that sparring when you were younger, Wu. It's affected your brain. One character: *family*."

Wu pored over the proffered photograph. The tattoo was there but he couldn't read it. "Family?"

"It's oracle bone script, maybe two thousand years old. This isn't my dad's 'Fight the Communists' tattoo or your son's broken heart tattoo. I wouldn't have recognized it myself if I weren't blessed with a little book learning."

"Oracle bone script? Like on actual oracle bones? Are you sure?"

"I'm sure. As for Chiu, it was again as the renowned Detective Wu inferred. Cause of death was a single gunshot to the forehead. No water in the lungs, so he went swimming post-mortem."

"Any signs of a struggle?"

"None."

"All very professional. And since when has Taiwan had such professional killers?" Wu stood to leave, still muttering under his breath.

Yang called him back. "Wait a minute. Aren't you due to retire soon?"

"Ten more days. I'll see how far I get with these two."

"What, I'm just helping you while away the days till retirement?"

"Got to admit, Yang, I'd hate to leave an unfinished case."

Yang stopped him again as he reached the door. "I forgot to mention, when Chiu's wife was identifying the body, she said something about a threatening phone call."

"Threatening her?"

"Him. He was shouting down the phone. All he'd say was that it was a senior officer."

"Now that's useful. Don't suppose Chiu had a tattoo as well."

"Unfortunately, no."

Wu's mobile rang as he walked through the bureau entrance.

"I'm here. Coming right up."

"Faster!" Egghead yelled.

"What's the hurry?"

"I'm on my way to the airport, to Rome. You're in charge."

"Rome? I didn't know you had a holiday booked."

"Have you not seen the news?"

"No. What's happened?"

"Chou Hsieh-he, a military consultant to the government, was assassinated in Rome just a couple of hours ago."

7

Manarola, Italy

DESPITE THE DETOURS, he reached home in Manarola, a small fishing village on the Ligurian Sea, by dusk. Manarola was one of five such villages, known as the Cinque Terre, nestled into the twisting mountain coast that ran north from La Spezia. The second of the five, Manarola could be reached only via a railway tunnel through the hills or by boat.

He jumped down from the ferry, the Adidas holdall slung over one shoulder. A narrow road chiselled from the rock took him upwards to the cliffside village. A pot-bellied man lay on a bench by a restaurant, shaking the street with his snoring.

He kicked the bench. "Up you get, Giorgio. Moon's already out."

Giorgio's bloodshot eyes cast about in confusion as he watched him skip lightly up the stone steps.

This was the village's main street, with steps running up to the train station and cramped roads leading left to the church and right to houses. His place was halfway up the steps to the hilltop church that overlooked the harbour far below. The lower floor of a three-storey building, so battered by wind and corroded by salt it looked like the lungs of a century-old smoker. The interior was twenty square metres at most, a wooden counter he'd made by the door, the kitchen behind that.

There was no sign outside, just a picture in the window of an egg frying in a wok. Someone trying to relieve boredom had sketched a few pentagons and hexagons onto the egg, turning it into a football, with the unexpected result that passersby had stopped in to see what kind of establishment fried footballs. They had become his earliest customers.

There was no seating. He sold takeaway fried rice — and only takeaway fried rice.

It was Gramps's recipe. Gramps had driven buses after leaving the army, and if traffic was bad he would come home late. First he would feed him a biscuit to keep him quiet and then take his time over the rest, placing the wok on the stove, selecting four eggs from the fridge. There's nothing more pleasing to the taste buds than fried rice — or easier to make. All perfection requires is a little practice.

He had been away for two days and the door was covered with notes, mostly enquiring when he would be back. Some of the older folk couldn't be bothered with cooking three times a day and had become very fond of his fried rice.

"Alex, you're back!" A small boy was hanging head-down from the second-floor balcony, his feet hooked through the railing.

"Come down. I'll make you egg fried rice." Alex beckoned as he opened up.

The boy landed beside him with a thump.

"Help out and get the rice from the fridge."

Alex shoved his luggage up into the mezzanine living space and fired up the gas stove. He was hungry too.

"I want shrimp in it!" Giovanni lived on the second floor with his grandparents. Both were in their seventies and lacked the energy to deal with a nine-year-old boy.

"There's no time to go and buy shrimp. We'll have salami."

Within three minutes the eggs and rice were hopping about in the heavy iron wok, as if trying to prevent their feet from burning.

The orders from two days ago still hung from a rack above the stove — eleven of them, five with shrimp, two with salami. He charged fair prices — 5 euros or 8 euros — and gave fair service. He wasn't getting rich, but it was enough.

He claimed the addition of salami to egg fried rice as his own invention. Here on the northwest coast of Italy there was no char siu pork to be had, and the flavour of Italian hams didn't suit fried rice. Then he had tried salami, the Italians' favourite. They loved it. The pork fat in the salami released its fragrance as it melted in the wok; the salt in the meat removed the need to add more.

Unusually, no tourists arrived in search of sustenance, and the two sat, man and boy, eating their fried rice. Giovanni, delighted with the meal, expressed his admiration for Alex in the form of questions. "Why do you use eggs?"

"Dante said that one day, when he was sitting at his door, God walked past and asked him which was the most delicious of all foods. And Dante replied, 'Eggs.' A year later, Dante was again sitting at his door and God again walked past and asked, 'But Dante, what is the most delicious way to eat eggs?' And Dante said, 'With salt.'"

"Impossible! Why would God ask such a silly question?"

"Don't mind that. The moral of the story is that eggs are tasty."

"But your eggs are fried, not salted."

"I add salt while frying."

"But that's not the same. It's not like Dante's eggs."

"Eggs are eggs."

Setting up a village fried-rice shop had been Paulie's idea. He'd said there were so many Asian tourists in Italy now that he was starting to confuse it with Hong Kong, and Chinese-style fried rice would sell well. Alex didn't have any other ideas, so he fried and fried and looked on in surprise as the orders poured in. He sold dozens of portions every day, which did wonders for his upper-arm strength.

Giovanni was summoned back upstairs by his grandfather, leaving Alex in peace. He collapsed on his mattress and slept.

Alex woke during the night and climbed down in search of water. A spot of light outside caught his eye, and he went to the window to gaze past the frying football. Nobody in the street, no illumination but the streetlights.

He was thinking more clearly after some water. A spot of light? He found his night-vision goggles and sat motionless. The night was rich with noises: a tap not fully closed, an elderly cough, someone waking from a nightmare and fetching water, the typing of an Internet all-nighter, the scrape of chair legs on wood, the pattering of rain at the window.

There it was again — a small red spot of light. A laser sight.

He reached out for the smaller wok, balanced it on the handle of a mop, and slowly raised it over the counter. It swung back and forth in search of balance.

He pulled his bag down from the mezzanine and assembled the M21 before squatting in the corner, watching the now-settled wok.

All remained quiet. His eyelids drooped, the gun resting in his lap. A cold breeze woke him; he'd left the vent above open and the wind had set the wok swinging again. He reached out to steady it. As he did, a puff of air tore across the back of his neck and sent the wok clattering to the floor.

Alex hit the ground, moving slightly to silence the wok and keep the neighbours safely in bed.

Gun over the shoulder. Arms up, he hauled himself onto the mezzanine. A bullet slammed into the opposite wall, sending plaster flying.

The shop sat halfway along a lane that was less than two metres across. Opposite, another old three-storey building made of brick and stone. Too close for those angles; the shooter had to be farther away, on high ground. There was only one place it could be.

He pulled on the night-vision goggles and wriggled through a small window to climb the metal steps attached to the rear of the building. The space between the buildings was barely enough to accommodate a cat — assuming the cat wasn't claustrophobic. No chance of being spotted.

The second floor housed Giovanni and his grandparents, who all went to bed early. The owner of the third floor headed inland every November to avoid the cold sea winds. The eaves of the tiled roof extended far enough beyond the walls to provide cover. Alex surveyed the higher ground through his sights.

Take the right set of steps on the way up from the harbour and you ended up at a group of older buildings. He'd been in all of them, delivering food. Only the top floor of the westernmost building, one hundred metres distant, had a view of his shop. He raised his gun, but he had no clear view and no target. *This*, he realized with a start, *is no longer home.* It was a battleground of his enemy's choosing.

Back on the mezzanine, he threw a few things into a bag and eased open the door. Another bullet slammed into the wall. Alex rolled into the lane and headed for the higher ground, bag over his shoulder, bullets cracking off the stones underfoot. *Find a more advantageous position, then counter-attack*, he thought.

He ran head down, vaulting a gate and sprinting along a hillside trail he knew well. The Via dell' Amore linked Mana-rola with Riomaggiore, a kilometre away, and was a favourite with sunset-watching tourists. It was closed now — too wet and windy for tourists in winter.

He stopped behind a small rise just before the path reached Riomaggiore. Steadying his breathing, he aimed his rifle down the oncoming path. The rain had stopped and the moon was out; despite the wind, no pursuer would make it past. Then he realized his error. All it would take was a second shooter at the other end of the path and he was dead.

He remembered Ironhead's story about Yang Youji.

—

"History tells us Yang Youji was a gifted archer who lived around 560 BCE. He was said to be able to shoot a hundred willow leaves from a tree at a hundred paces with a hundred arrows. The king at the time dispatched troops to put down a rebellion, but the rebel leader was himself a feared archer, causing unease among the soldiers. The king offered riches and honours to anyone who would confront the rebel general."

"Eventually a common soldier, Yang Youji, stepped forward. The match did not seem fair, but the rebel general accepted the challenge: an archery duel, three arrows each, the general to shoot first, the result to decide the battle. The two men stood between the massed ranks of two armies who were waiting for Yang's death.

"The rebel leader's three arrows missed. Yang killed him with a single arrow — just one, you hear? He was known as "Yang One Arrow" forevermore.

"And why did the great general lose to an ordinary soldier? I'll tell you: He missed the first time because of arrogance. He missed the second time because of anger. And he missed the third time because of panic. Once you panic, your body stops following orders, and you become a sitting duck, like the rebel leader."

—

Alex knew that was where he was now — panicked. He forced his breath to slow. He pressed his ear to the ground. Footsteps? One person. He could deal with a single opponent by waiting him out there, but if there were reinforcements he was trapped.

He grabbed his gun and ran, bent double but still exposed on the moonlit ridge. A sudden sting in the right shoulder — the enemy had him. Alex dove forward to crawl through the mud, pausing only to lift the sight to his eye and check that no ambush lay in wait ahead.

He had to flee — flee far — and then decide what to do. This was home, and he could not risk losing it.

He smashed a car window and got in, hotwired the engine. He had to misdirect the enemy, and the farther away he could send them, the better. As the car pulled away, a bullet punched silently through the door and into his left leg. No time to examine the wound. He spun the steering wheel; tires screeched.

The road went east to La Spezia. His injured left leg struggled with the clutch as he sped down the twisting mountain road. As he rounded a curve, he spotted headlights behind him.

The road split as it left the mountains, offering two options: left to La Spezia, a big port city, and right to Porto Venere, a small harbour town — and the potentially life-saving Church of San Lorenzo. At the junction Alex raised the handbrake and spun the wheel right, sliding into the right-hand road. Would Paulie be at the church?

The moon had disappeared. Now it was raining again, pouring through the shattered window and soaking him.

Porto Venere had a single main road that followed the harbour, with smaller streets leading off to residential areas. The harbour was silent, the moonlight ebbing and flowing as it reflected off waves of sea and rain. He left the car blocking the road and ran up a steep street, keeping his footsteps light to avoid attracting attention from the few illuminated windows. He would settle this in the square in front of the church: a clear outlook, higher ground, and the wind and rain at his back.

The church stood on a long, narrow hilltop with a stone staircase leading up to its doors. He stopped to fumble for his phone, briefly forgetting his atheism as he offered a prayer for God's aid.

God was, on this occasion, listening. Paulie picked up after a single ring. "Where are you?" he asked Alex, his voice quiet and deep.

"Outside the church."

"How many?"

"One, a sniper."

"Come up. I'll look after you."

From another pocket Alex retrieved the Nokia he'd obtained in Rome and called the sole saved number. Again it was answered after a single ring.

"I told you to get rid of that phone." Her voice again.

"Get Ironhead."

"Problems? Go to the first safe house."

"Baby Doll?"

Silence.

"Why are you on this phone, Baby Doll?"

"Ironhead gave you the address. I'm sure you remember."

The call ended. No time to reminisce about the owner of that familiar voice. Alex had pressing matters to attend to.

Looking down, he could see headlights moving along the harbour road. Alex shouldered the M21, measured his breathing, and took aim at the car he'd stolen, which was still blocking the road. *Breathe, relax the left arm, hold breath, gas tank, trigger.* The bullet rushed from the barrel. He watched unblinking through the sight until flames engulfed the vehicle and a boom rolled across the town.

In the firelight Alex could see the pursuing Citroën brake and a figure roll from the driver's seat to the roadside. Lights came on in nearby houses and boats. He lost sight of his opponent, but Alex presumed he was being tracked up the hill. He wiped rain and sweat from his eyes and winced as a tearing pain in his right shoulder forced him to lower the rifle. His sleeve was soaked with blood; his left leg refused to move. He looked back at the church to see the lights of the steeple obscured by a shadow.

The shadow spoke. "Here, take my shoulder. You can tell me all about it inside."

Paulie, as solid as the stone church itself, took his weight. Alex let himself be dragged up the steps, his eyes closed against the wind and rain. Paulie carried him through the church doors, which he closed against the sound of sirens and the light of flames licking at the sky.

A church of plain stone, unadorned, cold, damp. Alex was shaking violently.

Saint Lorenzo himself, haloed and carved from dark rock, sat erect in his chair, one hand clutching two keys, the other pointing to heaven with the index and middle fingers. In the third century CE San Lorenzo — Saint Lawrence — had been martyred for distributing the Church's wealth to the poor rather than handing it over to the Roman prefect. He was said to have been roasted over hot coals and, after enduring great agony, to have joked, "I'm done on this side. Turn me over." And so he became the patron saint of cooks and comedians. Alex was a cook. Was he a comedian as well? He hoped so.

And now he was feverish, desperate to claw at the hot needles of pain in arm and leg.

"I disinfected the wound, used battlefield dressings; both bullets are still in there. How's your strength? Do you remember where my boat is?"

Alex nodded.

"Put on this robe. Head down from the statue of Mother Nature watching the sea."

Another nod.

"Whoever's chasing you is on the steps. It's just the one. I'll take care of him."

Paulie kicked the M21 over to the wall and pulled on a rope. A bell rang out above.

Alex pulled on the robe and picked up his bag, now much lighter. From the side door he edged his way along the church wall towards the cliffs. The rain bounced off everything, off the wall, off the path, off his bloodless face.

The blaze at the foot of the hill had been extinguished, but Alex knew it would have destroyed any trace of him, and the rain would take care of any blood he'd left climbing the hill. With a bit of luck, the police wouldn't notice the bullet holes in his shop.

The moon broke through the clouds and Alex saw how exposed he would be on his climb down the cliff. But he carried on, dragging himself to the foot of the statue and then along the cliffside. There it was — the rope.

He looked back to see Paulie standing tall in front of the church, hands tucked into his wide sleeves. The dying ringing of the bells was drowned out by approaching sirens. The wind tore at the hem of Paulie's robe.

His right arm was no use, but he managed to descend the rope by gripping it between his thighs, using his left hand to lower himself towards the sea. Blackness swirled as his strength failed him. He recited the address of the safe house, a mantra to keep himself alert. He'd been leaving Taipei to join the French Foreign Legion, and Ironhead had driven him to the airport. "If you're ever in trouble, you can hide there — and just wait. I won't give up on you, so don't you give up on yourself." And now, five years later, he was in trouble. Ironhead's every word came back to him.

The boat was moored to the cliff. When he first got to Manarola, Paulie had taken him out fishing. He'd asked why

Paulie had become Brother Francesco. Paulie just shrugged. "No point in questioning fate, Brother Alex. I just accept it."

The boat could take two passengers and was powered by a small outboard motor at the stern. He had no fear that the motor would not start or that he would run out of fuel. Brother Francesco took care of his brothers.

He steered the boat around the peninsula, heading east, aiming for the castle on a promontory overlooking the Bay of Lerici. Paulie's friend Mario would be waiting there.

He was burning up, despite the wind and rain scouring his face as the boat picked up speed. But at last he had time to think. Where the hell had he gone wrong?

8

Taipei, Taiwan

WU STAYED LATE AT THE OFFICE. It seemed likely that Chiu's death was linked to his job, so he was going over the military's big procurement projects for the past few years. Plans to buy the M1A1 Abrams battle tank weren't popular with the government. Plans to buy submarines were stalled because the United States and the European Union refused to sell, and the Ministry of Defence was hoping to build its own. Plans to buy the F35 fighter . . . Again the U.S. refused the sale, offering only an upgrade to Taiwan's existing F16s. Chiu was Army, so he would have worked on the tank procurement. If that didn't go ahead, a lack of parts would see the current tanks pulled out of service and the Defence Minister — no Army fan — would take the opportunity to cut back on its armour. And once that budget had gone to submarines or advanced fighters, there was little chance the Army would ever get it back.

Losing two armoured brigades and their budgets would mean cutting two major generals. And with that, the Army would lose standing relative to the Navy and Air Force, a loss it would struggle to recover from. So the Army would be looking for expensive weaponry to spend its money on. A lot of weight on Chiu's shoulders. What did the Army plan to buy? What had Chiu been about to do?

As for Kuo, he might have been a non-commissioned officer, but he had a record that would put many high-ranking officers to shame. Minesweeper training in Germany in 2005: there weren't many non-coms who had the necessary English, but Kuo did, and the Navy had pulled strings to get him into German courses at an intelligence training school. He'd re-enlisted twice already and had requested a third stint. A specialist in anti-submarine warfare, Kuo had served on Cheng Kung– and Chi Yang–class frigates and Yung Feng and Yung Ching minesweepers and was most recently a petty officer first class on a Kee Lung–class destroyer.

Wu googled that last one. The Kee Lung class was known as Kidd class in the U.S., where Taiwan had bought them. Old, but at 9,800 tons they were Taiwan's largest frontline warships. Given his experience, Kuo would have been captain of the ship in all but name. He'd applied to re-enlist only the month before, and there seemed no risk he'd be denied. So why kill himself when everything was going so well? And where was the link with procurement? Kuo was still far too junior for any involvement at that level.

A television on the wall interrupted Wu's line of thought. A news broadcast, showing footage caught by a tourist in Rome. Chou Hsieh-he, his body suddenly falling onto a café table, the foreigner in a fur-lined coat next to him staring in shock.

What was a military adviser to the government doing in Rome? And who was taking the time to assassinate advisers?

They didn't have any real power. The government had dozens of them, mostly unsalaried — it was an honorary title.

Wu did a little research. Chou was forty-three, unmarried, a university professor. Lived in a grand villa off Ren'ai Road, though. *Universities must pay a lot better than the police*, he thought.

But what had Chou been doing in Rome? That was the question. And who was that foreigner with him?

It was past ten when Wu got home. His wife, as usual, was on the sofa with a box of tissues and a Korean soap opera. She waved in greeting. "There's dumplings in the fridge."

The light in his son's room was on. *Studying this late?* Wu put his head around the door. "Studying for the exams? Hungry?"

Keeping his eyes fixed on the screen, his son raised his mouse and shook it from side to side.

"Quick nightcap with your old dad?"

The mouse declined again.

I'd get more response from the furniture, Wu thought.

Ten dumplings and two nightcaps later, his wife joined him at the dining table, red-eyed.

"Why do you watch those shows if they just make you cry like that?"

"You wouldn't understand." She took his glass and sipped. "There's something I want to talk to you about."

That didn't sound good.

"Your dad was here again."

Wu's father had been an elementary school teacher. He'd retired at fifty-five and then enjoyed two happy decades with Wu's mother. She'd died two years before, and shortly afterwards he'd arrived at their door one evening with containers of food, saying he'd cooked dinner for his grandson. He was a fine cook and it was good to see him busy, and it saved Wu's wife the trouble. But it was happening every day. Nobody felt able to go out because they had to be home for dinner. Finally, one day his son had spoken up: "Grandad's food is great, but I'd like to go for a burger with my friends now and then."

The day after, Wu had arrived home at nine. His son's bedroom door was closed. Their bedroom door was closed. And in the kitchen, a table full of uneaten food. So his son had opted for a burger. The wife? She appeared, leaning on the door frame. "I was out. I phoned your dad and told him to take a day off. He said he'd already made the food, so he'd bring it over."

Thankfully his son had gone to stay in the university dorms for a while, so Wu had been able to tell his dad to take a break: no need to spend an hour on the bus bringing dinner. His dad hadn't said much, and he hadn't turned up the next day. No more cooking for them unless they went to visit at New Year's or a holiday. Back then his dad was out hiking or swimming every week with old colleagues, so Wu hadn't worried about him. And work had been busy. Now that he thought about it, he hadn't seen his father since a Mid-Autumn Festival visit.

"Your father's spent the last six months taking cooking classes at the community college. He's got a certificate. He says he wants to try out his new skills and make sure his grandson's properly fed. So he brought over all the ingredients and got here about four. I got home at five. So he was sitting at the door, waiting, for an hour. How do you think that made me feel?"

Wu noticed a big pot on the stove.

"A stew. Want to taste it?" She fetched him a spoonful anyway. "That's . . . salty."

"That's what your son said. Your dad was not amused."

"Do you think he's lost his sense of taste?"

"That's not the worst of it. He wants a key."

Wu's phone rang. The bureau chief, summoning all the section heads back for a meeting, orders of the Presidential Office. Chou's assassination was to be given top priority, with a report to the National Security Council first thing. Another all-nighter.

"I'll phone him tomorrow."

Setting aside thoughts of his father, Wu went to the computer to check the files they'd sent through. The Italian police were focusing on one suspect, a Korean man who had been staying nearby, at the Hotel Relais Fontana di Trevi; the hotel had reported him as failing to check out that morning. But a review of all the security camera footage from the square failed to reveal any suspicious-looking Asian males. Wu watched some of the footage: blurry and confused, as it always was. And a rare sleet storm, so the square was blotted out by umbrellas.

Egghead should still be on the flight to Rome — and in economy, given the bureau budget. He grinned, remembering how much Egghead hated the foil-wrapped mush the airlines served as food. He messaged him: *Have a look at the man in the baseball cap in the footage. Everyone else is panicking, but he's calmly making his way out of the square, not bothered about who's been shot or where.*

It'd be ten hours at least before Egghead saw the message. Wu pulled his coat back on and eased the door closed behind him. An early start for him.

It was just after midnight. Three months ago he'd been griping about the time dragging. Now there were only nine days left and time was flying. And he couldn't stop it.

9

Budapest, Hungary

ALEX WOKE UP in a truck, in a car, in a train. Then he left the train, took the Budapest metro, and was now making his way through Danube-side streets, reciting an address under his breath, holdall over his shoulder, wincing as his wounds made their presence known.

He remembered Paulie and that deep voice: "I'll look after you."

But it had been Mario who met him. Alex knew the man, a local with a thick beard who had once joined them on a fishing trip. "Super, super Mario," Alex had said in greeting.

Mario had clapped his hands to Alex's cheeks. "Humble, humble Mario. Paulie sends his regards. He's fine, by the way. You're not. Whoever's after you got away."

He tried to sit up. He was in a bunk in the sleeper cab of a tractor-trailer. Next to the bunk was a washbasin and a table laden with food, including a plate of scrambled eggs.

"Paulie said you like eggs. Get up, eat something."

Declining Mario's offered hand, Alex swung his legs

from the bed and leaned on the basin as he shuffled towards the table. He had no appetite but sat down and shovelled in mouthfuls of food. He needed the strength. Mario had added milk — it made the eggs silkier. But Alex had an unadulterated love for unadulterated eggs.

Mario held out a fist full of calluses and roughened skin, opening it to reveal two deformed bullets. "This is the one from your shoulder. This other one looks like it hit the ground and ricocheted into your leg; didn't get much farther than the skin. The doc just dug it out with his fingers. Keep 'em as souvenirs. You're young enough that the wounds will heal quickly."

Mario rolled the bullets onto the table. "Every cop in northern Italy's in Porto Venere right now. We need to get you away. Finish your eggs and we'll get moving. And take these."

Alex, still dozy, took the pills and was soon asleep in the back seat of a car. He dreamed of Ironhead. *"Remember Yang Youji. Marksmen always know where they are, and they never stand out."*

Alex awoke, wondering why the car was swaying so violently, and found he was already on a train, Mario stroking his hair. "You're doing fine. I need to get off at the next stop, so you're on your own from here. You were muttering an address in your sleep. All I understood was 'Budapest,' so I put you on a train to Hungary."

Where had he gone wrong? Who was hunting him? The fever only added to Alex's paranoia. And then he fell into a long, deep sleep.

—

"During the time of the Warring States there was a great Wei archer, Geng Lei, who bet the king he could bring down a bird merely by drawing back his bowstring. As the goose approached from the east, Geng raised his bow, drew back the string . . . and on hearing the twang of the released string, the goose fell to the ground as if struck. The Wei king asked how."

Ironhead was marching back and forth in the mud in front of a row of prone snipers.

"Geng explained that he had seen the goose was hurt. It was flying slowly because it was wounded, and calling out in distress, as it had lost its flock. It had panicked at the sound of his bowstring, reopened its wound as it tried to flee, and so was brought down without a single arrow."

"So what am I trying to tell you?" Ironhead demanded.

—

Alex found the safe house and the key under a stone slab on the second step. He replaced the slab and took the elevator to Apartment 315 on the third floor. A keypad lock. He tapped in his birthday and the door opened with a buzz.

A small apartment, maybe fifty square metres. An open space, except for the bathroom. A bed and a window opposite the door. Recalling the tale of Geng Lei, Alex took two more pills and lay down to sleep.

He dreamed of a woman, not clearly seen, who pinched at his arm. *"I like you too. But can we just be friends for a while?"*

He woke up, his wounds sore and itchy. He looked

through the bag Mario had given him, then removed his dressings in front of the bathroom mirror. He wasn't sure who'd done the stitches, but they sprawled messily from the central wound, a spider on the move.

He changed the dressings and left the apartment. Snow carpeted the lane, and it was a long walk before he found a shop where he could stock up on essentials. Then he explored for half an hour, feeling inexplicably well.

He ate a sandwich and then searched every inch of the apartment. Nothing behind the print of Rembrandt's *Night Watch* on the wall. Nothing in the fuse box by the door. Nothing in the toilet tank. He patted down the pillow — there it was. Alex memorized the address on the slip of paper he pulled from the pillowcase, then burned it.

A safe house was only safe for three days, then it was time to move on to the next one. And he'd found no gun.

More pills, then he collapsed on the bed, soaking the sheets with sweat as he slept. Up, instant noodles, back to sleep. Eighteen hours later he got up, the fever gone. He was still weak but no longer feeling faint. He pulled on all the clothes he had and shuffled his way through the grid of surrounding streets like a vagrant. An old habit: learning the local environment.

His window looked out to the side of a casino across the street, about six metres away. The top floor of the five-storey building was a hotel: eight windows, all tightly closed. In front of the casino was a park and the road along the Danube. Two lanes north there was a noodle shop named for Momotaro, the Peach Boy of Japanese folklore. He checked the menu on the door. They had sashimi, tempura, noodles, xiaolongbao, Yangzhou fried rice.

The hot, humid air of a Chinese restaurant swaddled him. Car horns could be heard from the direction of the river; condensation streamed down the windows.

Yangzhou fried rice bore only a passing similarity to fried rice as Alex made it. Put yesterday's rice in a wok, add a little water, cover until the water is absorbed. Only then add the eggs and stir rapidly. Softer rice, stronger egg flavour.

One large plate of Yangzhou fried rice later, Alex stood on the street, taking deep breaths of cold, clean air. The chef, outside for a smoke, nodded upwards twice in greeting — a Zhejiang mannerism, he remembered — and proffered a cigarette. He accepted and gazed down the street: the river, hemmed in by buildings, and the chain suspension bridge linking Buda with Pest. The snow still fell, the bridge still stood, and silhouetted figures hurried back and forth. Maybe he should just stay there. Get a job helping out at Momotaro, perhaps.

He waved thanks to the chef and received another upwards nod in return.

No suspicious people or vehicles on the way back to the safe house. He ate six kiwi fruit for the vitamin C. He knew that guavas, kiwi fruit, sugar apples, and oranges were best for vitamin C, but he'd found only kiwi fruit.

He had trouble sleeping. Getting up to read, he noticed that the far right window of the fifth-floor hotel across the street was open but dark. The others were all lit up or showing traces of light through drawn curtains. Alex knew the city was quiet year-round, but the casino seemed to be doing great business. And last night there'd been lights on in all the rooms. Now one looked empty. But if it was empty, why was the window open?

He moved away from the bed, turned off the lights, and crouched in a corner from where he could watch the open window.

Then he pulled the dark bedspread from the bed and hung it from the curtain rod to block any view of the interior, and he cut the power at the fuse box. Slipping out the building's rear door, he found a spot in the shadows where he could observe the open fifth-floor window. He spotted smoke drifting outwards.

He called Tsar, and after a lengthy tram ride reached the northern suburbs.

"I need a gun."

Tsar ignored the request and pulled him in for a bear hug that left him breathless. "Anything you need. Water pistols, if you want them."

Tsar was Moldovan, not Russian. A country slightly smaller than Taiwan, west of Romania and south of Ukraine, with a population of 3.5 million. It had, after the breakup of the Soviet Union, stolen Albania's crown as poorest country in Europe. "The young folk go abroad in search of money. The old folk sit at home scared to spend it," Tsar had once said of his homeland.

Tsar had left the Foreign Legion a year earlier than Alex and returned to Moldova. He endured it for several months, then spent some time in Romania before making it to Hungary, where he had married and settled down. Tsar had been one of the four in that mess in Ivory Coast, and he had come out the worst of all, as his flattened nose still testified. Tsar, Paulie, Necktie, and Alex.

They drove north towards the border with Slovakia, to Tsar's house hidden in the forest.

Tsar tossed him a rifle. "Dragunov svu, Russian. You know it. I can give you a suppressor for the noise and flash, a pks-07 sight, and a ten-round magazine."

He'd used the svu. Light, didn't jam, didn't break, easy to clean.

"And don't worry about where I got it. A souvenir from Afghanistan." Tsar threw his arms open, an expression of generosity. "Or a CZ?"

The CZ was Czech-made, a fine gun at a good price. But the svu was a better weapon than its size suggested.

"Haven't fired a gun since I left the Legion, myself," Tsar said, wondering at how times had changed. "Prefer the smell of tobacco to gunpowder now."

Tsar sketched three concentric circles on a piece of paper and attached it to a tree thirty metres away. Alex took three shots, each landing high and left. He adjusted the rear sight and landed three more, dead centre.

"What's the range?"

"The Russians claim twelve hundred metres." Tsar waved a finger of warning. "So, eight hundred at most."

That should be enough.

Alex made fried rice. No wok, so he had to use a flat-bottomed pan, and he could only stir with his left arm. He chopped and parboiled whatever vegetables Tsar had in the fridge — Gramps would have shaken his head in dismay at some of the ingredients — before frying up a bit of bacon for the grease, then adding the egg and rice, and finally the veggies and a sprinkling of salt and pepper.

Tsar's wife beamed as she ate. It occurred to Alex that it was good for a woman to be a little plump in these cold climates.

"Paulie said someone was trying to kill you. Shouldn't you be lying low? Who is it?"

Alex shook his head. They were sitting out on the porch after dinner, Tsar leaning back in a wooden chair and stretching out his legs.

"If you need a gun, I assume you're not running."

"No. I can't figure out how they knew I was in Budapest. Which means I'll have to ask them."

"If they tracked you from Italy they must be good."

"The best."

"Give me your phone."

Tsar took the iPhone from Alex's hand. "There are three kinds of people now," he said. "People who use Apple phones, people who use other mobiles, and people who don't use any." He placed the phone on the ground as he spoke, then crushed it like a cockroach under his boot. Stamp. Stamp. Grind.

"Ashes to ashes, dust to dust," Alex recited.

"That'll make it harder to find you." Tsar said. "Oh, and I meant to say the night vision on that scope's no good. Don't go trying to send anyone back to ashes and dust after dark."

"How wide's the Danube at the chain bridge?"

"Maybe four hundred metres. Planning to go swimming?"

Alex glanced down at the rifle in his lap as Tsar leaned over to slap him on the back. "You've not changed, Alex."

"What's on the other side of the bridge?"

Tsar stood up. "It's a long time till morning. We need a drink and a map."

—

"During the Three Kingdoms period, the general Taishi Ci arrived to rescue his besieged friend Kong Rong. He learned Kong Rong had not dispatched messengers in search of reinforcements, as nobody dared travel through the siege lines."

Ironhead loved a little speech before dinner. The extra food laid out for the Mid-Autumn Festival wasn't going to change that.

"The next day, Taishi Ci took a squad of soldiers out to the moat, where he placed a large target on the ground. The enemy army assumed an attack was imminent and prepared accordingly. But Taishi Ci merely rode his horse back and forth in front of the target, firing off ten arrows, each of which landed true. The next day and the next, the same performance. By the fourth day, the enemy no longer expected an attack . . . and Taishi Ci charged the enemy camp, a single man on a single horse. The enemy soldiers, knowing he never missed, let him pass. Those few who dared approach fell dead.

"Do you get it? A sniper has to be so deadly that the enemy panics at the whisper of his name." Ironhead grabbed a chicken leg from a serving dish. "Eat, then!"

—

Heavy snow had closed roads, and it took Alex several buses to make it back to Castle Hill, on the west bank of the Danube. He followed the castle walls south to a hotel, where he slipped past a busy receptionist into the toilets and then moved upward to the roof. He rolled out the white sheet Tsar had donated and settled in to observe the hotel. The overnight wait was bound to be making his opponent anxious, assuming that his absence had not been discovered.

Directly across the river was the Baroque magnificence of the Four Seasons Hotel, and next to it the casino and top-floor hotel he was interested in. Through his binoculars he had a clear view of the far right window on the top floor. Still open. The dark cloth he'd used to cover the apartment window, combined with the grey skies and snowy ground, would turn the glass into a huge mirror.

"Think," Ironhead used to say, "as if you were the enemy." And if he was a sniper looking out from that fifth-floor window at the safe house, with a bad angle and no visibility? There was only one choice: to the roof, as in Rome. Climb out a skylight and hide behind the ridge of the roof. No chance of being spotted, and a better view through the higher ventilation windows of the safe house.

Or he might just cross the road and kick in the door. No. This was a sniper, not a killer. Snipers think in terms of distance, camouflage, field of view, wind, and weather.

He thought back to his survey of the nearby streets. The casino looked sideways onto the river, a narrow alley behind it, with a steep roof to prevent snow accumulating. Four skylights on either side of the roof, closed because of the cold. A layer of snow on the roof.

If he was in that situation — couldn't use the skylight of his own room because it opened to the front, too visible; couldn't break into one of the rooms at the back, too risky — it'd have to be the skylight over the staircase, the one at the back. And at the staircase there were no walls between the front and back skylights. He shifted the binoculars. Sure enough, he could see through the front skylight to the back.

Alex thought back to the attack in Manarola. His opponent had opted to shoot from distant high ground and through a window. He was clearly worried about being spotted — no doubt particularly worried about being spotted by Alex. Perhaps someone like Alex, with an Asian face, someone who knew he would be noticed, would be mentioned to Alex by gossipy locals. But opting to keep so distant had been an error. And after the attack failed he'd chased Alex — to the hiking path, to Porto Venere, to Budapest. This was someone determined to see him dead.

His opponent would be more cautious now, having failed once, knowing that Alex had been warned and could counterattack. Or perhaps the room opposite the safe house had been empty all along and Alex was just being paranoid.

Three hours later, Alex was massaging some feeling back into frozen legs and considering withdrawal. But if there was someone after him? Someone also lying on a frozen rooftop, massaging frozen legs? Would he be climbing down from the roof?

Alex waited.

A big tourist coach pulled up to the Four Seasons and a dozen passengers disembarked. Two of them, men, stood smoking at the hotel entrance. A ponytailed woman jogged around the park. Traffic backed up on the chain bridge.

Seven smokers now.

A woman with a camera, taking shots of the bridge in the snow.

A man on his phone, wrapped up in a warm coat and woollen hat.

Traffic on the bridge still motionless.

The jogger ran onto the bridge.

Half an hour later Alex caught a momentary flash of light on the casino roof and immediately swapped binoculars for rifle. He blinked to moisten his eyes and fixed the skylight in his sights, his reasoning now justified. He shifted the rifle slightly. Distance of 650 metres, slight breeze, humid, a little snow. He chambered the first round and lowered the muzzle a fraction.

Outdoor tables were being set up at a restaurant across the river. A black-suited waiter erected canopies with practised motions.

The man on his phone strode into the hotel.

The smokers changed shifts: two men, one woman.

A white hat poked over the ridge of the roof, then a silencer.

Alex held his breath. Barrel resting on the parapet, stock tight into right shoulder. The hat again, two eyes. Squeeze the trigger. And . . .

With both a flash suppressor and a silencer, the svu did no more than puff and press back against his shoulder. But a flurry of snow had obscured his vision at the last moment. A spurt of snow flared up from the casino roof. He'd missed.

Alex rolled twice to the right, to the edge of the roof, ignoring the pain from his shoulder. He knew his opponent would be rolling too, but likely to his left. Left-handed or right-handed, snipers always shoot with their right hand, and an empty left hand made rolling in that direction easier.

No sign of White Hat. As Alex ran his scope along the roof, he felt a puff of air pass and instinctively shrank back. A few inches away, snow flew from the parapet.

A man wearing an apron and carrying an aluminum food container appeared and headed for the Four Seasons. A waiter from Momotaro. Sunlight glinted from the metal box.

A man in a blue ski jacket sat down at one of the riverside tables. A waiter fetched a cup of coffee.

No sign of the jogger.

The traffic on the bridge started edging forward.

Alex chambered a second round. He couldn't see the shooter, but through the two skylights he could make out the reflection of a rifle barrel. He shifted slightly and took aim.

Alex waited.

The gun in his sights shifted. He saw light glint from the lens of his opponent's scope.

Alex waited.

With his eye tight to the scope, Alex had a momentary glimpse of his opponent's telescopic sight — and the eyes behind it, snowflakes melting on eyebrows. It was Fat!

Fat's barrel jerked upwards and Alex's trigger pulled back. Two bullets pierced snowflakes, passed over a snarled-up bridge, flew by each other above crawling cars, a returning jogger and her swaying ponytail. The waiter from Momotaro continued on his way, oblivious.

A bullet sliced past Alex's right ear with a quiet breath. His own bullet had missed its target too . . . but it hit his target's gun. A puff of snow rose up over the ridge, a gun barrel briefly discernible before disappearing. Had he dropped the gun? Was his opponent disarmed?

Alex chambered a third round and shifted to view the skylight. The light was poor, but he could make out the movements of a dark figure. Unhesitating, Alex took his third shot.

The glass in the front skylight shook for a moment, falling from the frame in one piece before shattering as it fell, a wave breaking. He now had a clear view as the rear skylight did the same, falling backwards into the alley behind the casino. There was no sign of Fat.

The jogger, earphones in, continued to leave her footprints across the snowy bridge. Clouds of vapour poured from her mouth.

A couple were now sitting outside, drinking coffee in the snow. No, not coffee; red wine. The waiter brought them blankets to keep their legs warm.

The tourist coach outside the Four Seasons had been replaced by a Porsche. A man, also ponytailed, got out, along with a woman who clearly didn't care if her legs got cold.

The Momotaro waiter emerged from the hotel, hurrying to light a cigarette.

Alex packed away his gun, made his way down a fire escape on the side of the building, pulled on a black woollen hat, and raised the collar of his coat. He headed for the western side of Castle Hill, away from the river, then over a road and through a park. At the Budapest South train station he jumped onto a tram.

Twenty minutes later he crossed to the eastern side of the Danube again and made a call from a kiosk next to the city's iconic symbol, the Basilica of St. Stephen's. "Well?"

Tsar laughed. "Not seen the news? Some tourist managed to film someone jumping off the roof of a casino. The reporter wanted to know if he'd gambled away his return fare. Come and have a drink. My wife's hooked on your fried rice."

He didn't go. He took the subway to the western train station, heading for the next safe house. He spent the journey awake and jumpy, clutching the old Nokia that Tsar had let him keep.

Why Fat?

10

Taipei, Taiwan

THE CHIEF SENT WU to speak to Chiu's widow. The street in front of the house was filled with reporters and satellite trucks. As he approached the house, the grieving widow emerged to speak in front of dozens of microphones.

"I'd like to thank the Ministry of National Defence for my husband's posthumous promotion, the President for the flowers, and all the members of the public who have offered their sympathy." She bowed to the cameras, two children about the age of ten following suit. "But I do have one more thing to say. The Army and the Ministry owe me an explanation. Why was my husband killed? And where is his killer? I will not rest until I have the answers."

With that she turned and went inside, ignoring the shouted questions from the press.

Wu waited for the reporters to disperse and then made his way to the door.

⊕

"Ching-chih never discussed work with me, and I've got no idea what he was working on. You should be asking the Ministry. . . . Ching-chih didn't have enemies. He wasn't always popular at work, though; he liked to follow the rules. Maybe you should ask the Ministry. . . . It's obvious Ching-chih was murdered. Don't go thinking the police can smear his name like the Ministry. . . . He got a phone call from an old commanding officer before he died. They argued, but I don't know about what. He never spoke about work. . . . I don't know which officer. Ask the Ministry. Check phone records. Have you found his mobile yet? He died almost a week ago. Don't keep telling me you're 'actively investigating'. The police, the Ministry — you're as bad as each other!"

Wu travelled across the city to Zhongshan North Street, not stopping for muffins or coffee, to ring the second doorbell of the day. No answer, but a question from behind the door: "Who are you looking for?"

The woman he'd seen smoking in the fourth-floor window the day before was sitting in the small streetside park. She was still smoking.

"Detective Wu, Criminal Investigation Bureau. At your service."

They bought convenience store coffees and sat by the road.

"I can't talk to you. That other man, Chiu Ching-chih, got promoted to major general after he was killed. Do you know what that means?"

"No."

"That means a major general's pension and bereavement pay. The Ministry is treating it as death in the line of duty. But if my husband killed himself, there's no pension. Not even life insurance."

Wu nodded.

"I'm begging the Navy to show some mercy and not record it as a suicide. But they won't listen. Even his best friends ignore me. That's up to the police, they say. So, Detective Wu, my future and the future of my two children are in your hands."

Wu was careful not to nod again.

"He never argued with anyone. The Navy wanted him to do more training so he could become a commissioned officer. He refused, said he was happy as a non-com. That's not the kind of man who makes enemies."

Kuo's widow fell silent. Wu thought it might be his turn to talk, but missed his chance.

"None of that rubbish in the papers, about him meeting a lover, is true. I know him better. He never stayed away longer than he had to; he'd come home as soon as he could and take our son out to play basketball. He loved to cook. I hardly set foot in the kitchen —"

"As far as the police are concerned, there was no lover," Wu told her.

"Then what did happen?"

"Mrs. Kuo, did your husband know Chiu Ching-chih?"

"Not as far as I know."

"Was he involved in procurement at all?"

"Of course not. He was a petty officer."

Wu thought that was all, until something else came to mind. "He had a tattoo on his arm. Do you remember it?"

"*Family*. He got that when he was seventeen or eighteen. A bunch of them from school got them, because they were as close as family. All that 'one for all, live and die together' nonsense. You know what young men are like."

Wu was due back in the office for a call with Egghead, but Mrs. Kuo showed no sign of going home. She lit another cigarette and offered one to Wu. "Detective, he couldn't have killed himself."

Except maybe with the cigarettes, Wu thought.

By two that afternoon Wu was in the office, looking at an image of Egghead on a computer screen. The hospitality of the Rome police seemed impressive: Egghead was slurping through a large bowl of Chinese noodles, a bottle of red wine sitting to the side.

"Luckily a cleaner at the station found the suspect's wig and clothes. He was disguised as a foreigner."

"Anything from the station cameras?"

"Here, take a look." The video Egghead sent over was clearer than the last. An Asian man, facing away from the camera and drinking coffee, clad in a black jacket and hiking boots and carrying an Adidas holdall.

"Where'd he go?"

"Took a train to Naples."

"Anything from there?"

"No. He got off along the way, crossed the platform to come back to Rome, and then we lost him. We're assuming he kept heading north. The police here are going through video from other stations, and I've just been going along with that. You should come sometime and see how they do things, Wu. They're almost as good as us."

"You can write up a report when you get back: a comparative study of investigative practices in Italy and Taiwan."

"Good idea. And that reminds me, I need to update the Chief on my progress. Could you type something up? Don't make that face; you type faster than I do. Tortoises type faster than I do. I'll bring you back some Italian ham and red wine. I'll even spend some hard-earned cash on a silk scarf for your wife. Something for the whole family."

The first promising lead was a video shot by some tourist that had ended up on the news: a café waiter's scream, Chou Hsieh-he's body slumping to the floor, his hand brushing against an English girl, which caused another scream, and then a chain of screams as the seven friends she was travelling with saw Chou's corpse. And then chaos in the square.

A Taiwanese tourist, a Miss Zhao, happened to be taking a 360-degree selfie at that point, spinning with selfie stick in hand. She caught the crowd as some crouched, some fell prone, and one man — just one man, a large American — made his way towards an alley. No concern for the screaming girls, neither rushing nor dawdling, as if bound for an appointment he was in good time for.

"How do you know he's American?"

"Shorts. Only the Americans wear shorts on holiday."

"Only Americans wear shorts on holiday?"

"More than the Europeans, I mean."

The local police's first port of call had been the hotel by the alley entrance, the Hotel Relais Fontana di Trevi, where they inquired about the whereabouts of the guests. Of three travelling alone, a Mr. A was found drinking in the hotel bar; a Miss B contacted the police that evening, had a good alibi, and could not recall the Asian man the police asked her about. Only Mr. C could not be found. The police searched his room: empty. Walls and floor still damp after being wiped clean, not even a fingerprint left. A professional.

A copy of Mr. C's passport, taken at check-in, was sent to the Korean embassy and quickly declared a fake. So no fingerprints, but a sample of handwriting from the signature in the hotel register, a sloppy English scrawl.

Meanwhile, other officers were at Roma Termini, collecting security camera footage, when a cleaner reported finding clothes in a garbage bin. Interviews with train staff led to a conductor who reported seeing some kind of temporary Chinese-character tattoo stuck to a toilet wall. Egghead was able to identify it: *zen*.

An alert was sent to every hotel in Rome. The Hotel Tokyo, a backstreet guesthouse behind the station, reported a guest who had disappeared without settling up, leaving a suitcase behind. No passport copy had been taken, but the receptionist remembered that the room had been booked by phone a day in advance by a woman speaking English. The police were working on tracing that call.

The Hotel Tokyo had only one security camera, at its entrance. It had captured an image of the suspect's back, no more. And a bicycle had been reported stolen from outside the hotel that day.

Of most interest was an empty suitcase left behind a newspaper kiosk at the Florence bus station. The kiosk owner had spotted it when closing up and reported it as a potential terrorist bomb. And so the police obtained security footage from the Florence bus station.

To date four images of the suspect had been found. All fuzzy, and all from the side or back.

"And here ends the report. What do you reckon, Wu?"

"He's Taiwanese."

"How do you figure?"

"The tattoo from the train. The cartoon bear logo on the case from the Hotel Tokyo — that's a Taiwanese make. And the victim was Taiwanese."

"That's what I thought. Let's try a harder one." Egghead slurped up some noodles. "Where do you find a sniper in Taiwan?"

"The Army."

"It's a pity you're retiring, Wu, with that brain."

"Don't forget to stop eating now and then to breathe, or you'll end up with brain damage. And I'll just let you lie in the hospital, because I don't have time to come in and turn you off. I'll see what I can find out from the Army. You send me over a nice clear photo of the suspect."

A few minutes later Wu received three photos: a rear shot from the train station in Rome; a side shot from the bus station in Florence, but without enough face to be useful; and a selfie of Egghead, noodles hanging from his lips.

His email pinged again. A new file, several photos: a corpse face-down in snow; the corpse rolled onto its back; a closeup of the face; a rifle broken in two. And a note from Egghead: *Asian male, fell from a building in Budapest. A sniper. If this is our suspect we're out of luck.*

But who killed the killer?

11

Telč, Czech Republic

SEVERAL TRAINS LATER, Alex arrived in the Czech Republic. It was dark by the time the local train from Brno dropped him in Telč. A tiny town. The station opened onto a divided highway, much like Taiwan's provincial routes. The sky was black, the pavements white with snow. Cars sprayed slush as they passed. He took care not to slip, and so almost missed the gate into the old town centre.

It was not the grand city gate he had been expecting, more of an archway between buildings. The view changed as he passed through: an oval town square dating back to the Middle Ages, surrounded by Renaissance-style buildings.

According to Ironhead, relations between the Chinese nationalist government and Germany had been good before the Second World War. Large quantities of German equipment were purchased, and there was talk of Germany dispatching military advisors and fitting out forty infantry divisions. Property was purchased in Europe to accommodate officials travelling back and forth. Then Hitler allied with Japan, and China declared war on Germany.

After the war the nationalists were defeated by the communists and fled to Taiwan. The government properties in Europe were taken over by intelligence agencies, and more were acquired during the economic boom of the 1970s. The existence of those properties was a state secret, missing from any official ledger. And with the end of martial law, the advent of democracy, changes of government, and a rapid turnover in intelligence chiefs, the buildings soon disappeared even from the unofficial ledgers. They were known to only a select few and very rarely used. Somehow those properties became safe houses for intelligence agents.

Risk of exposure meant that a stay of no more than three nights was permitted at any one safehouse. The attack in Manarola meant Alex's cover was blown, so he had to keep moving. But for how long? Would it ever be safe to return?

The safe house was tucked down a small lane, the surrounding houses mostly unlit. Barely six thousand people lived there, and most of those outside the old town. Tens of thousands visited during tourist season, but in winter the town was deserted.

The safe house was the upper apartment of a two-storey building, more welcoming than the place in Budapest. A stove in the kitchen, a cushioned cover on the toilet seat for warmth, a curtain on the shower, even flowers, albeit wilted, in a vase on the table. The front door opened onto the living room, which led to two bedrooms. Alex automatically planned escape routes, pushing open windows at the back of the house. A lake or river, no boats visible.

The apartment downstairs was empty, the owner perhaps in Brno for the winter.

A wooden rack on the back of the front door held a number of local tourist maps. Telč's old town lay on a peninsula, connected to the south by the archway he had come through. Lake to the east and west, a narrow channel to the north, crossed by a bridge. Too far. If things went wrong, he'd have to get wet.

A remote town, empty in winter, and an obviously foreign face. Not ideal. Ironhead would not be impressed. And surrounded by water on three sides — dead ground. Where was the next safe house?

Not under the bed. Not in the pillowcases. Nowhere. He boiled some water; the Darjeeling tea bags in a box on the table smelled fresh enough. He fired up the stove and took cheese, ham, and bread from the fridge to make a toasted sandwich.

Tea and the sandwich helped him relax. He looked again at the rack behind the door. Alongside the local maps and brochures was an English guide to Poland. He read as he ate, but most of the pages were missing. The section on Warsaw had been left, though, and beside the map of the city an address had been written in Polish.

He rearranged the back room to his satisfaction, turned off the light, and crept down the staircase. The door to the lower apartment stood to the left of the main door. He tested it, then pulled a Swiss army knife from his back pocket and picked the lock.

Nobody home. Not for months, judging by the cold and the smell of mould. A different layout from upstairs, with only one large bedroom towards the back. Alex dragged the mattress and blankets into the living room. Cold as it was, he wouldn't be able to hear movement outside if the window was closed.

He looked at his Nokia. Should he get in touch with Taipei, ask what his next move should be? He had to know how Fat had ended up in Budapest.

———

"Soldiers should read books when they have free time, not chase after girls in clubs. You'd get too used to that. Who wants to hold a cold, hard rifle after a soft, warm body?"

Stifled laughter.

"There was a man once by the name of Ji Chang, a pupil of master archer Fei Wei. Fei Wei told him that before learning archery, he must learn to focus. Ji Chang caught a louse, tied it to a roof beam with a hair from an ox's tail, and watched it every day until it came to seem as broad as a cartwheel. And then he shot that louse — one arrow, to the belly."

Ironhead squinted at the barrel of a gun.

"If you enlisted for the sake of a job and you're happy to man a guard post and draw your wages, that's fine by me. But if this is a calling, you need focus. Focus until a louse seems as big as a cartwheel, you hear? And whose gun is this? See that rust? I don't want to hear it. Confined to base for a week, and no visitors."

———

Alex let his eyes adjust to the dark before reconnoitering the rest of the apartment. A simpler kitchen than upstairs, with a smaller table, separated from the living room by a wooden partition. In the living room, an old-style television, short and squat, and a hi-fi with cassette player. The fridge in the kitchen appeared empty until he spotted two bottles of wine in the bottom drawer. He made himself at home and opened one.

As expected, not far off from vinegar. That was disappointing. Alex sat down to relax long-tense muscles. Something didn't make sense. Where had the fresh cheese and ham upstairs come from?

Back upstairs he placed a pillow under the blankets and shifted a clothes rack to beside the window. He assembled the svu and left it by the clothes rack.

Back downstairs to an old laptop he'd seen by the bed. No Wi-Fi; it needed to be connected to the phone line. Would it work? It did. He bent over the ancient Acer, struggling to get the machine to respond to his commands. Thankfully no password was needed, but he knew no Czech. It was several minutes before he managed to bring up an English-language news page.

He was right. Fat had been found in an alley behind the casino in Budapest. There were three photos: Fat's body lying in the snow; his battered face, eyes bulging; a broken M82A1 sniper rifle. Again the question: Why Fat?

He tried a Taiwanese page. The assassination in Rome had been the lead story for days. He settled down to read. Chou Hsieh-he, a military advisor to the President —

That was not possible. He'd been ordered to kill a presidential advisor? Had he got the wrong man?

He found the photograph he'd been given, now heavily creased. It was the right man. But things had gone very, very wrong.

PART TWO

家, now translated as "family," has a simple definition in the Shuowen Jiezi, a Han Dynasty dictionary dating back to the second century CE: "to reside." The even earlier Erya, which dates back to the third century BCE, describes 家 as "that which is inside the walls of a home." The former is a verb, the latter a noun. A number of 家s can join to form a city state or a nation state, and so the character is found in both those words: 邦家 and 國家. Without 家, there can be no nation. 家 implies warmth, intimacy, and marriage. An ancient poem speaks of the plight of a young spinster: "I alone have not been wed (家) and fear the loss of youth." 家 can also refer to the conscience. So, in a sense, no matter how alone you may be, you carry a family with you.

12

Taipei, Taiwan

THE POLICE IN ROME seemed to be keeping Egghead well informed as well as well fed. He sent Wu another set of photos: images from the autopsy of the Budapest sniper.

The Hungarian pathologist confirmed the cause of death as a broken neck resulting from the fall. No bullet wounds. A broken M82A1 sniper rifle was discovered at the scene; bullets and empty shells were found on the rooftop. The shells belonged to the deceased's weapon; the bullets were identified as Russian-made 7.62 mm rounds, as used in the Dragunov SVU.

"Snipers on both sides now, Wu. It's getting exciting. Do you think we'll get to be in the movie?"

The other sniper's position had been identified: the roof of a hotel across the river. No shells found, only a rapidly filling outline in the snow.

So the shooter on the east bank of the river had, despite freezing conditions, clambered out of a skylight and hauled his M82A1 up the thirty-degree slope of the roof to lie on snow-covered tiles. The other sniper, on a hotel rooftop on the west bank of the river, had a Russian-made svu. A gun-fight across six hundred metres of Budapest sky.

"Does that still count as urban warfare? Or is it air-to-air?"

"If I told you to shut up during a video conference, would it be cyber-warfare?" Wu retorted.

"You shut up and think. Is that how you'd settle a grudge? Why not make it personal, face-to-face, a switchblade each? Worried about the laundry? It's bizarre. Anyway, Wu, how hard can it be to track down snipers trained by the Taiwan-ese army?"

"No trouble at all for you, if you're sitting on your ass in Rome eating pasta and ordering me to do the running about."

"Ah, Wu, you'll miss me when you retire."

"I think we'll find they're both Taiwanese army–trained."

"That's more like it, Wu."

No authentic Italian pasta for Wu. He took a mouth-ful of Din Tai Fung shrimp fried rice from a takeaway box instead. A few tough days was no reason to let standards drop, after all. The two wonders of Din Tai Fung's fried rice: each grain of rice remained separate and firm to the bite; the eggs were fresh and deliciously . . . well, eggy.

"Seriously, Wu, I don't want to see you go. Why not think about signing up again? You're young enough. I'll back you up, tell them you're a gifted detective, the best we've got. Your retirement would be an irreplaceable loss to the nation."

Egghead did talk a lot of bullshit.

Taiwan had 100,000-plus serving or former soldiers, but surely only a few hundred had been trained as snipers. With a photo to go on, it wouldn't take long.

Wu sat in a meeting room at the Ministry of National Defence. Hsiung Ping-cheng walked in with a new and easy-going persona.

"What, the boy's not brought you afternoon tea? The chef here is from a five-star hotel. One of the advantages of military service — we offer an easy posting and get the pick of the bunch. A French macaron? Scallion pancake, made with Yilan's finest scallions? Something German, a pork hock?"

Another master of bullshit. "No need, thanks."

"Well, let me know if you change your mind. We're all on the same team."

"I'm grateful for your concern." Wu seemed to be bullshitting too.

Hsiung handed over several photographs, still warm from the printer. "We went through our records with the photos you sent and found the guy in Budapest. Chen Li-chih, nickname "Fat," Marine Corps, rank of sergeant when he was discharged. And he did do sniper training."

"And now?"

"Didn't take any of the training Veterans Affairs offers, and we've had no news of him. I've got people working on it, but it doesn't look promising. His national identification number and last known address are in the file. The police can find him more easily than we can; you've got better databases."

Wu thumbed through the file. If Hsiung thought he was going to get away with handing over a few sheets of paper, he was wrong. "Can you tell me more about the Army's sniper program?"

"Of course, Detective. Your esteemed bureau has our full support."

Wu foresaw a promotion to general in Hsiung's not-too-distant future. He had the same gift for bullshit that would see Egghead chief of a major bureau soon enough.

With pressure from above for a resolution, Wu got moving. He drove to the address in Chen's file. No sign of him. He'd rented the place three years before but moved out before the lease was up. A search of household registration information found nothing. He'd disappeared.

Chen had grown up in an orphanage, parents unknown, and had been adopted at thirteen by a Chen Luo. As for Chen Luo — retired soldier, last address a veterans' home in Hualien, died seven years before of respiratory failure, aged seventy-six.

Fat, as Wu now thought of him, had vanished the day he'd quit the Army. No recent address, no taxpayer records. Only a passport, obtained the year he'd been discharged.

Taiwan was an island. How could he just disappear?

Wu called Hsiung. "We can't find him. We need a closer look at your snipers. Can we meet?"

The Ministry offered what was meant to seem a helpful introduction but was as dull as it was unrevealing. There were three military units training snipers: the Navy's Special Operations Group, the military police's Special Services Company. and the Army's Guguan Special Training Centre. Snipers were selected over three stages: extra preparation during infantry training, sniper warfare training for those deemed suitable, and Guguan for the elite. Weapons used included the American-made M107A1 and M82A1 and the Taiwan-made T93. There were no current figures on how many had completed the full process, and no information about where those who left the military had ended up.

Back in the Ministry of Defence meeting room, Hsiung treated Wu to a hearty pat on the back. "Here this morning, here this afternoon — you're like a bad smell, Wu. I'll get you a desk and you can set up an office here."

"Captain Hsiung, three people are dead. I do not have time to sit at a desk."

"There's a gym! Some yoga might help."

"I would like to meet whoever's in charge of sniper training for each of the three units."

"Go home, take a hot bath, relax a little. I'll make some calls."

Wu noted that this was not a direct response to his request. "How long will that take?"

"They named the Hsiung Feng missiles after me," Hsiung said. "I'm supersonic."

There was still work to do. A tattoo had been visible in the pictures Egghead had sent. A tattoo Wu recognized.

By sunset Wu was meeting with a Professor Wang, an expert in oracle script. Academics seemed much more inclined to aid the police than the military. First, a freshly ground and fragrant coffee, then a Nantou oolong tea accompanied by red-bean rice cakes fresh from Mrs. Wang's steamer. The professor's wife smiled as she set down the tray. "I made them myself, Detective. No chemicals or anything."

Wu swallowed a sudden rush of saliva.

"My love, it's past five," the professor observed. "Perhaps two glasses of wine to boost our morale?"

Wu made a note to try that approach with his own wife.

Professor Wang was seventy-two and retired; he boasted that his good health was down to plenty of reading and no exercise. There wasn't just knowledge and beauty in the pages, he told Wu, but the secret to a life of contentment.

The professor turned on his computer and pointed to an image on the screen. "Do you know the origin of this character, Detective?"

Wu answered honestly. "Treat me as uneducated, Professor. Illiterate, almost."

Wang laughed. "You police, always joking." He traced the strokes of the character with a finger. "You can see at the top there is a roof with a chimney. Archaeologists have found chimneys on dwellings in Shaanxi dating back to 5,000 BCE. Two walls supporting the roof. Underneath the roof is an ancient character meaning 'pig,' pronounced *shi*."

"Well, I've learned a new character. *Shi*, pig." Wu summoned patience, ensuring that his brow wrinkled with smiles rather than scowls. The face of an eager student.

"Now, as for why the character for *family* is made up of a roof and a pig, there are two schools of thought. One view is that in ancient times people kept livestock on the ground floor and slept in the roof space, away from dangerous animals like wolves or snakes. And keeping pigs meant an agricultural society, with surplus grain. Once the food supply was assured, families could grow."

Roast pig's head, Wu thought. *Boiled pork, sliced. Salted pig's tail. Pig's kidneys. Stewed trotters.* The rice cakes were stimulating his appetite.

"The second school" — the professor was a very slow talker — "says the ancients noticed that pigs live in groups, with sows feeding their young. My granddaughter once saw piglets suckling at their mother on the television. Now she cries if we give her pork. So they thought the pig has a strong sense of love and used the character to represent that. If you don't have intimacy, you don't have a family."

Wu decided to change the subject. "A fascinating analysis. I just had a thought. Why do we drink milk from cows and goats but not from pigs?"

Wang guffawed and slapped the desk. "Here, have some more. There's pork fat in the rice cakes, you know. Keeps them from tasting bland. I don't get to chat with strangers too often at my age, much less policemen."

"I hope you find us worthy of education."

"Anyway, before Qin Shi Huang unified the writing system, it was all very complicated. Oracle script, bronze script — all those different ways of writing one character. Visit the Palace Museum if you get a chance. The characters on the Zhou Dynasty cooking vessels are nothing like those on the Shang earthenware. All the way up to Qin Shi Huang. He burned books and buried scholars, they say, but his script unification changed the course of history."

"So, thanks to Qin Shi Huang, we all used the same script. Then when Mao simplified the characters on the mainland, it changed again."

"Another fascinating analysis. Now look at these four pigs."

Four pictographs appeared on the computer screen.

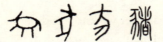

"I'll give you just a rough explanation — that wine's gone to my head. So, the first one's obvious: fat body, four legs. The orientation changes in the second; looks like it's up on its hind legs. Not because pigs evolved the ability to walk like us, but to make it neater when carved onto bamboo tubes. The third is the same, but more emphasis on the body. Up to this point, this is the only character for pig. The one we have now didn't exist."

"I see."

"The fourth is a pig on the left — standing again, four legs — with a stove to the right and a pot over it, steaming. That got simplified, and then the original *shi* character was added to the left, and that's the character we use today. No point in a pig without a pot to put it in. Or a stove. Language hasn't been kind to the poor beast."

Wu burst out laughing at that.

Another four characters appeared.

豦 豦 豦 家

"Next, let's take a look at *family*. There's a roof supported by two walls and a pig character inside. You can see that the first one's got a round stomach. The second one has a flatter stomach, but it's still clear. The third doesn't show the stomach, and the line across the top represents the head. It's seen from the side, so two legs are shown. The fourth is very similar to the character we know today."

"Four legs and a tail," Wu suggested, peering at the screen.

"You're right. I've never thought of that line as a tail."

Which of these characters was tattooed on Kuo's arm? The third, without the tail, Wu thought. Was the tattoo on Fat's body the same? And what were the chances of them both having the same character in the same script? That would be odd.

"So that's the origin of the character for family. A house has to have that familial affection, like the pigs, or it's nothing more than a building," Professor Wang concluded.

"So, a building full of love."

"You've got it, Detective!"

Wu declined Mrs. Wang's offer of dinner and hurried back to the office. As he was leaving, he noticed a framed photograph in their living room: a young couple with a small girl on a street full of English shop signs. Wang's son, perhaps, off in the United States, leaving Wang's house with fewer pigs, less love.

Back in the office, Wu's buttocks had barely hit the seat when a message came through from Hsiung, who had apparently been working at distinctly subsonic speeds: *Got it. The Guguan sniper trainer is Tu Li-yan, a lieutenant colonel. A messenger's bringing you his file. You owe me a drink.*

Sure enough, a manila envelope stamped CONFIDENTIAL lay on Egghead's desk. Inside, a file on Lieutenant Colonel Tu Li-Yan, commander and sniper trainer at the Guguan training centre. A handwritten note had been added to the last page: *Tu has files on all the snipers trained at Guguan. Told you we did things fast over here.*

He'd speak to Tu tomorrow. For the time being, Wu updated Egghead on his progress over a video chat in which Egghead was yet again eating.

"Italian pasta's similar to our noodles, but it's not the same. Firmer than noodles, chewier. I think I could live here."

Had Egghead decided he was working for the Culinary Investigation Bureau? Wu filled him in on Fat and Tu Li-yan, then got to the tattoos. "Fat had the *family* tattoo. So did Kuo, but Chiu didn't. If it was just the same word, you might call it coincidence, but they both used the same old-fashioned character. That's not coincidence."

"They're about the same age, they could know each other. Some kind of barracks brotherhood?"

"Kuo was thirty-eight, Fat thirty-six. Kuo grew up in Taipei, Fat in Chiayi — opposite ends of the island. Kuo was a navy sailor, Fat a marine. I don't see how they would have met."

A wet slurping noise came through the speaker. At least Egghead was showing the Italians how things were done in Taiwan.

Another mouthful. "Fat didn't kill Chou Hsieh-he. The Hungarians compared their bullets with the one from Rome. No match."

"And even if he did, then who killed Fat? The same man must have killed them both."

"No rush to decide that. The situation is dire, but Captain America and Ironman will stand beside us in our fight for justice." There were good reasons why Egghead was in charge. He had a talent for staying detached, and for making sure everyone else did too.

"Have we heard anything from the presidential office on what Chou was doing in Rome?" Egghead asked.

"The original story was that he was there on holiday," Wu told him. "Only took a reporter two hours to show that wasn't true. Then they said he was on a study tour, learning about the military in Europe."

Egghead held a forkful of pasta up to the camera. "Gorgeous, isn't it. All wriggly and shiny. Now, Taiwan's got only one ally in Europe, and I don't think Chou was having dinner at the Vatican."

"The Chief asked again what Chou was doing. It's —"

"A state secret."

"Clever. That's why you're in charge and I'm retiring."

"Don't moan. You've got the full pension coming."

Wu stepped away from his computer screen and walked over to a whiteboard covered in scrawled notes. He rubbed out an eight from the bottom right corner and replaced it with a seven. One week left to retirement.

He took a walk through the noise and dust of Zhongxiao East Road on the way home. He'd always thought retirement would mean being able to do what he wanted. But the call with Egghead had left him wondering if he could ever be happy without a job to go to. Not that he didn't have other options. A friend hoped to headhunt him for security work; two detective agencies had taken him out for dinner, with one promising a vice-president's title and salary. He liked the idea of being a private detective.

But he had two cases on the go: Kuo Wei-chung and Chiu Ching-chih. Plus two he was helping Egghead with: Chou's murder in Rome and the death of Chen Li-chih in Budapest. Was a week enough time? Wu had never complained about working twenty-hour days. And it felt as if policework was what kept his blood pumping, giving his vital organs reason to work. What would happen if he lost that thrill?

He crossed Dunhua Road and Fuxing South. He'd end up on Zhongshan North Street if he kept going. Thinking of Kuo's widow, he turned into a subway station and headed back to work. A report declaring Kuo murdered would save widow and children from a long battle with bureaucracy.

Just as he arrived, he received a message from the widow. *Detective Wu, has there been any change?*

He replied: *I'm classing it as murder*. Which made it sound a bit more immediate than was justified. First he had to go through the coroner's report and the statements taken at the scene, then come up with a way to track down the killer.

An immediate response: *Thank you*.

Wu recalled the sight of her blowing smoke from the fourth-storey window.

13

Telč, Czech Republic

WHY FAT?

The Ministry of National Defence had a program running that year, encouraging anyone up to the rank of major to acquire new skills. There were plenty of options: tae kwon do, boxing, swimming, diving, parachuting, outdoor survival, marksmanship. Alex had been a first lieutenant at the time, fresh from basic training and still clueless, though heading up a platoon and acting as deputy company commander. He didn't have the seniority to take advantage of the scheme, but Ironhead had asked for him personally, claiming he was a natural marksman.

Alex had heard that Ironhead put forward two newcomers: him and one other. He had called them both in for a pep talk that first morning. The memory of Ironhead's index finger jabbing at his nose as he spoke was still fresh. "I chose the two of you for one reason only: talent. Also, we're related."

Alex tried a sidewise look at Baby Doll, standing at attention beside him.

"Alex, your gramps was a big brother to me. I used to be scared of the water. He started me on the breaststroke, and by the time he was done I was the army's best swimmer. Baby Doll, your dad was like a brother to me, and I know how much you must miss him. I can't play favourites when we're training, but know that I promised your dad I'd look after you. Understand?"

Baby Doll had graduated from the Army Academy and had been assigned to electronic warfare operations at head-quarters. She had not expected to be summoned like this by Ironhead.

The sniper training course had an intake of fifty from the three branches of the military. Fat, a corporal in the marines, was among them. After three months most would return to their units, but ten would be chosen to stay on for a further three months and assignments to special ops or anti-terror teams. Alex and Fat made it into that final ten. Baby Doll returned to her original unit and entered officer training college the following year.

Alex had the bunk above Fat. He could feel the frame shake as he snored. He hated it at first but soon got used to it. The snoring became a lullaby — if he didn't hear it, he couldn't sleep.

The first day of training covered how to disassemble an M21. Alex was rushed and clumsy. Fat worked next to him, calm and methodical.

"Do what I do," Fat said. "Lay every piece in front of you as you remove it. Do it every time and it becomes habit, so you won't miss anything putting it back together."

The whole class was sitting on stools under the trees around the training ground. Baby Doll was on Alex's other side, nervous and copying his movements as closely as she could. Fat had spoken to him, but the message was for her.

"The trick to looking after your gun is the oil — not too much, not too little. The right amount looks oily but feels dry. Doesn't make sense at first, but it will."

Fat was a good man to know. He loved to sing, particularly Wu Bai's "Norwegian Wood." He never came back to base on a Sunday evening without food for everyone. In the evenings he'd find Alex and Baby Doll before lights out and take them to the target range to feed them beef pastries — his favourite — by moonlight. And he'd swallow down any of her leftovers.

Alex missed those days. Up, run, target practice, lunch, swim or tae kwon do, more target practice. No need to think about what to do with your time; just practise what they told you to practise. Any spare minutes could be spent telling jokes or chatting. Neither time nor need for worries.

Fat was the best sniper among them. Ironhead said his extra weight provided stability and his slow responses meant he was keeping his eyes open. "Remember, eyes open. If your eyes aren't open when you're pulling the trigger, how the hell are you going to see where the bullet lands?"

Ironhead was walking back and forth along the firing position, carrying a length of bamboo he used to poke at any trainees displaying imperfect posture. "Standard position: hands relaxed but firm on the gun; breath steady but prepared to stop; and absolutely no closing your eyes when you fire. If I spot you doing that, I'll clothespin your eyes open."

The bamboo stick clanged off Fat's helmet. "There are only three in this class that started out keeping their eyes open. Two of them because they're not scared of the noise, and Fat, whose eyes bulge so much his eyelids can't close."

Despite Ironhead's mockery, Fat was actually more focused than any of them. The barrel, the stock, his arms, his eyes at the sight — all one. Alex had asked him once how he was able to shoot so well with both eyes open. "I don't know what he's talking about. I close my left eye and keep the right open. Look, like this."

Regardless of how he tried, Fat was unable to close only one eye. Both open, both closed — those were the only options. A natural sniper.

Fat had an obvious affection for Baby Doll, as obedient to her will as to that of Ironhead. Alex was much the same. "Baby Doll's right," Fat would say, and Alex would nod vigorous approval. Fat made no secret of his affection. Alex kept his quiet.

"Of course I like her. Who couldn't like her?" Fat was sitting on the concrete slab covering the sewer at the back of the toilet block, blowing smoke rings into the air. "But that's as far as it can go. Look at us — no house, no savings. She's officer material. It's not even a Mercedes or a BMW picking her up at the gate, it's a Ferrari. I'm just going to enjoy her company before she gets married. And then it's 'Congratulations, all the best, and thank you for popping down from heaven to visit.' You like her too, don't you? Have you said anything? You've had three months. If you can't do it in three months, just keep quiet. Enjoy the three months of bliss like me, and be content. Getting your hopes up doesn't mean you get a chance."

Fat made it all sound so simple. He'd obviously given the matter some thought over those three months.

Baby Doll and the three other female trainees had struggled to keep up during the first week of training. Fat had slowed his pace on the runs, letting them catch up, then offering advice as he raised and lowered his M21: "Keep a count in your head: one-two, one-two. Don't look too far ahead, just at the ass of whoever's in front. That's what I do, stare at Alex's ass and count one-two, one-two. Try it and see if you can spot what's wrong. No buttocks! You can't trust a man like that. Now if you look at mine, that's a proper strong ass."

Fat moved to run in front of the four women as he spoke. Word went around later that he did indeed have the sexiest ass of the male trainees, buttocks pumping like pistons, left-right, left-right, one-two, one-two.

But Fat only had eyes for Baby Doll. By the eighth week two of the women had paired up with other trainees, and another was already engaged to a university sweetheart. Nobody felt fit to pursue Baby Doll. She stood apart, a goddess among trainee snipers.

Before training ended, Alex confessed his feelings. Baby Doll took his hand. He'd never forgotten her words: "Who knows what will happen after officer school? Why don't we just be good friends for now?"

He realized then why Fat had kept quiet. Speak up and you win or lose. Keep quiet and you always have hope. Fat's love for her was deeper than his own, Alex saw. Deeper than he could grasp.

At the final dinner she'd rushed into Fat's farewell embrace, eyes streaming, perhaps with sweat, perhaps with tears. Fat reddened, perhaps with alcohol, perhaps with love.

Alex recalled the eyes he'd seen on that morning in Budapest. Wide, bulging eyes. But he'd had no choice. Pull the trigger or plummet dead from the roof.

But why Fat?

Fat was still in the marines when Alex had left for the French Foreign Legion. A sergeant, but due for another promotion on next re-enlistment. Had he quit?

And how had Fat tracked him from Manarola to Budapest? There was no way he hadn't known who his target was. Fat had seen him in his sights and was still able to pull the trigger?

And why was Baby Doll handing out the orders? Where was Ironhead?

A noise outside. Alex closed the laptop and crept to the window. He could make out the silhouette of a small boat on the water outside. The boat was approaching, so slowly he was initially unsure it was even moving. He ignored it, listening for closer noises.

What was the number for the police here? 112? 911? 112, that was it, the standard for Europe. He dialled and set the phone aside.

He turned on the stove, not lighting the gas but letting it hiss away. He stripped, wrapped his clothes in plastic bags, and stepped out onto the windowsill, closing the window behind him. One jump and he'd slipped smoothly into the water. Freezing. How long could he last?

He had to move fast or the attacker would see through his plan. He submerged and swam to meet the boat. Sure enough, empty, a decoy to see if the apartment was occupied. The mooring rope at the stern had been cut.

Another underwater swim to the bank. On bare feet he snuck along the road, checking the hoods of parked cars.

The third was warm. In this weather, that meant it hadn't been parked long. His opponent's car.

No more time. He smashed the window, only noticing the key in the ignition as the glass shattered. Cursing, he opened the door and sped off, scraping along the sides of five other cars as he went, triggering a chorus of alarms. Bedroom lights turned on. He accelerated, then pulled in down the road when he had a view of the safe house.

One police car had arrived and another pulled up as he watched, the officers calling to each other. He looked at the window by which he had fled — open. Was his opponent equally keen on a midnight swim? No. Gunshots rang out. The police returned fire.

That took care of that. He started the engine, turned on the heater, and dried himself before dressing, scrubbing until his skin reddened. Still barefoot, he drove away.

The gunshots continued behind him, then an explosion. Flames illuminated the rear-view mirror. That'd be the gas.

Who was tracking him? He'd ditched the smartphone; he'd kept his eyes open on the way here. And who were they? Fat, this guy . . . Was there a third yet to come?

Alex knew there was no time to worry about who had just died in the gas explosion. Nor did he want to know. It might be another friend.

He recalled the first day of training. Ironhead leading the trainees on their five-kilometre run. His arms were failing, but Fat ran behind him, offering advice between huge breaths. "Concentrate your strength on one arm, then the other. Like you shift weight between your feet when at attention."

Alex had taken the advice and made the distance. His arms were limp and useless, but he finished, one of only eleven to do so.

Fat and Alex sat in the mess that day as the recruits who hadn't completed the earlier run made a second attempt, puffing around the training ground. Big white steamed buns, steaming-hot soy milk.

"I'll show you how to eat these. Eat the first bun with pickles. That'll get you eighty percent full. Then dip the second in sugar." Fat grinned through a mouthful of food. "I love sugar. Who doesn't, though."

Alex eased off the accelerator, realizing his speed had crept up. Not a good time for a conversation with the traffic cops.

He'd start dipping steamed buns in sugar, he thought.

He could see Fat's face. Two eyes, round and bulging. And he could see his own crosshairs between them and feel the trigger moving under his finger.

14

Taipei, Taiwan

WU WAS SAVED the trip to Guguan. Tu Li-yan was in Taipei and came into the office to offer his cooperation.

Tu had been in charge at Guguan for two years, prior to which there hadn't been an official sniper-training program. The training Fat had undergone had been arranged by a Colonel Huang Hua-sheng with special permission from the Ministry. Huang had trained three intakes over two years at a disused base in Pingdong. When Huang left the army, the training unit, never official, simply ceased to exist, though all the files were transferred to Guguan. Most of Huang's trainees had returned to their original postings, where some had been promoted and some had left the military. Others — those kept on for extra training — had carried on Huang's mission, becoming sniper specialists or sniper trainers themselves.

As for Fat, also known as Chen Li-chih, Tu didn't have much to say about him. One of the marines' best snipers, winner of several all-services competitions, and expected to re-enlist and be promoted before unexpectedly leaving the service. A talented soldier lost for no good reason. "Not much we can do, though," Tu acknowledged with a sigh. "Between his military pension and a job he'd have two incomes, his weekends free, and national holidays off. You can see why he left."

Tu didn't know anything about Chen's fellow trainees but offered to have a colleague locate the files and, if the Ministry didn't object, pass them along.

Wu, curious about what snipers could actually do, had questions. "From how far away can a sniper hit a target?"

Tu was in uniform, peaked hat in his lap and the two rows of decorations on his chest attesting to a glorious military career. He never relaxed. "That would depend on the weapon, the ammunition, the weather, and the skill and determination of the sniper."

He seemed willing to help. Wu pulled up the information from Budapest and Tu read it attentively. Meanwhile Wu decided to show the military a bit of hospitality and sent a colleague over to Julie's Café for coffee and cake. Julie took coffee more seriously than most men, as evidenced by her excellent java and miserable love life.

"Both experts," Tu commented, "shooting at that distance."

"Is there anything here an outsider might not notice?"

Tu sipped at his drink. "That's good coffee. Is it African?"

How am I supposed to know? Wu thought. *And when did the Taiwanese start caring where coffee comes from?*

Tu continued. "Chen had been out of the army for years, and his abilities would have suffered even after just a year without practice. You lose the feel for it very quickly unless you have extended combat experience. It was just the two snipers? No spotters you're aware of? They were professionals, practised, or they couldn't have made those shots. And the assassination in Rome: that's not just an expert, that's someone who is truly gifted. The news said there was sleet and nobody heard the shot. If it had been my operation, I'd have pulled the sniper out as soon as the sleet started. You risk failure when the environment turns against you. Better to pull back and wait for another chance. But he did it — with one shot."

"Forgive me, I'm no sniper myself. You're saying that —"

"I'm saying that if Chen did assassinate Chou, he'd been getting plenty of practice since leaving the marines."

"Is there anywhere in Taiwan he could have done that?"

"Nowhere open to the public. There are shooting clubs, but that's for Olympic events, air rifles, clay pigeons, short-distance shots. Not sniper training."

"And outside Taiwan?"

"There are shooting ranges in the Philippines. A forty-minute flight from Kaohsiung and you can fire as many bullets as you like."

All interesting, but not much help. "And Colonel Huang? What did he do after sniper training?"

"You'd have to ask the Ministry. I met him a few times. The Army had been grooming him for great things, but he passed up staff officer jobs at headquarters and the Ministry for combat command. There's a rule, though, that combat commanders spend time as staff officers at headquarters or group level, so they've got an overview of how the Army works. There was a rumour that Third Command smoothed that over."

"Third Command?"

"Military intelligence. Staffing is First Command, combat is Second, intelligence Third, logistics Fourth."

"He was an intelligence agent?"

"No, no," Tu corrected, waving a hand. "It's not the James Bond stuff you're thinking of. It's *military* intelligence. More like research, studying military tactics the mainland might use, that kind of thing. There's a different ministry bureau that does the 007 work."

"And why would an officer opt for Third Command?"

"Well, there's the possibility of being assigned overseas as an embassy military attaché."

"Is that good?"

"There's an extra stipend for overseas work. But if you go from Third Command to an embassy job, you're going to struggle to make it any higher than brigade commander."

"Was Huang ever a military attaché?"

"Not as far as I know. Joining Third Command doesn't make it automatic."

Wu took a chance on a sudden thought. "Forgive the personal question, but do you have any tattoos?"

Tu gazed back in surprise. "No, I don't. Just a birthmark on my scalp."

"Do many soldiers?"

"I suppose. The younger ones like to get something that looks cool."

"What are the most common types?"

Tu blinked. "Military insignia. Army Airborne Command has a winged parachute and a knife. Maybe someone gets drunk the night they quit and decides to get a souvenir tattoo."

"Are there a lot of tattoo parlours near the bases?"

Tu's concrete-hard face finally cracked into a smile. "Did you do military service, Detective?"

Did the police academy count?

Tu continued. "When you fill in the form on your first day, everyone exaggerates what they've done. Dishwashers claim they're chefs, and so on, hoping to get out of the physical training and sent to some easy posting. Anyway, there's bound to be some who were tattooists. So you find one and save some money."

Wu had hoped tattoo parlours might prove a fruitful line of inquiry. So much for that.

He saw Tu out. What now? He had reached a familiar point in the case: a good idea of who the culprit was and no idea of how to find him.

A message from Egghead: *The Czech police found a second sniper in some small town called Telč. An anonymous tip, a gunfight when police arrived. Details to follow.*

Yang, the coroner, must have gone mad. He was phoning Wu. "Hey, Wu, not retired yet? Let me buy you lunch."

"Sounds good. Let me know when."

"Will do. And I've got good news for you. A body's just come in from Songshan. There's a tattoo on the arm."

"*Family?*"

"You're obsessed, Wu. You need some time off. Go to karaoke, let a pretty girl sit in your lap. It's a dragon, on the back and reaching around to the chest."

"So? Every gang member in the city's got a dragon or a tiger somewhere."

"You're right, they love their tattoos. And you're in charge of investigating organized crime. If the gangs have got dragons and tigers tattooed all over, who's to say there isn't a *family* tattoo in there as well?"

Yang's suggestion got Wu moving, his coat trailing as he hurried to Julie's Café, second road down from the office.

Julie's dad had been a gangster since he was thirty, and he'd done three years during the crackdowns of the eighties. Retired now, he was an avuncular figure sitting by the door of his daughter's café like some guardian spirit. He'd know a thing or two about gang tattoos. Could you retire from organized crime?

Julie had never married. The café, the tabby sunbathing outside, her father snoring in a chair alongside the cat — that was Julie's life.

"Long time, no see, Wu. Don't tell me you've gone healthy. It's your vices that keep me in business."

"Just been busy. I'll have a coffee. African."

"You'll drink what you get. No fancy menu here."

Regardless of the season, Julie always dressed the same. Waist cinched in to emphasize hips and bust, short skirt, tights, and high heels that made her totter. The sexiness of the 1980s preserved as a relic for the twenty-first century.

"I hear you're retiring." Julie put down his coffee and sat opposite him, clearly intending to stay there until another customer rescued him.

"Seven days," Wu said, checking his watch. "Or six days and six working hours."

"You're really going? Men should never retire. It just annoys their wives."

"Annoying? Me?"

"An old man sits at home all day, nothing to do. Can't get him into bed because of his prostate, can't take him for a walk because of his joints. Won't go to the movies because it's expensive and there's a television at home. Wants breakfast in the morning, then it's the paper, then it's television, lunch, a nap, and dinner. And then he wants to know what's for breakfast the next day. Sound annoying?"

"Does sound like it," Wu allowed with a grin.

"Have a word with your boss. Stay on. You can stay until you're sixty-five, can't you?"

"I'd still have to retire then."

"That's different. Then you've got your bus pass, free health care. You'll be at the hospital all the time, bothering the doctors about your blood pressure and your sleeping tablets. Your wife'll be fine."

The bell over the door rang. Wu's saviour — another customer.

Wu carried his coffee out to the sidewalk. Julie's dad sat in his chair, enjoying a rare patch of sunshine with a woollen blanket — purchased by Julie on a trip to the States — over his knees. Eyes closed, motionless.

"Help yourself to a cigarette, Detective. But I'll tell you now, I've been straight for fifteen years, ever since the diabetes kicked in."

"Just here for a chat."

"Now you're misleading the public. Cops drink and gamble when they've got free time. They don't chat with us old folk."

Wu tried not to laugh.

"And don't stifle a laugh like that, it's bad for the lungs. So, what can I do for you?"

"A simple question. Which gang has *family* tattoos?"

No reply. Eyes still closed. A mole on the left side of his jaw twitched.

"*Family*, oracle script pictograph," Wu added.

"Oracle script, pictographs — all just tattoos. Doesn't ring any bells, but I can ask around."

"I'd be grateful. A nice Scotch in return?"

"A present from the police? Here I am, out of the game, being an upstanding citizen, and you're trying to turn me into a snitch. That'd ruin my good reputation if it got out."

"An official commendation for assistance with an investigation?"

"Nothing, thank you. Come for a coffee when you can, keep my girl in business."

"That's easily done."

"I'll be in touch tomorrow whether I've heard anything or not. I know the police — not good for much, but very good at bothering folk till they get what they want."

Wu went inside to settle up, leaving the old man sunning his eyelids. Julie pulled him in for a hug. "Remember, don't stay at home bothering your wife. Come talk to me. Retirement will make you old if you're not careful."

Still plenty to do. No rest for Wu while Egghead was absent.

Reports came in of shots fired on the expressway. A police car whisked Wu to the scene. An old story: racing, the loser taking a couple of shots at the winner, missing but sending the driver into the barrier. The shooter had sped off but had been stopped at Linkou Junction. Three in the car, three guns sighted so far.

There were already a dozen police cars on site, from Taipei, New Taipei, Traffic. All surrounding a black BMW reported stolen three months earlier. A temple charm hanging from the mirror. Dashcam. Two bags of pills on the dashboard, most definitely not prescribed by any pharmacist.

Wu stood behind the ranks of police cars and shouted, "You fuckers in the car, put your guns down and give yourselves up! Three minutes, starting now!"

The other officers stared at Wu, too stunned to challenge him.

"Fifty-nine, fifty-eight . . ."

"Fuck off! It hasn't even been thirty seconds yet!" Someone in the BMW could count.

"Thirty-five, thirty-four . . ."

Wu took a Type 65 rifle from the man next to him, checked the magazine, and flicked off the safety. "Eight, seven, six, five . . ."

Wu strafed the bottom of the car, sending twenty rounds bouncing off its wheels and underside.

"We surrender!" Five guns were thrown from the windows; three men climbed out. Wu peered into the BMW as the handcuffs were going on. Drugs again, ten bags of red and white pills. Where were all the drugs and guns coming from?

Every police officer on the scene — Taipei, New Taipei, and Traffic, wielding rifle, pistol, or mobile — was staring awestruck at Wu and his borrowed Type 65. *If you're going to be a cop, act like a cop.* That was Wu's philosophy.

He tossed the weapon to a passing uniform and, catching the eye of the officer in charge, gestured towards the plastic bags of pills. "All on drugs. Not thinking straight. Just needed a scare."

It was almost five in the afternoon by the time he got back to the office, and by rights he should have been finished for the day. But Tu Li-yan had kept his word. A list of snipers trained at the same time as Fat was waiting in his inbox. The papers, television, and websites were all featuring a picture of Fat from his army days, and the switchboard was busy with people who knew him offering info.

And now the shit jobs. He divided the list of names among five juniors. Anyone who couldn't be found or who'd gone overseas would warrant a further look. Wu himself sat down to sift through the callers. There wasn't much information to be gleaned, but one lead was promising. An old army buddy of Fat's claimed to know his girlfriend, who ran a backstreet karaoke joint in the Yonghe district.

Yonghe was small but crammed full. Thirty-nine thousand people in a square kilometre, officially, and over forty thousand when those in illegally rented rooms were factored in. Not many places in the world packed them in like Yonghe.

It took Wu's driver fifty minutes to get him there over the Yongfu Bridge. Cars were backed up getting onto the bridge, cars were backed up getting off the bridge. Wu lay on the back seat in a dreamless sleep.

MIMI'S KARAOKE, SNACKS AND DRINKS the sign said above the door. A place for the local retirees to pass the time and have a singsong. Eighty for a beer, a hundred for fried noodles. Nothing flashy.

Mimi herself caught him at the door. "Detective Wu? Let's talk here. You'll scare off the customers."

Mimi looked to be a little over thirty, hair blow-dry puffy with a single green streak. Younger than the women who usually ran these local joints. Pink Chanel suit (fake) over a white strappy top; bare, pale calves. Cleavage proudly displayed despite the cold, but that did not prevent Wu from noting the worry on her face.

"You've seen the news about Chen Li-chih?"

"What's happened to Fat?"

His own girlfriend hadn't heard? Wu toned down how he'd died, telling her only that he'd been killed in Budapest.

"That's not possible. It can't be." Mimi held her face in her hands. "He was a good man. Who'd want to kill him?"

She led him inside out of the cold, past a dozen or so old men and women taking turns on the microphone, into a cramped kitchen. Mimi ran the place single-handed, Wu realized. Greeting customers as they came in, singing a song or two herself to get things started, cooking up simple meals and pouring drinks. *No money after rent for a cook*, he thought.

"This place was his idea. He pays the rent."

"To give you a new start? Keep you off the drugs?"

Mimi blew smoke towards the extractor fan.

"Sorry." Sometimes Wu hated what being in the police had done to him. Why go for the weakest spot first? "It can't have been easy, getting clean."

"I used to work as a hostess when I was younger. Drank too much one night and passed out. Two customers, nasty types, managed to get me out of the building. I woke up as they were trying to get me into a motel, realized something was wrong, but they wouldn't let me go. Fat was walking past. He rescued me."

"When was that?"

"Five, six years back."

"Does Fat have any family, close friends?"

"He was an orphan. He never talked about anyone."

"So you've been together since then?"

Mimi didn't answer, head lowered, shoulders shaking. Wu watched her. The extractor fan ground on.

He made it home at 11:17 p.m., his wife waiting up at the dining table. She gestured for him to sit. "No more dumplings for you. I'll make you noodles with your dad's stew and bamboo shoots."

"He's been back?" He'd completely forgotten about his dad.

Wu changed, poured himself a drink, and sat down in front of the promised noodles. His wife sat opposite him, cupping her chin in her hands and showing no signs of turning on a Korean soap. "I think we should talk," she said.

"About my dad? I'll have a word with him tomorrow."

"Good. But that's not all."

"What else?"

"What are you going to do after you retire?"

A lifetime of questions in the time it takes to eat one bowl of noodles, Wu thought. *What to do about my dad? What to do about my wife?*

His wife reassured, Wu looked in on his son. "Your dad's inviting you for a nightcap again."

His son held up his mouse and answered through it. "Mum'll have one with you."

"Keep staring at the screen like that and your eyesight will be worse than mine."

"At least I'm still young at heart."

Why had he had a son? Wu couldn't recall. "Is it a pain having your granddad here every day?"

"It's okay."

It had been years since he'd set foot inside his son's room. There was hardly space for him to do so: computers, wires, extension cords. "Come find me if you get hungry."

"Aren't you going to bed?" his son asked, face still fixed on the screen.

"Got work to do. Don't stay up too late."

The mouse shook head and tail.

15

Eastern Europe, Route E59

SOMEONE HAD BETRAYED HIM. He had two choices: fight and win or give in and run.

He'd run already. He was tired of running. Had this new guy they sent seen the gun he'd left? Bet he hadn't expected the old phone-the-cops trick. Had the cops caught him or had he died at the scene? Regardless, Alex knew he needed to protect himself. Baby Doll had sold him out, that was clear. Or, more optimistically, someone was manipulating her to get to him.

None of it made any sense. Not even Ironhead had known about his bolthole in Manarola. And he hadn't been in touch with Ironhead, much less Baby Doll, since joining the French Foreign Legion. They must have been tracking his phone. But she had warned him to lose the Nokia. He hadn't. Was that how they'd found him again? Or had Baby Doll given the attacker the safe-house address? If so, why?

Baby Doll was in army officer training when he'd left. She'd taken him out for dinner, a Western-style place, fancier than anywhere he'd been before. Huge T-bone steaks, wine at four thousand a bottle. Fat declined the invitation, claiming he couldn't get leave. Alex knew he just didn't want to see her.

They had lingered over the meal. She knew of his plan to join the Foreign Legion, the only one who did except Ironhead. She made no mention of it as they ate, but as they were parting she made clear that she knew. "Be careful out there. Remember when I said we could start again when I graduated officer training?"

Those words had given him hope. Two years of chewing them over and he'd decided it was just her way of telling him to take care, not to play the hero. Simple concern for a friend.

They had not spoken for five years. And now Fat was dead.

Alex hadn't understood why Ironhead chose him. "Wouldn't this suit Fat better?" he asked.

"He'd be good, but I'm cheating a bit. Your gramps and I were good friends, remember?"

Ironhead had never explicitly stated that Alex remained on the payroll of some unit or other back home. But every three months money arrived in his bank account. Orders came only from Ironhead, presumably to keep his actual employers and the government safe from involvement. But he knew that only the Military Intelligence Bureau kept agents in the field.

But if Ironhead had passed over Fat, how did Fat end up taking shots at Alex? Who was he working for?

Fat.

The Czech police would be setting up roadblocks soon. He sped up, figuring a hundred kilometres should get him clear. The highway led north, towards Prague. Not good, he thought; the police would close that route first. Can't have terrorists reach the capital. A U-turn and Alex was heading south on the E59, bound for Vienna. With his face, he had to be where the tourists were. Then he'd work on getting back to Italy.

He thought back to the two people sharing the table with Chou that day in Rome. An older Asian man and a big European in a fur-lined coat. If he could find them, perhaps he'd learn why someone wanted him dead.

The three men hadn't met out of friendship, Alex guessed. A business meeting. The Asian man, the one whose eyebrows arched like Chow Yun-fat's when he grinned, was likely Taiwanese. That'd make him easier to find. And from there he could track down the foreigner.

A blizzard struck as he sped through some anonymous town. Too good an opportunity to let pass. Alex parked and searched the car. Some receipts, a bottle of water, a greasy sandwich wrapper. No clues to the assassin's identity. He pocketed the receipts and abandoned the car.

He swept the snow from the driver's window of an old Lada. The car and the snowdrift on the roof spoke of an older driver who hadn't been out in a few days. And the fresh snow would keep him indoors tomorrow, hopefully. With a bit of luck it wouldn't be noticed missing.

He was in Austria by daybreak. He took a little time to find a Vietnamese-run shop. They were the safest option, not ones to gossip and no fans of the authorities, and they sold everything you might need.

Resupplied, Alex took a closer look at the receipts. The assassin had set out from the airport in Vienna and stuck to the expressways, spending a night in somewhere called Znojmo on the way. Looked like someone with a single task: to kill Alex.

Alex dialled a number on the Nokia as he devoured a banh mi sandwich. Number unavailable. Too risky to hold on to it anymore. He pried loose the back of the phone and spun the SIM card into the back of a passing truck. His next call, from a public telephone, passed through five different people before he finally reached the weary voice he wanted.

"Yes?"

"Necktie, it's Alex."

A long silence, a wary response: "I'm not sure how happy I should be. Time to repay a debt?"

"Afraid so."

Back in the car he changed plans; no need for Vienna now. He stopped in another town to change cars again.

Back on the road, wipers sweeping back and forth cleared oncoming snow from the glass. He had forgotten to check the tank; he was running out of fuel and couldn't risk filling up — there'd be cameras. Yet another car was needed. Exhaustion dragged down his eyelids.

16

Taipei, Taiwan

THE TV NEWS SAID the United States had agreed to sell Taiwan the Avenger surface-to-air missile system but was holding out on the M1A1 tank and submarines. Who would be dealing with the Yanks now that Chiu was dead?

In Egghead's absence, Wu was honoured by a meeting with Egghead's own boss, the bureau chief. Wu explained his theory: that the deaths of Chiu and Kuo were linked to some secret hidden within the military, and cracking the case would require figuring out what that secret was. The Chief made no comment, but his expression told Wu what he already knew. Without orders from the President or the Ministry, the military wouldn't talk.

A dead end. Back to a detective's old tricks: put the victim's life back together piece by piece and see what looked odd. He couldn't get any more info from Hsiung on Chiu and Kuo, but they couldn't stop him from working on Chen. *Build a picture of the man's life and there'll be a clue in there,* Wu told himself.

His wife went to bed at midnight, ceding control of the dining table. Egghead's face shone from the laptop screen, flanked on either side by Wu's files. What was he eating now?

"Can you believe it? I knew you could get bubble tea in London, but it turns out you can get it in Rome too. Got it for free because I'm from Taiwan. And they told me about this Taiwanese bun place."

A meat-stuffed bun gyrated about the screen as Egghead bit into it. "Pork belly," he reported through a mouthful. "Real Taiwanese cook."

"Let me guess. The bun people told you about an oyster omelette place."

"Do you ever stop thinking about food? Anyway, no. It was a stewed meat place, Taiwanese-run."

"Hence why you're stuffing your face."

"Not my fault they're so hospitable. And I'm spreading it around: they sent a load of buns and bubble teas for the station. The Italians are loving the pork belly. Didn't used to be much of a fan myself, but it's grown on me today. Let me tell you why: I hadn't noticed how well the cilantro and peanuts go together, or how sticky the meat gets in the cooking wine. Then you put it in this white bun. It's rich, but there's a sweetness as well. I guess I shouldn't be so picky about my food. I miss out on a lot of good stuff, and that's a waste. Not eating yourself? What did your wife make you tonight?"

Wu waved a bottle at the screen.

"That's what you need, Wu, a woman who doesn't mind you drinking at home. Of course, if you had something to go with it —"

"Stop gibbering and wipe your chin. You'll get my screen dirty."

"See, it's like I'm in the room with you."

"Right. I've got something. I'm going to start with Chen Li-chih, also known as Fat."

"Old-style?"

"Just putting the pieces together."

"You go first. You've got more to work with there."

"Right. And please back off from the camera before I get sick." Wu made a show of arranging his notes and began his report:

"Eleven p.m., August 14, 1981. Staff at the Chiayi Chen Children's Clinic are awoken by the police. Two officers are responding to a call from nearby residents. As reported, an infant, no more than three months old, has been left wailing in a cardboard box by the clinic gate.

"The police ring the clinic doorbell. Doctor Chen himself, sixty-seven, lives on site. His wife, sixty-two and a nurse at the clinic, comes to the gate. Concerned for the child, she summons her husband, who declares it in good health. A boy. The box contains nothing else but the blanket the infant is wrapped in and an empty bottle of milk.

"In Taiwan in the eighties and nineties, young women did not always know how to avoid pregnancy, and when pregnant they may even have thought they were simply putting on weight. It was not uncommon for newborns to be abandoned in public places by desperate teenage mothers. Fat's mother may have been one of those young unmarried women. The blanket and bottle indicated she had done her best. But, overwhelmed, she presumably had decided a children's clinic was the best place for her child.

"The police took statements from the Chens and were about to take the infant to social services when Doctor Chen objected, fearing that a child so young would not be cared for properly. He offered to keep the baby for a while. After all, the mother might regret her decision and return. The police consulted social services, and all agreed that the child had a suitable temporary home.

"The Chens had two children of their own, a girl, married and living in the U.S., and a boy living in Taipei, also a doctor. Their empty nest became a loving home again. Baby Fat spent a happy and peaceful week there. He didn't even cry —"

"How do you know he didn't cry?" Egghead interrupted.

"Hush, Egghead, or I won't tell you the story."

"Let me just check something online. Are you sure it was August 14, 1981?"

"That's what the police files say."

"Wu, guess what day that was."

"August 14? A summer public holiday?"

"The fifteenth day of the seventh month of the lunar calendar. Ghost Festival."

"Spooky . . . Anyway, a week later nobody had claimed the child and the government was set to take custody. However, Mrs. Chen, enjoying a maternal renaissance, hoped to keep the child, if only until the parents could be found. Social services were happy to be relieved of the problem and offered an allowance to help with the costs. The Chens refused any assistance.

"Six months later the child was adopted, officially by the Chens' daughter, as the Chens themselves were too old. The necessary formalities were carried out and the child was named Chen Li-chih. Officially the Chens were his grandparents, but to him they were mother and father.

"Fat had an unremarkable childhood. He did not distinguish himself in elementary school, nor was he a troublesome pupil. He did excel in one respect: at the age of eleven he stood 171 centimetres tall, a fact generally ascribed to Mrs. Chen's insistence on buying various supplemented foods for him, regardless of the cost.

"Doctor Chen retired at the age of seventy. His doctor son declined to return from Taipei to take over the family business, so the Chen Children's Clinic lives on today only in the memories of the good people of Chiayi.

"Their new son brought the Chens great joy. They wished only for a larger household, for their children to return from Taipei and the U.S. with grandchildren in tow. Chen Li-chih was the same age as the grandchildren and they would have made fine playmates. And, if the gods were kind, perhaps the youngest Chen would discover more academic aptitude in high school and the family would be blessed with a third doctor.

"But suddenly sadness struck. Mrs. Chen began to lose her faculties — nothing serious, but she would often forget to turn off the gas. Dementia, the doctors concluded, and no way to treat it. Their son in Taipei arranged for a nurse to help care for her. But two years later it was Doctor Chen who passed away first. Heart failure. The family conferred. The house would be sold and Mrs. Chen relocated to the States, where her daughter could care for her. But where was Chen Li-chih to go? There was no place for him in Taipei, and as the daughter explained to social services, she could not look after both her mother and her younger brother.

"So Chen Li-chih, at the tender age of eleven, found himself cast out of heaven. Mother and father lost, rejected by his siblings, and, most unsettling of all, he discovered he had been an abandoned baby."

"An orphan in a cardboard box? Wu, have you got any happier stories? Maybe the one about the little match girl?"

"It fully accords with the facts as uncovered by my investigation."

"Let's cheer it up, make it uplifting! I think you're having a pre-retirement crisis. You want everyone else to be miserable too."

"Oh, you're a psychiatrist now? Let me finish. The neighbours remember Chen Li-chih as a devoted son to his adoptive parents. After school the boy would push his mother's wheelchair to the local park. There's no doubt they enjoyed happy and loving times together.

"The second adoption was closely documented by both the police and social services. As he was not a blood relation of the older Chen children, they had no obligation to care for him and he was sent to an orphanage, where he remained for two long years. Several families considered adopting him but always backed out. He was too tall, too inclined to scowl. What if he turned out to be a delinquent?

"The orphanage also kept excellent records. The boy was quiet and rarely spoke, and certainly never of his former family. He treasured the annual Christmas cards from Mrs. Chen, although a Miss Lin notes in the file that they were presumably sent by her daughter and contained no message beyond a signature. She could not have imagined that would make Christmas the saddest time of the year for the boy, who would clutch the card and weep under his blankets."

"You're putting me off my buns."

"Hey, Egghead, maybe that's what I can do when I retire — volunteer at orphanages and old people's homes."

"They've got professionals for that. You're police."

"Yeah, but I'd like to feel a sense of achievement."

"A sense of achievement! Yeah, I know how you feel."

"Two years later, Chen Li-chih was adopted by a former soldier named Chen Luo. There's less detail in the file about this. Strictly speaking, Chen Luo met neither the age nor income requirements to adopt. Perhaps someone who handled the case would be able to enlighten us as to how it was permitted. Chen Luo was fifty-three then, his Vietnamese wife thirty-one. Perhaps his sperm count had dropped and his young wife wanted a child.

"So young Chen had a new family, and according to the neighbours he was treated better than any biological son. Made the basketball team in high school, hung around with a small group of friends, got mixed up with a gang when he was sixteen and was sent to juvenile detention. Chen Luo got him out somehow.

"According to his classmates he spent all his time playing basketball or lifting weights, and he already had the nickname 'Fat' — all the makings of a sports science student. One of the school tough men; got a problem, go see Fat to sort it out. He ended up in juvie because of a friend named Zao, who had been tricked into losing big at cards in a gambling den. Some real gangsters were demanding he steal his dad's watch collection to clear the debt. Fat didn't think that was fair, so he went to have a word. Things got messy, and Fat took a beating and lost a front tooth.

"Soon after, Fat joined up with a different gang, looking for people to help him regain face. He and some older kids stole metal poles from a building site and smashed up the gambling den. It ended up with one dead and eight badly injured. Big case — seventeen arrested, seven of them minors. Juvenile court sent them to detention for six months each. Oddly, despite being the ringleader, Chen Li-chih was released two months later and did five hours a week of community service instead.

"Chen Luo was furious, and worried that his son was turning bad. He pulled him out of high school and sent him off to military school. Fat did well there and stayed away from his old gang friends. Being raised as an only child must have been lonely, and maybe he found a sense of brotherhood. Graduated no problem and volunteered for the marines. Boot camp was tough, but he liked it tough. Made it fun.

"His commanding officers remember him well: the leading light of their amphibious scouts, apparently. Wanted to do all the extra training he could: parachutes, mountain warfare, winter warfare, sniper school. Wouldn't be passed over for any of them. So they couldn't figure it out when he quit. He was a natural soldier, it seemed to them, set to make sergeant.

"One of his squad mates described Fat as always friendly and smiling, but never a talker, never close to anyone. Fiercely protective of his personal space. Someone once lay down on his bunk for a joke and almost got flattened. He had very clear boundaries, to be crossed at your own risk.

"Border records show that he travelled overseas a few times after quitting the marines. Chen Luo's wife moved back to Vietnam after they divorced, to a small village in the north. He visited. There's pictures of them together, so I'm assuming he found some kind of family there."

"I saw the photo in the files you sent over. Looks like a nice woman."

"She came to visit Chen Luo after he went into the veterans' home. According to Fat's squad mate, she turned up at the base with gifts. Fat got all excited and showed her around like a tourist guide. Apparently by then she was fat too, and they all thought she must be his real mother."

"Maybe things would have worked out differently for Fat if Chen Luo had lived a few more years."

"Did you see the photo of him giving his mother a piggyback ride?"

"How the hell did you find these? Don't go, Wu. You're a natural at this."

"There was little information on Fat's personal life. His wage from the marines was decent but nothing special. Rather than save for marriage and a house like his squad mates, he spent generously: his adoptive mother's expenses when she visited Taiwan, extra nursing care for his adoptive father. The occasional visit to a back-street brothel or a hostess bar, but no lasting relationship until he met Mimi.

"He and Mimi seemed to be roommates more than anything else, and even then Fat was often away. She'd ask where he was going and he'd say, 'Just things I've got to do. Responsibilities. It's best you don't ask.' Unlike most women, Mimi left it at that."

"Hey, we're figuring out the life of the deceased. Don't let your own experiences colour the narrative."

"How did I do that?"

"*Unlike most women?* We're talking about Mimi, not your wife."

"It's hard to describe the effect Fat had on Mimi's life, or how much she loved him because of it. She quit the hostess work and started helping out at a friend's clothing shop. Fat wanted her to have her own business, and Mimi's aunt was ill and couldn't manage her karaoke place. It was Mimi's for two hundred grand. Fat simply disappeared for two days and returned with cash. He took care of the monthly lease payments as well.

"She's never met a man like him, Mimi says. She was used to receiving cash and gifts, but that was just to get her into bed. Fat was different. She had to seduce him to get him into bed. It wasn't sex he wanted, she says, but love. But he was walled off, no way in unless invited.

"She did wonder why he never spoke of his work, or where he lived when not with her. Once she'd joked that he must have a wife somewhere, and Fat pulled out his ID card to show he was single. It also showed that he was adopted, the first she'd heard about it. He helped out at the karaoke parlour when he had the time, singing old Japanese tunes or Wu Bai's songs of melancholy men. The old folk adored him.

"But he never explained where he went. 'Something to do,' he'd say. 'Back in a week.' Mimi got used to it. She suspected he was dealing in black market guns, because she'd noticed him carrying a gun once. 'If he gets arrested,' she told herself, 'I'll open a new place near the prison, so I can bring him proper food.'

"I asked her if she liked running the place, as it seemed to be mostly old folks killing time. She said she didn't at first, but it grew on her. 'I can do proper meals now, though it was only noodles when I started. Some of the old men say I'm the only thing keeping their kids from putting them in a home. It's cheaper for them to eat here, where they can get lunch and dinner for a hundred. That was Fat's idea. He said an extra fifty won't make me rich, so keep it cheap so they can afford to come. He was like that, never concerned about making money.'

"Fat never spoke to her of his past, but there were traces of it in their apartment. Three photographs in particular."

"Three photographs?"

"She sent copies from her mobile. Here, I'll send them over."

"Any leads?"

"The first looks like him and two others from sniper training, one a woman."

"Good-looking?"

"Have a look for yourself."

"Just got them. Hey, not bad. A love triangle?"

"Good instincts. That was one thing he did tell Mimi. They were both in love with her. Fat never made a move. The other one, the one with the big grin, did. Got turned down flat and it broke his heart, never recovered. Left the military and went off to roam the world."

"The second photo. His first adopted parents? The Chens?"

"Correct. Mimi doesn't know who's with him in the third photo; he never said. Some old fart, a bit short but well-built. Dark glasses and a baseball cap, so you can't see him clearly. There are other pictures, but just of Fat with his second set of adoptive parents. I'll send those over tomorrow."

"Right. That's a decent picture of Fat's life."

"Your turn."

A hand delivered a cup of coffee to Egghead's desk. He mustered up a valiant effort at an Italian thank-you. "It's not as fascinating a story as yours, Wu, but I've got more detail."

"As you should, since you're in charge."

"There you go again, bitter because you're leaving."

"Hurry up. I could be in bed."

"Fat took the scenic route to Rome. Two days before Chou was assassinated, he flew Singapore Airlines to Singapore and then on to Barcelona. A train to Paris, then another train to Rome. Clearly trying to cover his tracks. Immigration records show that he left Taiwan five times last year, but according to the Italians this was his first trip here or to anywhere in Europe.

"We've no idea where he stayed in Rome. He crossed the border looking like a backpacker. The border guard remembered him: nasty looking, poor English, black woollen hat, dressed like he was off to climb the Alps. Using the description and the images from when he crossed the border, the police found another possible sighting at the train station in La Spezia, in northwest Italy. They were checking La Spezia in particular because it's close to Porto Venere, where a car exploded recently. Local police reckon someone shot the fuel tank. The car's owner is a painter and decorator in Riomaggiore, a seaside town nearby. He claims the car was stolen and has no idea how it ended up in Porto Venere.

"There were plenty of witnesses in Porto Venere, and all of them said the shooter was outside the Church of San Lorenzo. Another car, also stolen, was dumped in the middle of the street. That one was from La Spezia. Fingerprints matching Fat's were found on the wheel. So it looks like Fat knew what he was doing in Europe: cover his tracks, head to La Spezia, steal transport, and head for Riomaggiore. His target also stole a car to escape to Porto Venere, where there was a gunfight. They found bullets in the burned-out car, but no body.

"The Italians reckon Fat must have had help in Italy. He had to get the gun from somewhere. And there's no sign of him on hotel cameras in Rome, Pisa, La Spezia, or anywhere. Someone was putting him up.

"So his target got away and made it to Budapest, with Fat on his tail. One rooftop sniper shootout later and Fat finds out he's not as good as he thinks he is."

"I worry how Mimi will cope with all this bad news," Wu said.

"Never mind the sentimentality. We're police, not social workers."

"So we've put together the life and last movements of the deceased, one Chen Li-chih. Detective Egghead, what clues have you spotted?"

"I'm in charge, so you go first. Then I'll —"

"Pick holes?"

"Fill in the gaps. Am I such a terrible man to work for, Wu?"

Wu's son emerged from his bedroom. Had hunger finally lured him from the computer screen? "There's some of your granddad's beef soup in the fridge. I could add some noodles for you."

"Who's that?" Egghead asked from the screen.

Wu turned the laptop to face his son. "Come and chat to Uncle Egghead."

His son leaned into the camera. "Hello, Uncle Egghead."

"You've got taller. Do you want anything from Italy?"

"No thanks, Uncle."

His son went off to heat up some soup. Wu called after him: "Add some noodles — you're too skinny."

His son turned and spoke, for once, seriously: "You two are cool."

"How so?"

"Solving crimes."

"How do you know what we're doing?"

"I've been listening."

"Shouldn't be spying on the police. Did you hack my computer or something?"

"Dad, please. Who set up the network? I don't need to hack anything. It's just there."

"Oh, we've raised a spy? Keeping an eye on me and your mum, are you?"

"I've got to. You almost got divorced last year. You shouldn't fight with her like that."

"*I* fought with *her*? She was fighting with me, more like."

Last year. What had they been fighting about? Wu couldn't recall. But it hadn't been that bad, had it? "We'll talk about it later. So, what do you think about our case?"

"I liked hearing about Fat's life. The news always makes it sound like people are born criminals. But we're all onions."

"Onions?"

His son offered no explanation, returning to his room with a bowl of steaming beef soup.

Back to Egghead. "Did you hear that, Egghead?"

"I did. Computer hacking, breaching family confidentiality, breaching police confidentiality. You'd better get him a lawyer."

"He's never asked about my work before."

"And we're all onions? I think they must all be pasta sauce here. It's good he's showing some interest in your work, though. I never see mine; his girlfriend's family has as good as adopted him."

Wu fetched a bottle and poured himself a large Kavalan, his preferred Taiwanese whisky. "Where were we?"

"Leads."

"First, what was Fat's mission? He went to Italy to kill

someone and followed that target all the way to Budapest. It doesn't seem possible there was any conflict between the two that would drive Fat to murder, so he must have been acting under orders. Did that explain his lack of a job? Gainful employment as an assassin?

"If that was the case, he displayed a level of skill and professionalism that we haven't previously encountered. That means whoever was giving the orders was someone special, possibly even overseas. And the car explosion in Porto Venere happened the night of the day Chou was assassinated. That means there was a connection. There's something going on here," Wu said.

"Go on."

"The first sniper is sent to Rome to kill Chou, a military advisor. The second sniper is sent to kill the first sniper. It seems to me like they're trying to make sure Chou's assassin can't talk. So —"

"So whoever was giving orders to Fat was also giving orders to the first sniper," Egghead interjected.

"Brilliant, boss."

"Brilliant, my ass. We need to find the first sniper. He'll lead us to the people pulling the strings."

"Whoever is in charge is linked to Kuo and Chiu. They were both military. And Kuo and Fat had matching tattoos: *family*."

"This is getting exciting, Wu. Can you taste the adrenaline?"

"I'm not even sleepy anymore."

"I'll see what I can do here to track down the first sniper. You chip away at Fat's known associates. And get some sleep."

"Will do. And you go easy on the food. Your wife's too young for you to get fat."

"How do you know what my wife likes?"

His son's light was still on. Wu forwarded to his son's phone the three photos Mimi had supplied and tapped at the door.

"Still keeping an eye on me?"

"It's pretty exciting. Maybe I'll skip grad school and join the police."

"You haven't seen what it's like when there's nothing happening. The things boredom drives us to . . ."

"Like what?"

Like sitting in Julie's Café swapping stories, Wu didn't say. He pointed at his son's phone. "Something you can help with. Police business, so keep it quiet."

"Okay."

"I sent you three photos. See if you can figure out who's in them."

"Just from the photos? That's skilled work."

"Remind me. Who paid your university fees?"

"I'll see what I can do. Won't be quick, though."

"I've waited twenty-two years for you to become useful. I can wait a few more hours."

17

Taipei, Taiwan

Wu WOKE UP on his son's bed, still waiting. Shit, eleven already. And his son still on the computer.

The doorbell rang. Wu opened the door: his father, pulling a trolley bag full of vegetables. Playing chef again.

"How come you're not at work? Did you retire?"

"Six days to go, including today."

"You can't retire yet. Your son's still in school."

Wu's father's first task was to check on the boy; there was a bubble tea and rice cakes for him in the bag. Grandfather loved grandson, mother loved son. Sometimes Wu wondered if they had forgotten his role in the family, as both son and husband.

He'd promised to speak to his dad about coming around like that. He readied the words and walked into the kitchen, where he found his father bent over the sink, carefully washing and peeling cabbage. The words rearranged themselves as he spoke. "Dad, could you . . . put less salt in?"

"Oh, my food's too salty? Didn't do you any harm. You grew up on my salty food."

"Just try putting in a bit less. The boy'll be in working all day; get him to taste it and see what he thinks. Tastes are different now."

His dad didn't speak.

Wu grabbed his coat. A pile of things to do and twelve hours to do them in.

First, Julie's Café and the usual crushing hug. He ordered a coffee and added the most expensive thing on the menu, beef in red wine sauce. Still only 520 dollars, though. Enough to keep her dad on his side?

"Take a seat." The sunshine was gone, replaced by occasional light rain. Julie's dad had acquired a large umbrella and the cat now rested in his lap. The old man stroked the old cat, two veterans enjoying their comradeship. "Finish your coffee first," he told Wu.

The man had his eyes open this time, looking down at the cat, which in turn was relaxing under his fingertips. Wu took a sip of coffee and set down his cup. A beefy hand stretched out to silence Wu's opening mouth.

A few minutes later they were joined under the umbrella by three elderly gentlemen.

"Detective Wu, three friends of mine. You may know them."

Of course he knew them. Each one was a known crime boss. He shook hands and showed respect. "Stab, long time no see."

"It's been a while, hasn't it."

"Lucky, looking well."

"Thank you. I'm hanging on."

"Kong. I'm still grateful for your help that time."

"That was twenty years ago. No need to mention it."

Julie fetched a pot of tea, a fragrant oolong. He'd thought she sold only coffee.

"So I asked a few friends about that question of yours." Julie's dad indicated the new arrivals with a sweep of his hand.

Lucky poured the tea neatly into cups. Stab folded his hands over his stomach and gazed up at the sky. Kong wheezed at an electronic cigarette.

"And?"

"They think it'd be best if you didn't ask it."

No comment from the other three.

"The Heavenly Union? The Bamboo Alliance?"

"There's no name."

Still the three had no comment.

"The Triad with No Name?"

"You've heard of the Vast Family and the Green Gang?"

"Of course. Went straight years ago, even registered with the government."

"The Green Gang goes back as far as the Yongzheng Emperor, 1700 and whatever. A secret society; Sun Yat-sen and Chiang Kai-shek were mixed up with them. The Vast Family has been around just as long; tried to restore the Ming Dynasty when the Qing came in. Koxinga's Heaven and Earth Society is more or less the same people with a different name."

The three raised teacups in unison.

"Is it a Green Gang tattoo?"

"It's a gang that's much less well-known. There's no official name, but the members swear to be as loyal as to family. So that's what they get called — by the few folk who know of them."

Julie left a pot of hot water on the table.

"Family?"

"There's not many of them. Membership gets passed down through families, so they're all related somehow. They swear an oath of brotherhood, and there's no way for outsiders to get near them. The oldest member runs things. They call him Grandfather."

The three watched as Julie placed saucers of sunflower seeds and peanuts on the table.

"Well, that explains the tattoos."

"And they don't deal drugs, they don't run nightclubs, they don't run protection rackets. It's not a criminal gang. The police can't touch them."

Kong threw peanuts in the air and caught them in his mouth. Stab was still watching the sky. Lucky had crossed his legs.

"If there's no crime, where's the money come from?"

"It's not always about money. There's loyalty, a sense of family."

The three lifted their teacups in unison.

A sense of family? "How can I meet this Grandfather?"

Stab still looked at the sky. Lucky filled the teapot with hot water. Kong slipped off his jacket, removed his flannel shirt, and rolled up the sleeve of his thermal underwear. A tattoo on his upper left arm: *family*. "That it?" he asked.

Julie's dad was again engrossed in the cat.

"That's it."

Wu got the message but was unwilling to give up. "I need your help. If I can't meet the Grandfather, I can't close this case."

Kong put his clothes back on and finished his tea.

Julie called from inside, "Wu, your food's ready. Come eat it in here."

Wu took a seat inside by the window and ate. The four men outside sat in silence, drinking tea, eating peanuts, and cracking open sunflower seeds. Wu lowered his head to look at the sky beyond the umbrella. Rain pattered down. Had Stab been looking at the same patch of sky?

His mobile pinged. His son: *Dad, come home.*

Julie blocked his exit, jabbing a finger at Wu's dish. "That's my homemade beef in red wine sauce. I want to see a clean plate."

First lunch finished, he went home for a second. His dad had prepared three dishes: fish with tofu, dry-fried pork, and fried cabbage. And an egg-and-tomato soup.

His son called from his room. "Hurry up, Dad."

Seeing that his own dad was already serving, Wu called back, "Come and eat; your grandad's made lunch. We can talk later."

His son arrived at the table, clearly annoyed. Wu offered a warning look and his son took the hint. "Hey, Granddad, you made my favourites." The old man's face lit up.

Nor did Wu fail to show his appreciation, forcing the lunch down on top of the first one. He even let his father refill his bowl with rice.

"Ah, not so much."

"You're a growing lad!"

Had he forgotten how old he was? Or got him confused with his grandson?

His dad had been listening, though; the food was no longer salty. But Wu, watching the old man's jaw work as he carefully chewed, recalled that when people lose their sense of taste, they compensate by oversalting their food. And what would be next after taste? Then he thought about the abandoned infant Fat and his two sets of adoptive parents, and how each loss had led to a quest to fill the holes left behind.

His father refused aid with the washing up, so he followed his son into his room.

"I've found one of them but I'm still looking for the others."

His son had obviously been paying attention to his conversation with Egghead the night before. The photo of Fat and two other sniper trainees was displayed on the computer screen, with three smaller photos alongside it.

"I've found the man to Fat's left. That's Alexander Li, a sniper-training friend of his." He pointed to the three smaller photos. "This is him in these three photos. What's odd is that there's nothing about him online, apart from when he was in the Army. He's not on Facebook, doesn't use LINE or WeChat, and I can't even find an email address."

The first photo was from Li's induction into the Army, his head newly shaved. In the second, from his ID card, he looked older, perhaps just after he had left the service. The third, from his passport, was basically the same as the second. A bit more handsome in that one, though.

Wu checked his list of sniper trainees. Sure enough, there was Alexander Li.

"I can't find anything on the woman. I usually get a seventy-five percent success rate with this facial recognition program. Hey, Dad, I know the police have Taiwan's fastest computer . . ."

"Could it find the people in the photos?"

"Maybe not, but it's got a better chance."

"Don't worry about the woman; there were only a few in the class. I can work on that at the office. What about the other two photos?"

"I can't find anything on the guy in the sunglasses. And that's never happened before, Dad. Holiday snaps, dating profiles — nobody's completely offline. But the people you're looking for are as good as invisible. It's weird."

"Nothing weird about it. Good work. Finding Li is useful. Got anything else on him?"

"He left Taiwan five and a half years ago. As far as the immigration records go, he never came back."

"Watch who you're hacking, kid. We're putting more time and money into catching people like you, and the courts aren't going easy on them."

"It's not my fault their security's so bad."

His wife's voice came from the hall. "Oh, you're both home? Come and eat. I got squid soup and rice noodles from Shuanglian."

Another lunch? Father and son emerged as instructed.

"Was your dad here?"

Wu nodded. His wife glanced at their son, then rolled her eyes at him. "Eat it while it's hot. My hand's still sore from carrying it."

A glare from Wu stopped an imminent protest from his son. "Excellent. Let's eat."

And for once the whole family ate together.

"So how come you're home?" his wife asked him.

He looked at his wife, then at his son.

"Well?"

He nudged his son. "See, if I'm here for lunch your mother gets suspicious. If you're here, she's all smiles."

"You can always leave me and go live with your dad." His wife was struggling with the competition for her son's appetite.

"Oh, and there's something else you can do," he told his son. "There's some kind of secret society called the Family. See if you can find anything online."

"Okay."

"Don't you get my son involved in anything illegal!" his wife warned.

Her son?

Wu finished his third lunch and rushed out. Not to avoid his wife, of course. He had a new lead to chase: Alexander Li.

18

Rome, Italy

BACK IN ROME, Alex headed directly for his meeting with Necktie. He loitered, face half concealed behind a new hat and wig, by the Piazza della Bocca della Verità, with its marble sculpture of a face said to bite the fingers of liars. Eventually a small Fiat pulled up nearby. Alex walked over and got in.

Half an hour later they stopped in a dormitory town on the outskirts of Rome. He'd been watching the mirrors — no sign of a tail.

Necktie always kept an unlit cigar balanced on his lower lip. "What are you after?" he asked, offering no time for Alex to respond before he sent the cigar wobbling again. "A man, perhaps? An elderly Taiwanese gentleman who sat outside a Fontana di Trevi café, next to the deceased?"

"How do you know that?"

"Alex, a video of your display of marksmanship — in the sleet, no less — has gone viral. You'd be annoyed if I hadn't seen it. Bet you'd like to know who the Russian gentleman was as well. Anything else?"

"He was Russian? I just want the name and address of the Taiwanese man for now. And some cash."

Alex was pointed towards the glovebox, where he found a bundle of small-denomination euros and a brand-new Beretta Storm: compact, durable, twelve-shot magazine.

"Enough?"

He stuffed the cash into a pocket and returned the gun.

"No gun?" Necktie asked.

"Just the cash for now."

"And later?"

"I don't know yet."

"So my debt's not cleared?"

"I wish it was. But not yet."

"Got somewhere to stay?"

"I'll find somewhere."

"You're big news, Alex. The police are all over the place with five different photos of your back. You'll see when you're finding somewhere."

"Photos of my back?"

"Turin train station, Fontana di Trevi, Pisa —"

"They haven't got my face?"

"Not yet."

Alex smiled. "So, what's next for you?"

"Might phone the police. Might not."

"It's good to see you, Necktie."

"Better than seeing Paulie and Tsar?"

"I knew they'd do well for themselves out of the service. You, I wasn't so sure about. Glad to see you did."

"Ah, so it turns out there is some meaning to my life. Thank you."

The car made its way back to Rome, turning from one-way street to one-way street to stop at Piazza del Popolo, on the northern side of the old city. The Egyptian obelisk in the centre was, as always, surrounded by tourists.

"The Taiwanese gentleman lives up ahead, by Santa Maria dei Miracoli. His friends call him Peter; everyone else calls him Mr. Shan. An arms dealer, well connected. Used to be a master sergeant in your very own army. Then moved to Europe for a change of career and got rich."

"What kinds of arms? Big ones, small ones?"

"The Americans won't sell some things to Taiwan, right? Well, he works with the American dealers or gets them somewhere else," Necktie explained. "Keeps on the move; it wasn't easy to track him down. But be careful. If I could find him, other people can too."

"How do I get in?"

"Not going to knock on his window with your rifle?"

"Might not be a bad idea."

"It's arranged. Tell the guard you're Alex, Necktie's friend."

"He'll see me? Good work."

Mr. Peter Shan. Which Chinese character would the *shan* be, Alex wondered.

A four-storey townhouse, maybe two centuries old by the look of it. Shan had the top-floor apartment. On the ground floor stood two well-built guards, one on either side of the entrance. And two men in black suits, so fast asleep they were sliding from their chairs, each with a black lawyer's bag at his feet.

The guards blocked his way. He ignored an urge to ask if there were rooms to rent.

"I'm here to see Mr. Shan."

"And you are?"

He made it up. "His nephew, visiting from Taiwan."

That seemed to work. When the elevator doors opened on the fourth floor, he was greeted by that same face he'd seen through his sights, grinning that same Chow Yun-fat smile.

"Welcome, long-lost nephew."

Shan's residence was, as Necktie had put it, low-key luxury. The apartment was hundreds of years old, the rooms large enough and the ceilings high enough that in Taiwan it would have been divided into sixteen tiny apartments across two floors. It was furnished with the kind of high-backed chairs you saw only in movies featuring European aristocrats, curtains that looked thicker than blankets, and carpets deep enough to lose a shoe in. A huge oil painting of the Battle of Lepanto hung on the wall. There were crystal chandeliers, an unlit fireplace, and a white-gloved butler to bring them tea.

"So why did I let you in?" Shan asked rhetorically, sitting in front of Alex with his legs crossed to show off his brogues. "I watched on the cameras as you came up. I'd have let you in whatever you said — nephew, grandson, whatever. But why?" The old man raised a questioning eyebrow before continuing. "One reason is because you've got guts. I like a young man with guts." He indicated Alex with the toe of one of those eye-catching brogues. "I'm told you earn a living here by making fried rice. The kitchen's ready: cold rice in the fridge, plenty of eggs. If you'd do me the honour . . ."

Perplexed, Alex followed meekly as the butler led him into the kitchen. Another huge room, windows on two sides, ten metres of work surface, a range of pans hanging from the wall. He selected a wok and took the eggs and rice from the butler before looking through the fridge. Spring onions, as expected. How did Shan know about the fried rice?

Making fried rice wasn't hard. Just a matter of practice, Gramps always said. Oil, then eggs, then rice, then a fast stir. He stirred with his left hand, his right arm not fully recovered. Rice leapt through the air, and the butler grinned as he watched.

Sprinkle over spring onions and pepper, and done.

"We'll eat together," Shan told him.

And so they did, the old man and the young man, eating fried rice with soup spoons.

"Oh, I've missed this." Shan said.

"You can get it in any Chinese restaurant in Europe."

"It's not the same."

The butler fetched tea. Also Chinese.

"You must be confused. I'm the host, so I'll go first. I'll tell you what I can, but I can't tell you everything. You'll have to understand that. Pablo — you call him Necktie, I think. Because of his long neck? He said you were asking about me. Don't blame him; people will do anything for money these days, and you know he hasn't got any. So I said if you were looking for me, you might as well drop by. Try the tea."

Alex found himself following the old man's instructions. It was good tea.

"When you shot Chou Hsieh-he, I was expecting a second bullet for me. But you didn't shoot me. That's not why I invited you in, though. Back in — Where do you live?" Shan turned to look at the butler.

"Manarola," the butler said respectfully.

"Ah, yes. Lovely little harbour. Shame about all the tourists, or I might retire there. Back in Manarola, someone tried to kill you, someone you thought was a friend. That must have been terrifying, and it cannot have been a pleasure to defeat him. To be glad you survived, to mourn your defeated foe." The old man raised a teacup in salute.

"And now you need to know who gave the order to have you killed, and so you came to me. Unfortunately, confidentiality in all things is crucial in my line of work. So I'm sorry to disappoint you, but there's nothing I can tell you. My mouth, full of false teeth as it is, must remain closed."

Shan laughed at his own jest, then went on. "It's not just you. Taiwan sent a detective over and the Italian police brought him to see me. All I told him — through lawyers — was that my old friend Chou came to visit and I was showing him around, having a coffee by the fountain, and . . . disaster! Disaster being you and your bullet, of course. And though I'm meeting with you personally, I can't tell you anything more than I did him. Policeman or assassin, you get the same treatment. As for the Russian? Between us, another friend, no more. He thanks you for ensuring there was no collateral damage."

Alex sipped tea in unison with the older man, waiting for more.

"So, despite saying so much, I haven't answered your questions. I did try to persuade them there was no need to kill you, but they wouldn't listen." Shan carried on before he had a chance to speak. "It doesn't matter who they are. They're not the bad guys you might expect, but they've got their rules and they have to act accordingly. That's all. What does matter is what you do next. There are arrest warrants out for you here and in Hungary, and it's just a matter of time before they get your name. There could be a Europe-wide alert going out right now: Alexander Li, Taiwanese, ex–French Foreign Legion. Photos, contacts — they'd have it all and you'd have nowhere to run.

"I'm too old now to make this any more difficult than it has to be. So I'm going to offer you two possibilities. Stick with me and I'll get you to London safe and sound, and you'll come to understand the situation. And once you understand a bit more, you'll be free to do as you please. Or head back to Taiwan. Because if you don't, you'll get me involved, and that means I'll need you dead before the police catch you. You're only alive now because killing isn't my business."

How did the old man know so much? Alex wondered. This was far more than even Necktie could have told him.

"Of course, you could lie low and try to wait this out. A good chef can always find work, and maybe you can dodge the good guys and the bad. But I think you're the type who needs answers. Remember, young man, the police don't know you did anything but pull the trigger. They think you're the key to the whole case. And that's all I can say."

Shan pointed to his empty bowl. "See, not of a grain of rice left. You cook well. Don't be angry with Necktie, and give him a message if you see him: He needs to stay away from the drugs and gambling. Neither will do him any good and he'll end up controlled by moneylenders. Cockroaches live better.

"And well done yourself for playing dead. The Czech police think it was you who died in that explosion in Telč. The Hungarians and the Italians aren't so sure, and apparently the detective from Taiwan doesn't believe it for a minute and wants DNA tests. But that takes time. I'd say you've got three to five days."

The old man took out a snuff box and inhaled a pinch. "You're thinner than I expected. Rare to see a young man with the sense to keep a low profile like that, hiding away in a small village. 'We work at dawn, we rest at dusk; we drill our wells, we plant our field; what does the Emperor have to do with us?'"

And with that fifth-century quotation warning him to stay out of matters that did not concern him, the door behind Alex opened and he found himself flanked by two big men.

Shan raised his teacup. "As is traditional, I shall raise my cup as you leave. I'm sure we'll both remember this unusual meal. And if you find the world out there too fractious, do return. My door will always be open to you."

Alex had many questions that the two men gave him no time to ask. He was seized by the arms and escorted out.

Shan called after him, in a voice stronger than his age, "Your fried rice is just as good as your gramps's was, Alex!"

He called back, "You've got a mole under your hairline."

The old man rubbed the spot. "How did you know?"

"I saw it through my sights. You should get it checked. Skin cancer will kill you as dead as a bullet."

The door slammed shut against his heels.

Necktie didn't dare meet his gaze. Alex saw no need to make it harder for him. "I need a plane ticket."

"Check the glovebox." And there it was, ticket and itinerary.

"The old boy has a message for you: no drugs, no gambling."

Necktie did not reply.

"We're even now, Necktie. But don't forget the oath we swore after Ivory Coast."

Necktie turned to him. "Never."

Everyone's always looking for an angle. Shortly after the French Foreign Legion arrived in Ivory Coast, Necktie announced he had a lead on cheap diamonds and persuaded Paulie and Tsar to chip in and make the buy. Before they set off, Paulie found Alex and gave him a slip of paper with instructions. When they hadn't returned four hours later, he followed those instructions and the map on the slip of paper to a beachside hut made of driftwood. It was guarded by three locals, armed and wearing bandanas. His M82 took care of those three obstacles, and two more who emerged from the hut.

He burst in just as Paulie slipped his bonds, and between them they killed the remaining two. But there was a third body, a child who had been cooking at a fire, shot through the chest as Paulie and one of his captors struggled over a gun. That was one of the reasons Paulie had entered the Church; Brother Francesco was offering the remainder of his life to God in penance.

Tsar had taken the worst of the beatings, for talking tough while the others kept quiet. Thankfully his bones were as tough as his talk.

There were cameras in three corners of the hut. The plan had been to film Necktie's diamond deal and release the footage to embarrass the U.N. peacekeeping mission and the Legion, forcing the French to pull out. And it would have succeeded if Paulie hadn't sensed something was wrong.

Necktie, remorseful, made a promise as he thanked Alex. "I owe you for this. Anytime you need something, just ask." Then the four of them swore an oath: to live well, not to get greedy, and in twenty years to get drunk together while watching an ocean sunset.

Necktie had only pretended to keep his promise. He'd arranged for the meeting with Shan but also told Shan everything he knew about him. Alex didn't bother asking what the information had been worth. "Go see Brother Francesco in Porto Venere," he told Necktie. "He'll help you make a new start."

"He's asked me, but I don't want to get him involved."

Alex understood. Necktie was scared that his debts were too big to escape.

They drove in silence until they reached Naples Airport. It was an hour's flight to Palermo, where Alex would make the first of many changes.

"God watch over you," Necktie said, giving him a thumbs-up from the car window.

"Look after yourself, Necktie. There's plenty of meaning to life yet."

But Alex knew he wouldn't see Necktie again. If he was dealing with the likes of Shan, he'd also be dealing with worse people — and each time incurring a debt. When Necktie failed to pay those debts, there'd be no reason to keep him alive.

He called Tsar from an airport payphone and recounted his experience. Tsar got the message: stay clear of Necktie. "Hey, my wife wants to know when you're coming back to cook for us."

Alex boarded smoothly and watched an ocean sunset. It was a shame more people didn't know how to enjoy the moment the way Tsar did. Dreams of the future were just another burden. Necktie had always talked about his dream: to buy a nice big house on the Côte d'Azur and dive and fish every day. But there would be no diving or fishing: Necktie hadn't been free from drugs since Iraq.

Alex drifted off as the sun sank below the sea. He had his dreams too. But Baby Doll just seemed to get farther away.

19

Taipei, Taiwan

MINISTRY OF NATIONAL DEFENCE: Alexander Li, born 1983, blood type A. Graduated Chungcheng Armed Forces Preparatory School aged eighteen and entered the Army Academy, then joined the 333rd Mechanized Infantry Brigade before leaving the Army in 2010 with the rank of lieutenant.

Ministry of Foreign Affairs: Li left Taiwan on September 10, 2010. No record of re-entry. Passport expires 2016. No record of any contact with embassies or consulates overseas.

Ministry of the Interior: Alexander Li, parents unknown, no siblings, raised in an orphanage; adopted by Pi Tsu-yin in 1988 but retained his own surname. Pi Tsu-yin died of an illness in 2005. No current registered address; formerly registered with Pi Tsu-yin in army housing, but that was cancelled by the Ministry of Defence on Pi's death.

Another orphan? Wu went out onto the balcony and watched the busy traffic below while having a smoke. His phone buzzed.

His son. *Found it! Have a look.* A mobile phone video clip: the Fontana di Trevi, Chou Hsieh-he's head slumping forward. Beside him two men, one Chinese, one foreign.

Wu replied: *Find the Chinese one.* He received a smiley face in return.

Wu headed to the household registration office. Things would happen faster if he turned up in person.

Pi Tsu-yin, unmarried, no children. Formerly a sergeant in the Army, retired from the bus company in 2001 at the age of seventy-one. Older than Li by fifty-three years, and fifty-eight when he adopted the boy. Far too old, according to the regulations. So, what had happened? And a birth certificate should have been put on file when Li was registered as living with him. Where was it? Nobody could tell him.

Pi had died in Taipei Veterans General Hospital. That was the nearest thing Wu had to a lead.

Wu phoned the hospital to see if they would help. They would, and he drove over at full speed. Pi's records showed that he had died of a combination of cancer and organ failure. The nearby Heavenly Funeral Parlour had handled things from there.

He turned up unannounced at the funeral parlour. The owners were co-operative and pulled up their records on the computer, explaining that all ceremonies were videoed to ensure that everything was handled properly and to avoid any later disputes. The video of Pi's funeral was easily found. A small hall, no more than twenty guests.

"We have our own hall. The city doesn't have many and they can be hard to book. So if there aren't many mourners, it can be easier for the family to use ours."

A camera fixed over the main door had captured it all: the Daoist priest reciting scripture, the mourners bowing, Li kneeling in the black robes of a bereaved son. The seats filled up as the ceremony proceeded. Only back views, but military bearing, Wu thought. They came forward in three groups to make offerings of incense. Wu kept a silent tally: seventeen in total. And not a single look at Li's face.

Then a brainwave. "Do you have a camera at the front door?"

"We do."

"How long do you keep the footage?"

"We wipe it every month."

Wu's last hope died too.

"Although we might have some from elsewhere."

"Where?"

"There's a VIP waiting room."

"Why doesn't that get wiped?"

"Maybe the boss likes to keep a record of his VIPs."

The young man behind the computer had pulled up the VIP waiting room footage from the relevant day as he spoke. "The camera's only on when the room's in use, and that isn't often, so the archive's not very big."

There wasn't much. Two men in uniforms were shown in by an usher in a black suit.

"Pause."

The image froze. Wu took note: two stars on one man's shoulder, one on the other's.

"Play."

The two generals changed into their mourning robes. Relatives of the deceased? Then more people arrived: four younger men with an older man in a wheelchair. The two generals kneeled in front of the wheelchair. Then the whole party left, the two generals pushing the chair.

The video picked up again after the ceremony: the two generals changing back into their uniforms. No sign of the others. And no view of the generals' faces.

"Any way you can enhance the image?"

The man laughed apologetically.

Wu re-watched the footage of the ceremony. He saw now that the generals had led one group of mourners. The man in the wheelchair stayed at the back, not getting up or bowing, and was pushed out at the end. Li did not greet him. It was as if the old man in the chair had been passing by and just popped in for a look. Who was he? Someone important, if it took two generals to push his wheelchair. Some retired senior officer?

Wu copied the file to a memory stick. Time for yet another visit to the Ministry of National Defence.

"Remember, Wu, I offered to get you a desk here. It's a waste of fuel driving back and forth."

Hsiung seemed in good spirits, even discounting the jokes. He went off to the kitchen himself and came back with coffee and French biscuits. "Take a seat. I'll see if I can find what you're after."

Wu paced. Time was short. After several minutes of waiting, he asked a guard where he could smoke. He should have quit ages ago, but stress always made him reach for a cigarette.

Hsiung returned more than an hour later. "Might I borrow a cigarette?"

Wu tossed him the pack.

Hsiung was visibly unhappy. He lit a cigarette, inhaled, and blew out a long cloud of smoke. "I gave up eleven years ago and just have the occasional one now. Mostly social smoking when one's offered. It seems rude not to, sometimes. This is the first one I've asked for."

"Go on."

"As direct as ever. Both the men in your video have left the army. Lieutenant General Zhi left first, four years ago. He got too old for promotion, so of course he retired. He and his wife moved to the United States, where his son is a chemistry professor. I can put you in touch if you want. Major General Lin was head of the Marines amphibious scouts and died three years ago, buried in an army grave. As for the old man in the wheelchair, I'm afraid we couldn't identify him from behind. Are you sure he's military?"

Wu nodded. Hsiung took a second drag on the cigarette before stubbing it out. "I took your photos to three generals and four field officers. Perhaps he's just too old for them to have met him."

Wu sighed.

"Is this connected with the Kuo and Chiu cases? The Ministry chiefs are keen to see those closed. It doesn't look good if they drag on."

Wu changed the topic. "I've been watching the news, and it seems like you've been busy. Have the Americans agreed to sell you anything?"

"They don't want to sell what we want to buy. We can keep making do."

Wu wasn't in a position to give away any more, and he still had two places to go. Kuo's widow had phoned the police, complaining of a threatening phone call.

They met in the park. Her sons were at home, and Wu had to admit it would not be ideal to discuss their father's murder around them.

"It wasn't really threatening," Mrs. Kuo said, pale. "A man's voice telling me not to worry, that Wei-chung was loyal and my sons and I would be taken care of. But also that it would be preferable if I didn't speak to the police again."

Wu became alert. He knew what that meant. "Did they say how you would be looked after?"

She pulled out a manila envelope. Inside, a bundle of U.S. hundred-dollar bills. "That's a hundred thousand, left in our mailbox. He phoned back later to check that I'd got it, and said it was for the boys' education."

"Could it have been raised by Kuo's colleagues?"

"No. I knew all his colleagues. Any funeral gifts wouldn't be in dollars, or anonymous."

"Some friend who would rather stay behind the scenes?"

"I don't know. I thought I knew him — until I counted that money. Where did it come from? What was he keeping from me? And should I keep talking to you?"

Someone Wu hadn't yet identified was closing doors he needed left open. He took his leave, advising the woman to use the money. It wasn't stolen, after all — at least, not by her. And for safety's sake it would be best if she wasn't in touch with him, barring emergencies.

Back to Julie's Café. Her father was eating inside. A lifetime of gangland friends and adventures and there he was, enjoying the attentions of a dutiful daughter.

"Sit down, Detective, and order yourself a beef in red wine sauce. And a bottle of red wine to go with it. My treat."

"Ah, how could I let you do that?"

The old man cast a wary glance at the kitchen and lowered his voice. "She gives me watery slop three times a day. Fine, I know my blood pressure's high, my blood sugar's high. But what's the point of living if I can't eat properly?"

Wu obliged. "I'm warning you, if my father gets so much as half a bite of beef, you're barred!" Julie told Wu as she took his order. Nobody knows a father like a daughter.

Wu got to the point. "Could you arrange for me to meet someone from the Family?"

Julie's father set down his chopsticks. "Four of Taiwan's best-known criminal bosses sat down for tea with you. Did you not get the hint?"

"I'm grateful for your concern, but I have a case to solve."

The chopsticks jabbed at Wu's face. "Do you know why these are called chopsticks? The triads didn't just appear out of nowhere and start beating people up, you know. We've got our history. Back in the Ming Dynasty, the north of China was plagued by drought. At great expense the Grand Canal was restored to bring water and grain north to Beijing. There were ten thousand government boats alone. Think how many crewmen there were."

Wu was not sure where the history lesson was going.

"Over time those crewmen banded together. We'd call it a gang today, but it was an underground union. The canal flows south but the goods had to go north. If the wind was wrong or the water was low, those men had to haul their boats from the bank. Back-breaking work, and if they died they got wrapped in a grass mat and were buried where they fell. When your fate is in the hands of the gods like that, you get superstitious. The old word for chopsticks was *zhu*, the same sound as 'stop.' Boats stopping, life stopping — bad news for those men. So they used a different word: *kuaizi*. Sounds like 'fast,' doesn't it."

"I'm not sure I see —"

He placed the chopsticks on the table. "If you want to stay lucky, stop."

"I'm grateful for the warning, but I'm a detective. This is what I do. My conscience won't allow me to waste the money of good taxpayers such as yourself."

"No wonder nobody likes the police," Julie's dad said with a glare. "Bringing up my taxes — you're liable to cause me heart trouble."

Wu's beef in red wine sauce arrived. Julie had vetoed the bottle of red wine but gave Wu a single glass on the house. "You're not getting any younger, Wu. Take it easy on the drink."

Wu did not complain and set about enjoying the meal, slipping bits of beef into his companion's bowl when Julie was busy with other customers.

Sated, Wu made to leave for the office. Julie's dad refused to allow him to pay, but he insisted.

"Okay, I'll see what I can do," the old man said. "Old lives are worth less money, and I'll die sooner or later anyway. What are they going to do to me?"

Back in the office to an inbox full of updates. His men had been in touch with fifteen of Fat's army mates, and everyone had the same story: they'd lost contact with Fat once he left the Army. The woman in the photo with Fat and Alexander Li was Luo Fen-ying, an officer school graduate who worked at the Ministry of National Defence. She hadn't yet been reached. Wu copied down the name. Time for another heart-to-heart with Hsiung tomorrow.

Egghead had little to report during their scheduled video chat. He was planning to return to Taipei in a day or two. He couldn't use up the bureau's entire travel budget so early in the year, after all.

"The Taiwanese man on the scene when Chou was killed has an English name, Peter Shan. Check with the passport people; see if they've got any dual nationals with that name. The locals took me to see him but he refused. Doctor's note — apparently he's too frail. He sent two lawyers to waste my time. And the Italians have decided to try to force Li to the surface. They've issued a Europe-wide alert. He can't hide for long."

Wu took over. "I've made a bit of progress here. The tattoo belongs to some gang known as the Family, dates back three hundred years. Kuo and Fat have to be connected to it somehow. Someone, presumably the Family, has been warning off Kuo's widow. And Li was an orphan too; looks like rules were broken when he was adopted but nobody can explain why. Hang on, message from my son . . ."

Wu checked his phone and then looked back at the screen with a huge grin.

"He's getting married? What's got you so happy?"

"No, he's asking if we're working on Li's life this evening."

"I hope he likes prison food. Soon I'll have to arrest him for obstructing the course of justice."

"He wants to know if he can join in."

"What does he think this is, a sleepover?"

20

Taipei, Taiwan

"ALEXANDER LI was born in Tainan in 1983. His parents, father Li Tzu-hsiang and mother Chao Ting, raised him at first. But his father, an Air Force fighter pilot, was killed in a plane crash when he was four. His mother suffered a breakdown as a result and after several failed courses of treatment was committed to a psychiatric hospital. Li was initially taken in by his paternal grandfather, who died of an illness only three months later. Without consulting Chao Ting or her parents, social services agreed that Pi Tsu-yin, a family friend, would adopt him."

"Hang on, dear nephew. Are you making this up?"

"Of course not, Uncle. I found it all online. They've scanned in a lot of old handwritten records. Li's file was last updated in 1999, a year after Pi adopted him, and it said his parents were unknown. But then I looked at the older files. Those were harder to find and I don't think anyone uses them. But I got in."

"Got in? What with? A crowbar?"

"Let him finish, Egghead."

"Pi was a non-commissioned officer in the vehicle maintenance corps, never married, drove public buses in Tainan after the Army, then switched to maintenance before retiring at seventy-one. He adopted Li when he was fifty-eight. For the first three years a neighbour, a Mrs. Lin, looked after the boy; then he took over. There's a picture of him and Li in Li's elementary school yearbook. Li wrote a caption for the photo: 'Gramps and me.' I can't find any contact between Li's mother and Pi. She was released from the hospital in 1999 but killed herself the same year.

"Li went to Chungcheng Armed Forces Preparatory School after middle school. I don't have much on that because I didn't want to hack the Ministry of Defence. He went to the Army Academy after Chungcheng, then into the Army. Shortly afterwards he was selected for sniper training, where he was an exceptional student. Second only to Chen Li-chih, also known as Fat.

"The sniper trainer, Huang Hua-sheng, wrote in his assessment that Chen Li-chih was a gifted sniper but Li was more reliable. He and two other officers recommended that Li be sent for language training at the intelligence agency training college. Normally only officers get sent there, so this was unusual. And they usually study English. Li was one of only two students studying French."

"I thought you said you didn't hack the Ministry of Defence. Where's all this coming from?"

"I couldn't help myself."

"Wu, I'm not sure I can stop myself from arresting your son. Could be a bonus in it."

"Don't go arresting him yet. Remember, Kuo Wei-chung did that language training as well. I'll check to see if he overlapped with Li."

"Li left the army when he was twenty-eight, as a lieutenant. He had to pay back training costs to the Army Academy, as he didn't serve his full ten years. I'm not sure how much it was, but he paid and left for Paris. There are immigration records of him leaving Taiwan.

"The next bit comes from France. He signed up for five years with the French Foreign Legion, where he was a sniper in Ivory Coast and Iraq. Then he spent six months as an assistant sniper trainer at a base in Nîmes. Reached the rank of corporal. Going by the Legion's records, he was an outstanding sniper. When he left the Legion, he was given French citizenship but didn't take any government help with education or employment. At this point, he disappears.

"If he does have a woman in Taiwan, it's likely to be Luo Fen-ying. They spent three months of sniper training together, but she wasn't put forward for the second stage. She went to officer school and is now a lieutenant working at the Ministry. Unmarried."

"So much for Hsiung being straight with me. He's hiding something. I just don't know what," said Wu.

"Don't expect any help from there. Everyone who's died turns out to be connected to the Ministry."

"You're in charge. Can't you get the Chief to twist some arms?"

"Fine for you, you're retiring. I've got to keep working. Let's just be happy the Ministry isn't twisting our arms."

"Why's it so hard?" Wu's son asked. "Shouldn't everyone be working together on murder cases?"

"Ah, Wu, look at your son. Such youth, such a sense of justice. An innocent spring flower. Look how you and I have been corrupted —"

"I'll explain later, son."

"Okay. Who's next?"

"Me — the special envoy to Italy! There was an explosion yesterday evening in an apartment in Telč, a small town in the southern Czech Republic. The town was quiet; no tourists in winter and most of the residents go somewhere else to avoid the cold. The apartment belongs to a ninety-two-year-old Czech woman who lives in Karlovy Vary, a spa town in the northwest. According to the woman, her late husband was Chinese; arrived there seventy years ago, took her name when they married, and got citizenship.

"On the scene they found one badly burned body and two sniper rifles, a fire-damaged AE and an intact Russian SVU. The Italian police are working with the Czechs to compare the ballistics with the bullet that killed Fat. They think it's the same SVU. The Italians also think the body on the scene is whoever killed them both, an opinion to which the talented senior detective from Taiwan has objected. Why? Because there are two rifles. A suspect already identified, Alexander Li, uses an SVU. That means there's another gunman about who's using an AE. It also means Li probably blew up the place in the hope the police would think he was dead.

"The explosion was caused by a gas stove left on in the ground-floor apartment. The Czech police were not stingy with their bullets when they opened fire, and one went astray and set it off. The owner of the ground-floor apartment lives in Prague and says he hasn't been there for ages. There was no way the gas was left on — at least, not by him."

"Thank you, Detective Egghead. The facts are now clear."

"Clear maybe, but do we have any leads?"

"Li was hired to kill Chou; we don't know why. Two more assassins were sent to kill him, both failed, and we don't know who sent them. Where will he go next? All of Europe is looking for him, so he hasn't got many choices."

"Dad, Uncle, he's been sold out. That means he'll want revenge."

"On whom?"

"Whoever hired him."

"Have you hacked that yet?" asked Egghead.

"No, but it must be someone Taiwanese. Nobody else would want Chou dead."

"Your son's better at this than you are, Wu. Those detective novels he reads must be more useful than all that historical stuff you like."

"Never mind stirring the pot. What do we do next?"

"I'll be on a late flight back. What do you think?"

"Son, what do you think?"

"Find Luo Fen-ying and the sniper trainer, Huang Hua-sheng."

"Why?"

"All three are his students."

"According to the Ministry, he's retired."

"Yeah. He's got a catch-your-own-shrimp place in Jinshan."

Both Wu and Egghead stopped to stare. Wu spoke first. "Son, I'm glad I spent all that money on your education. I'm also worried about my investment. Do you actually do any proper studying, or is it all hacking?"

"Ha! Send him to police college," Egghead interjected. "He can be my protégé. Probably do better than you have, Wu."

21

Jinshan, Taiwan

WU LEFT THE EXPRESSWAY and passed through Wanli on his way to Jinshan, not far from where Chiu had been found at Midpoint Bay. The hilly roads twisted a few times before delivering him to a modest brick building in front of a shrimp pond. No sign explained what it was, and as far as he could see, nobody had been inclined to brave the cold winds for the sake of catching a few shrimp.

A middle-aged man wearing a baseball cap decorated with military insignia waved to him. "Let's catch some shrimp, Detective. Then we'll barbecue them and have something to wash them down with." Huang Hua-sheng seemed to be enjoying life.

Wu rubbed his hands together for warmth, then sat on a plastic stool and took the offered rod. He'd never fished for shrimp before.

"See that bird on the roof over there?"

Wu followed Huang's pointing finger. "The one with the orange head?"

"A Japanese robin. It migrates south in late autumn. Rare to see one in Taiwan at this time of year."

"Too early for spring, too late for winter."

"Did you know that autumn is salmon season in Japan? But you can catch the odd one in summer. They say those ones must have read the calendar wrong. They sell for a good price; there's not much fresh-caught salmon to be found in summer. I suppose that robin can't read a calendar either. You're lucky to see one, though. Look how it's puffing out its chest. Must be ex-military."

"Do you know a lot about birds, Colonel?"

"Not much. But live somewhere like this and you get to know them. Like neighbours. Birds, snakes, wild dogs, squirrels. Now, where would you aim if I gave you a rifle and told you to shoot it?"

"It's tiny. Its belly?"

"No, the tip of its beak. See how it's ruffling its wings, getting ready to take off? Aim for the beak and you'll hit the right spot."

Wu noticed a thick scar snaking down Huang's left calf, maybe six inches long. And the steel-toed army boots on his feet, rather than the sandals worn by most folk out there.

Huang noticed the gaze. "From the U.S., while I was training."

"You got the scar in training?"

"I meant the boots. The scar as well, though. A mine caught me on a training exercise."

"The Ministry of Defence tells me they've lost track of how many snipers you've trained, and every one an expert. Quite the legend. And the trainees call you Ironhead?"

Huang laughed, pleased with what he was hearing. "Hardly. That's the recruitment people — they love a good story to get the kids signing up. I like the nickname Iron-head, though I might have stayed in longer if I deserved it. I couldn't stand the bureaucracy, so I quit and opened this place. Business is like the birds: seasonal. Save up a bit through summer, live off it during the winter cold and spring rains. We get six to eight months of business here on the coast, enough to get by. You said you want to talk about Li and Fat."

"Alexander Li and Chen Li-chih, yes. They were involved in an altercation overseas. Fat's dead."

"Yes, I heard. They were the best two I ever trained." Huang sighed. "I'll tell you a bit about snipers." He passed Wu a cigar and lit one for himself. Wu could hear the tobacco rustling as it burned. "An old army habit. I can't go back to cigarettes. No flavour."

Sparks flew from the burning tip and Ironhead began his lesson. "With a handgun you can shoot accurately up to about fifteen metres. Don't believe the westerns with cow-boys shooting revolvers off into the distance. You won't hit anything that way, except maybe by luck. Revolvers are the worst of any gun. With a rifle, you've got three hundred metres. With a Berretta .50 cal sniper rifle, over a kilometre. So snipers keep the infantry safe by killing the enemy before they're in range. In ancient times they'd train the longbow archers first, because the longbow had the best range. Then the short bow, then the crossbow."

Huang lifted a shrimp from the grill by its bamboo skewer. "Here, eat. Of course, the farther away the target, the more obstacles get in the way. Winning means dealing with those obstacles, and that's what we train snipers to do. That's why they're feared. Fat — Chen Li-chih — was good because he was accurate and steady, like a machine. Have you ever played golf? You need to practise every day until your swing is the same every time, so the ball stays on the fairway. And you need to practise that over and over to keep your handicap low. Fat ranked top in that first batch of snipers because nothing changed how he moved. Didn't matter if he was ill, nothing changed.

"Alex was different. He had the instinct for it, he was the best at planning things out, but he couldn't necessarily make the shot. Imagine they both had to shoot that bird. Fat would be trying to hit a target; Alex would be trying to kill. And that's not the same thing. The Ministry told me Fat is dead, and now you're telling me Alex might have killed him. I'm not surprised that's the way it went. He has more combat experience. If Fat had taken the first shot, Alex wouldn't have escaped. But if Fat lost the initiative, Alex would have a good chance."

Huang tugged at the rod in Wu's hands. "It's too cold for the shrimp to be swimming about. You've got to move the bait to lure them out." He threw a scoop of shrimp food into the pond before continuing. "The news really played up the drama — a bloodthirsty sniper battle. The two of them would have been up there, looking at each other across the Danube, and Fat would be thinking about how to hit his target. Alex would be thinking about how to kill Fat. You see, Fat would have been aiming at him, but he might not have been aiming at Fat. It could have been a brick he was standing on, or a light over his head."

Wu was fascinated.

"The best snipers can pull the trigger and watch as the bullet emerges from the puff of smoke and arcs through the air and into the target. It takes a long time to get the right amount of pressure on the trigger. If you get it right, you remove any excess energy that might move the gun or your arm. I trained them so their fingers barely moved. I also heard they think Alex killed that government advisor . . . What was his name?"

"Chou Hsieh-he."

"And in sleet. Fat would be more likely to fail if he had to deal with a sudden change like that. He would consider the increased risk of failure and adjust for it. That was another difference between them."

Huang pulled another shrimp from the pond and threw it to sizzle and twist on the barbecue. "But you didn't come all this way just to hear that."

"I want to know more about Alex. Why he might have killed Chou."

"I was a soldier all my life, and that doesn't do much for your imagination. So there's not much I can tell you. His gramps was my senior, treated me like family, so I took care of him. That's how he got chosen for the training."

"And when he went to France?"

"That was my idea. He was lovesick, depressed. It's still soldiering, I told him, but overseas. Told him the change would do him good. And after you finish five years in the French Foreign Legion, it's not just citizenship you get. There's a pension: 1,500 euros a month, for life. That's as good as anything we get here."

"All because of Luo Fen-ying?"

"I can't go criticizing the youngsters at my age, but it was like he was pinned down by an enemy sniper. He had to break from cover and find somewhere new or he'd be stuck there, too scared to move. Going overseas meant a new place to regain his confidence. It's all part of growing — which it never helps to hear when you're going through it."

"And Luo?"

"Still in the Army. I haven't seen her for a long time. Attractive, capable, a whole infantry brigade of admirers, none of whom ever suited."

Huang went inside and returned with a fish for the barbecue. "A black chub I caught in the sea this morning. Just needs salt and a stove, that's all. Good and fresh."

The two left their rods and busied themselves with grilling mushrooms and peppers to go with the fish.

Wu couldn't help but ask, "Where do you think he will go?"

Huang blew on the pepper smoking at the end of his chopsticks. "Where will he go? That I do know. He'll come back to Taiwan — if he's not here already."

"Why would he come back? He must know that every policeman in Taiwan will be looking for him."

"Snipers have their rules. I've seen the pundits on the news saying whoever ordered him to kill Chou whatever-his-name-was must be Taiwanese. And snipers don't have to kill people from hundreds of metres away. Get as close as is safe, we tell them. The closer you are, the better your chance of success. I never cared about how accurate they were at a kilometre, but I made damn sure they hit every shot at six hundred metres. And there's another side to that. We're shooting people, not deer. Being closer means a greater chance of success and a greater chance of a counterattack. That's why you need to hit with every shot."

"Was Alex sent to France with any kind of mission? From what I've found out, Colonel, your status in the army was . . . complicated."

Huang's hand flew to his mouth to prevent a shrimp escaping as he laughed. "Soldiers go where they're told. It could be Military Intelligence, it could be Logistics; it's not up to us. We don't get a say, so it's hard to explain why it's complicated. But I'm out now, so maybe I can be a little freer — on the condition that this doesn't go any further, Detective. Revealing military secrets is a serious crime."

"Of course."

"The Ministry of Defence programs for training young officers go far beyond what the public might expect. Take the Hsiung Feng missiles we make. Look them up in Janes and it's there in black and white: copied from the Israeli Gabriel missiles. And how did we copy the Israeli design? Do you think Israel sent us the blueprints as a gift? Nobody is that generous. But they let us send an observer over there once, and that observer paid attention and made some rough guesses at measurements, and then he came home and we worked from there. That's as much as I can say. Any more and one of us will suffer for it — and it's more likely to be me."

"Did Alex get that kind of training?"

"Well, you get assigned where your talents are most useful. He was a top sniper but he wanted to quit, and we couldn't keep him. So I suggested we let him go and develop his skills, and maybe one day we could make use of him."

"So was he still in the Army when he left Taiwan?"

"No. Out of the service and off the payroll."

"Had he and Fat fought at all?"

"No, they were like brothers. A bit of a spat over Luo Fen-ying, maybe. Everyone had a thing for her: best-looking woman in the Army. You should have seen her when she turned up for sniper training. Think of Brigitte Lin before she was discovered."

"Would one of them kill the other, even if ordered to do so, if they were such good friends?"

"Depends who's giving the orders."

"Do you think Fat might have been taken on by someone as a professional assassin?"

"I haven't heard anything from him since he left the Army. What does that old monk on the television say? 'Fate has already written the script. All we have to do is play our parts.' Friends come, friends go. No point in dwelling on it."

Huang escorted Wu back to his car.

"Do you think he'll visit you if he comes back to Taiwan?"

"Why would he? I'm just an old retiree. If he does come back, he's out for revenge. What am I going to do, feed him shrimp? But Alex — Have you heard of Guan Zhong?"

"Of the Spring and Autumn Period? Chancellor to Duke Huan of Qi? Of course."

"He wasn't just a politician; he was also a great archer. Once, while out hunting boar, he pinned a wolf to a tree trunk with a single arrow. He used a huge, stiff bow that took great strength to draw. Once he was helping the ruler of Qi, Duke Jiu, fight a younger brother, Xiao Bai, who hoped to usurp the throne. Guan Zhong shot Xiao Bai at a great distance and thought the foe was defeated. But Xiao Bai was playing dead — the arrow had hit a buckle on his clothing. He sneaked away, rushed to the capital, and claimed the throne. Meanwhile, thinking the usurper dead, Guan Zhong made a great show of escorting Duke Jiu home, but when they arrived in the capital, Xiao Bai was on the throne and Guan Zhong was arrested."

"I didn't know he was a man of arms as well as politics."

"He was too confident in his own abilities. If anyone else had international arrest warrants out for them, they'd be hiding. But Alex is confident and skilled. I think he'll come back for revenge. And I think that overconfidence means you'll catch him."

Wu drove back along the coast road, risking a breach of traffic rules by texting as he went. *Alexander Li may return to Taiwan. Alert airports and ports, and watch the cameras.*

The police at Taiwan's four international airports went on high alert, checking every passenger list and assigning more eyes to the CCTV screens. Wu took five men to Taipei's Taoyuan Airport, the largest. Their best chance by far would be to catch Li at an airport.

The description: 175 centimetres tall, thin, slightly darker than average, always monitoring his surroundings, travelling alone. Possibly using a French passport. The French had supplied photos from his Foreign Legion identification and passport, but what did he look like now? Wu ordered that anyone vaguely fitting the description be hauled in for a chat.

Huang's guess had been right: Alex *was* coming back to Taiwan. And Wu was also right: Alex was passing through Taoyuan Airport on a French passport. He carried his bag past washrooms and duty-free shops and went straight to Immigration. The guard scanned his passport, took his photo, and then gave him a closer look. Several closer looks. Then a thump as his passport was stamped and he was free to take the escalator down to reclaim his luggage, changing 500 euros on the way.

He had walked past more than fifteen cameras since exiting the aircraft, all of which sent their images to a command centre, where the deputy head of the airport police, Wu, and twelve others sat watching the screens. In a police van in the airport car park, a SWAT team waited to arrest Alex when he was sighted, with extra men nearby to control the scene. Weapons carried included seventeen Smith & Wesson semi-automatic pistols, twelve Heckler & Koch MP5 assault rifles, and seventy-one T65K2 rifles. In addition, snipers located on high ground were armed with four SSG69s, three AWs, and two SSG2000s. Everyone was wearing bulletproof vests and carried helmets and gas masks, and a thirty-strong detachment of riot police stood ready to encircle Alex. Two fire engines had been seconded from nearby towns to serve as water cannons if necessary.

Alex pulled his German Rimowa suitcase through Customs. He headed for the airport buses rather than the taxi stand and had a cigarette while he waited, asking an airport employee for a light. He took several drags before flicking the remainder of his lipstick-stained cigarette into the smoking-shelter garbage bin.

It was late evening and the trip into Taipei went quickly. He left the bus at Minquan East Road, walked across to Longjiang Road, and disappeared.

Wu kept everyone in front of the screens until the final flight of the day had landed. And as it did, he noticed a poster by one of the immigration desks: WELCOME, RUNNERS IN THE TAIPEI NEW YEAR MARATHON.

He froze for a second before leaping to his feet. "Go back, go through it again! There was a woman — tall, leggings under a short skirt, running jacket."

They soon found what he wanted: footage of a young foreign woman, tall and thin, with short blond hair and wearing leggings, standing at an immigration desk.

"Look at those calf muscles!" If that was a woman, she'd been training pretty hard.

"Where'd he come from? Where'd he go?"

The last arriving passengers were forgotten as everyone focused on footage from Customs, the banks, the taxi stand, and the bus station. It was two in the morning when they got the footage from the airport bus. He'd gotten off at Minquan East Road. Traffic cameras on the junction caught his back as he walked into Longjiang Road.

Alex was home.

Wu had forgotten to check his phone in the panic, and he'd missed dozens of messages.

Egghead had boarded a plane in Rome six hours earlier, texting *Coming home! Got you a Leaning Tower of Pisa fridge magnet to remember me by*. Egghead hadn't even been near Pisa.

Then his wife: *Your dad came to cook again. But I think we should just let him. We can tell him if we aren't going to be home and he'll just have to like it*. His dad would definitely not like it.

The Chief's secretary: *The chief will see you in his office at ten tomorrow morning. Don't be late. He needs an update on progress and wants you at the press briefing*. He'd need to get his wife to iron a suit and tie.

And a photo from his son, with a message: *Dad, take a look*. It was a U.S. M1A2 tank, with a caption explaining that the Americans had agreed to sell it to Taiwan to replace the older M48.

So what? he texted his son.

I was checking recent arms deals. Everyone on Facebook says it'll be useless.

Again, so what?

It's too heavy for the expressways or provincial roads. It won't be able to go anywhere outside its base. Plus it costs a fortune.

We'll make do. Think of it as protection money for the Yanks.

It was the first time his son had ever sent him a link to an annoying news story. But happy as he was to be communicating with his son at last, Wu couldn't spare any more time.

One more message, from Julie: *Come for a coffee tomorrow, my dad wants to see you. I think he'd like to set us up but I told him you're married. And that I've given up on men.* Good news? Or Julie's dad tricking him into drinking more coffee than his bladder could handle?

Where would Alex go now that he was back in Taipei? No parents, no siblings, no girlfriend. Time for a sweep of the hotels.

22

Taipei, Taiwan

IDENTIFICATION MUST BE SHOWN when staying in a hotel in Taipei, but not when renting an apartment.

Alex had rented an old studio apartment from an agency before leaving Taipei. The landlord was on the mainland and had no interest in meeting his tenant, as long as he continued paying the rent every month. Which Alex had, for over five years. Their only contact had been via a text message from the agency, informing him that the landlord wanted to increase the rent. The increase never happened. Perhaps the owner realized that a tenant who never complained about the lack of maintenance would be hard to replace. His children could worry about the repairs when he died.

The building was at least thirty years old: rusty window frames, an unkempt stairwell with flickering lights, shoe racks cluttering the landings. And all on a back street equally uncared for.

Shame there's no money in stealing shoes, Alex thought as he ascended the staircase.

The window creaked as he opened it to let in some air — the apartment was mustier than the safe house in Telč. He retrieved a bundle long concealed inside the bathroom wall: Gramps's vintage M1, safe under a thick layer of grease and still in fine condition. The firing pin had been removed before Gramps received it when he retired from the Army. But Gramps knew how to look after machines and had kept the rifle as good as new — and he'd replaced the firing pin. Alex had fitted telescopic sights and a silencer when he inherited it. He'd enjoyed the few test shots he'd taken. Nobody knew he had it. Nobody except Ironhead.

His first trip to Taipei in years. He allowed himself a trip to the Ningxia Night Market for a good feed and two local beers before returning to his plan. How was he going to find whoever had given Fat the order to kill him?

Baby Doll had passed on the order to kill Chou Hsieh-he. How could he find Baby Doll? And Ironhead?

He pulled an old laptop from its hiding place, the blue skies and green hills of the Windows XP desktop unexpectedly triggering a pang of nostalgia. He managed to get it online via his mobile and started catching up on five years of news.

He slept snug in a sleeping bag until nine, then took a bus to a breakfast place he remembered for its xiaolongbao. A police press briefing on the Chou Hsieh-he case was on the television news. Some senior officer was speaking, but he found himself watching the man standing behind him. Alex knew how Taiwanese bureaucracy worked. The man in front might be doing the talking, but it was the flat-topped detective behind him who actually knew what was going on. He was standing ready to help out if the boss got any tricky questions.

Alex checked him out online: an organized-crime detective named Wu. His mobile number wasn't hard to find, and that led to his home address. Google Maps let him reconnoitre the area: nice views of the nearby river and a park. Not a bad place to retire.

Now to find the shrimp place Ironhead had talked about opening.

The television was now showing clips of an M1 tank in action during the Gulf War while a reporter explained that Taiwan was to buy 108 of them from the United States. An initial outlay of thirty billion Taiwanese dollars and ongoing costs for parts, maintenance, and training. That was big money, even for the Army.

Tainan's military housing was all gone. Kaohsiung's military housing was all gone. Military housing in Taipei and Taichung had become artists' colonies for tourists to wander around. He grabbed his coat and headed out. Gramps's fried pancakes had been almost as good as his fried rice, and Alex had a craving.

Wu got up early to iron his suit and tie, as his wife was off hill-walking. His son appeared, massaging bleary eyes, and asked if he wanted any breakfast. He did but didn't have the time to eat. So, while he was making coffee, his son ran downstairs to buy turnip cake and a pastry. The pastry would have gone better with tea, but today was a day for an awful lot of coffee.

Working together on the Chou Hsieh-he case had helped thaw relations between Wu and his son. "Do you still play basketball? You need to exercise as well as study."

"Not for a long time."

"Wait till I've retired. I'll play with you."

"C'mon, Dad, you'll break something."

"Scared?"

His son hid a grin.

Wu walked into the bureau three inches taller.

The Chief wanted an update. His face lit up when Wu told him the Italians were working under the assumption that Li had died in the explosion in Telč. Wu was quick to point out that Egghead believed the body actually belonged to another assassin who had been sent to kill Li — and failed. The Chief became glum again, looking at Wu as if he had ruined his morning.

The press briefing started on time, the Chief dashing in a slim Hugo Boss suit, his shirt collar open to appear more casual. His explanation of the case was calm and methodical, and he assured the reporters that a resolution was not far away. Wu stayed behind him, gazing out at the room rather than interrupting as the Chief made promises the Bureau couldn't keep. His role was merely to show that the Chief was important enough to have a senior detective standing there, motionless, for no good reason.

A reporter asked about the Kuo and Chiu cases. The Chief did not consult Wu before offering further reassurances. "The guns belonging to the suspect killed in the Czech Republic will be examined, both by ourselves and by the Europeans, and compared with the wound to Chiu's head. But my colleagues assigned to the cases do not think the assassination of Chou Hsieh-he is as closely linked with the murder of Chiu Ching-chih as media speculation might suggest."

And how was that comparison going to happen? The Army had cremated Chiu — without the Bureau's permission — and held a memorial service, giving him a posthumous promotion and granting his widow a hefty pension. And he'd been shot at close range and dumped in the sea, not taken out by a sniper. It would have been a huge waste of Wu's time. Thankfully, it was also impossible.

But whatever the Chief said was right, and the job of subordinates was to repeat it until the waft of bullshit emanating from his Hugo Boss suit drifted away.

Egghead was due back in the afternoon. Wu sent someone to meet him, because he had to meet Julie's dad.

A rainy day meant good business for Julie as passersby popped in for a coffee and to keep dry and warm. Julie's dad sat in the corner, peering at a book through a pair of reading glasses. *The Five Young Gallants*, Wu saw. Well, what would gangsters read about if not outlaws? At least it was more literary than Egghead's pulp novels about hard-boiled private investigators. Wu's son was a fan of Japanese mystery novels. What were retired policemen meant to read? he wondered. Something about a corruption-fighting magistrate in ancient China, perhaps . . .

And the cat? Ah, yes, curled up in a blanket-lined basket at the man's feet.

"Julie said you have news."

The old man looked at him over his glasses. "News indeed. Grandfather will see you."

"Good news."

"Not necessarily. There are conditions: the meeting is secret and you cannot make any notes or tell anyone where he lives. Grandfather is old and finds speaking tiring. He will decide when he talks or does not talk."

"Conditions accepted."

"I'm told he's even older than me. Take him a gift, something to keep him warm in this miserable weather. And be on your best behaviour. The four of us have all vouched for you. You'll wreck our standing if you offend him. And men our age get offended easily."

"Understood."

"Good. I'll be in touch. It could be as soon as tomorrow, so make sure you're ready."

Dozens of updates awaited him back at the bureau. One email in particular caught his interest: *I did sniper training with Alexander Li and Chen Li-chih. I've left the Army and I don't want any trouble, but if you can promise to keep it quiet, we can talk.*

Wu replied immediately, offering to meet where and when the writer wanted and providing his mobile number.

The Chief summoned him before he had a chance to catch up with the rest of the team. Wu hurried into his office. Both the Presidential Office and the Legislature wanted to know why Chou had been killed, and immediately.

"You might not know, Wu, but Chou wasn't just an advisor. He was also a distant relative of the President. The media and their pundits are repeating rumours and tracking down the President's third cousins twice removed. He's not happy, the Premier's not happy, the Minister's not happy. Nobody's happy. Tell me what you reckon, provable or not, and we'll see what we've got."

"My section head's back from Italy this afternoon. If we wait we can report together."

"You can go first."

"Chou was definitely in Rome for business, not pleasure. The identity of the old Asian man having coffee with him is under investigation but assumed to be an arms broker, meeting with Chou and the unidentified foreigner about something to do with Taiwan.

"Chou was shot by Li, formerly a sniper in the Taiwanese marines. He joined the French Foreign Legion more than five years ago. There's no evidence to suggest he knew Chou or had any connection with him. He only killed Chou, not the other two. That indicates that whatever deal Chou was in Rome to discuss was a problem for someone powerful, someone with the resources to have him killed. So, Chou was killed to stop the deal from happening. And it was done in full public view, likely as a warning to others not to try again."

"What do you think?"

"It's a gang tactic, boss. A shop doesn't pay protection money, you smash it up and let the police fine a couple of kids with no record. But it's not about the shop. It's about showing all the other shops what happens when they stop paying."

"So they decided to carry out an execution in the middle of Rome."

"And then Chen Li-chih, another Taiwanese sniper, turns up to take out Li. Obviously they want to keep Li quiet, to tie up loose ends, but he ends up killing Chen. He makes it to the Czech Republic, where another assassin catches up with him. So they're tracking him somehow, but he's ready and dodges death a second time.

"Now Li's slipped back into the country, using a fake passport and wearing a disguise. And the only way he can sort this mess out is to kill the people who want him dead. Because if he can't, then he's dead."

"He's in Taipei?"

"Came through Taoyuan yesterday, dressed as a female runner here for the marathon."

"What do you need?"

"The key, sir, is whatever deal Chou was in Rome to discuss. I believe that will lead us to whoever killed Kuo and Chiu here in Taiwan."

"Whatever Chou was up to is classified. Politics. You're going to need to work on the other two first."

"What happens if we get Li and he implicates the President?"

The Chief stretched out a hand. "Got a cigarette?"

It was a non-smoking building. The Chief's idea. Wu passed him a cigarette and lit it for him.

"Was Chou in debt?" the Chief asked.

"I know he liked women who liked expensive dresses and handbags."

"Do the media know that?"

"Give it a couple of days and they will."

The Chief picked up a photo of Li. "Does he still know anyone in Taiwan?"

"I don't think so. He's an orphan, no relatives."

"How do you plan to catch him?"

"Once my section head's back from Rome, we'll sit down with the team and work out the details."

"Get him, I don't care how. Dead or alive. Then we'll decide what comes next."

Dead or alive? Where had that come from?

In a music shop, Alex purchased a Chinese zither case that could hold the dismantled M1. The sights, the silencer, and six rounds went into his pockets. Then he took a bus. Taipei's buses all had cameras, one at the front, one at the back. Fortunately, it was also common in Taipei to wear a mask to avoid catching a cold.

He wore both a mask and a baseball cap, making doubly sure he wouldn't get sick. He took a seat at the back of the bus. He'd replied to Wu's message with a time and place and would, as always, be there early to make sure the battleground was laid out to his satisfaction.

Wu was about to drop in on Julie to see if there was any news. Her dad refused to use a mobile phone, having been a criminal so long he was convinced that every law enforcement agency on the planet had nothing better to do than listen to his calls. But a shout stopped him as he passed a meeting room on his way out. Why was his son there?

"Good lad. Brought me lunch?"

His son accompanied him out of the building. "Dad, someone hacked into our router."

"How do you know?"

"It's . . . hard to explain. I don't think our phones are safe either."

"That's not possible. You need a judge to agree to a phone tap."

"Well, we were definitely hacked. So be careful what you say on the phone."

Wu threw an arm round his son's shoulders. "It's okay. Your Uncle Egghead's back today. No more need for evening video chats."

"And —"

"Don't worry about it. I'll tell you just as soon as Egghead and I have made some progress. Join me for a coffee?"

"Can't. I need to get to the library."

"Did your granddad come around to cook again?"

"Yes. I was going to tell you."

"And?"

"Wasn't great."

"How so?"

"I want to lose weight but I don't have any time to exercise. And he keeps insisting I eat more."

"I'll have a word with him."

At the junction with Zhongxiao East Road Wu watched his son walk towards the metro station. He'd need to do something about his dad. If this kept up his son would lose his patience and his dad would take offence. That'd be even harder to fix.

His mobile buzzed with a new message: a time and place from his mystery source. Riverside Park. Right next to Wu's apartment.

He turned into Julie's Café. Her dad and his three pals were all there. Stab was lifting the lid from a teapot to sprinkle in more leaves.

"Time's fixed, and you'll be glad to hear it's sooner rather than later. Eight-thirty tomorrow morning. Take the high-speed rail to Hsinchu. There'll be a car there to meet you."

"Tomorrow, eight-thirty a.m."

"The high-speed rail, not the suburban line."

The other men pointedly looked away as his phone rang. Egghead. "Are you at the airport?" Wu asked.

"Waiting for my suitcase. See you at the Bureau?"

"Later. I've got something to do."

"I've got Italian ham, sausage, bread, dates, and wine. We can have a midnight feast!"

Wu put his phone away and puffed on frozen hands. He hailed a taxi and had it take him to Riverside Park. The meeting was by the basketball courts, right on the river, and windy. Was he destined to freeze?

Alex was an hour ahead of Wu, braving the wind and rain to survey the land. A grassy park separated from the river by an embankment. On the east side the Grand Hotel lay to the north, to the south a lake. On the west side, the Fine Arts Museum to the north, Songshan Airport to the south. The best outlook was from the pleasure-boat pier by the basket-ball courts — nothing to spoil his field of view. He concealed himself behind a storage shed, using a tarpaulin to cover the M1. Five in the afternoon and getting dark, but not so dark the streetlights were on.

Wu entered the park and a cold wind rushed down his collar. He was almost at the basketball court when another text message arrived: *Go to the pier*. Fuck's sake. The windiest spot.

Nobody at the pier. Had he been stood up?

His phone rang. "Detective Wu, apologies for the choice of location. You must be freezing."

"Where are you?"

"Nearby. I need some information."

"And here I thought you wanted to give me some."

"Do you see that tree three metres to your left, Detective?"

Wu turned to look. A newly planted pongam oil tree, thick as a man's thigh. "I see it."

"Look very closely."

Wu looked, unsure what game was being played. The tree trunk shook and raindrops thrown from the leaves splattered his face.

"See the stone stool two metres to your right?"

"Yes."

"Look very closely." Dust flew from the top of the stool and a chunk of stone vanished.

"Now look at the brick near your foot, the one covered with leaves."

Leaves that had recently been shaken from the nearby tree. "I see it. I'll look very closely."

A bullet shattered the brick and turned the leaves to mush. The cloud of dust rose almost to Wu's eyes.

"Threatening police officers has consequences."

"You're investigating the deaths of Chou Hsieh-he and Chen Li-chih, as well as two others I'm not so familiar with. So you're the only person who can help me."

"Alexander Li?"

"Correct, Detective. I'm afraid I can't meet you in person at the moment, due to being a suspect in said homicides. And please don't do anything rash. I'm on the other side of the river and have an excellent view."

"What do you want to know?"

"Who's trying to kill me?"

"That's what we're trying to figure out. Look, if we could talk in person —"

"I'm in charge just now, and I'll ask the questions. You get to ask them when you catch me. And I promise I'll be honest if you are."

"Go on."

"Which unit was Fat working for?"

"Hadn't he left the Army?"

"He must have been working for someone or he'd have had no reason to kill me. I knew him. A born soldier, a born order-follower. So who was giving the orders? Believe me, I've thought about little else. It has to be someone official."

"I don't know. We hadn't considered that he might still be working for the Army."

"Really? I'm a desperate fugitive, Detective. Don't make me do anything stupid."

"Really. All we know is that he'd been running a karaoke place with his girlfriend."

"You're an honourable man, so I'll take your word for it. Next question: who is Peter Shan?"

"The old fellow sitting with Chou the day he was shot? We're looking into him, but there's not much so far. Ex-military, left ages back, lives overseas, has a U.K. passport."

"Peter Shan is an arms broker. He told me himself."

"That's useful information."

"Why was Chou in Rome?"

"I don't know."

"You don't know much, Detective."

"You know a lot more than I do. That's why we're so keen to find you."

"I killed Chou Hsieh-he, a government official. That's twenty years inside. So you'll forgive me if I don't rush to give myself up."

"Undercover informants get lighter sentences."

"I was already undercover, remember. Look where it got me."

"So who do you work for?"

"Not a question I'm allowed to answer."

"If you won't talk, how do I find whoever wants you dead?"

"You're the police. Do your job."

"Were you working for them when you joined the French Foreign Legion? Were you on a mission?"

"See the streetlight behind you? See the bulb at the top? Look very closely."

Wu complied. He stared at it for a minute . . . two minutes. But Alex was gone. Wu pulled his coat tighter around himself. A cold was the last thing he needed.

So, Li was as lost as the police. At least the destruction of park property hadn't been for nothing. Wu was now sure that Li was working for some official unit, and likely so was Fat. He just had to find out how many of those "units" military intelligence had.

Could he nip home to change into dry clothes? No, no time.

Wu hurried to the Ministry of National Defence and was glad to find Hsiung still in his office.

"Detective Wu, look at the state of you — you're soaking! I'll have them bring in some ginger tea."

"No need, Colonel. But I would like to talk with Luo Fen-ying."

Wu recognized the expression that appeared on Hsiung's face. He'd first seen it at the Laurel Hotel.

"We'll need an official request from the Bureau. Which case is this regarding?"

"Luo did sniper training with Chen Li-chih and Alexander Li, the two snipers in Europe. I'd like to know what she can tell me about them, and if she's been in touch with either of them recently."

"Off the record?"

"As a personal favour."

"I'll ask her tomorrow."

Wu gulped down half a cup of ginger tea and took his leave.

Hsiung waved him back. "I hear you retire in four days, Detective."

"Three, according to the labour laws," Wu said, pointing at his watch.

A cold and rainy rush hour. There were no taxis to be had, so Wu joined the crush on the metro. He had thought about telling Hsiung that Li was back in Taipei. He wanted to know who Li might turn to for help. Was he correct? Would it be Luo Fen-ying? Or was there more to Li's life in Taiwan than his son had been able to discover?

He'd hoped to visit social services and check the records of Pi Tsu-yin's adoption of Li, but they would be closed. Back to the office to see Egghead, then.

Through his sights Alex could see a man in his fifties with a greying flat-top standing erect despite the wind and rain. He hadn't flinched once during the three shots. He didn't seem the type to lie. And if he had, so what?

He broke down his gun and left the park. Wu had nothing useful to tell him. Who was next? Who else did he know?

He'd missed Taiwan every day of his five years away. Now he was back and utterly alone. The language might be familiar, the food might be familiar, but the constant sense of threat made everything seem alien.

Alex pulled up his hood and walked through the rain, past bus stops and metro stations. He passed a police station, a new "most wanted" poster in the window. Top of the page, there he was. There were rewards offered for information leading to an arrest. All generous, and for the most wanted of all, Alexander Li, ten million Taiwanese dollars.

Egghead wasn't in the mood for the usual banter, and Wu was busy sipping hot ginger tea. Neither spoke for five minutes after the Chief left.

The Chief's instructions were simple: Without adequate grounds to link them, the three deaths in Europe and the two in Taiwan were to be investigated separately. All the evidence pointed to Li's having killed Chou Hsieh-he. A Europe-wide warrant for his arrest had been issued in connection with the deaths of Chou, Fat, and the as yet unidentified man in Telč. And naturally the Taiwanese authorities had issued their own warrant. As for motive, perhaps a grudge, perhaps a dispute over money. Wu had no evidence for his theory of a rogue intelligence unit, and it was not to be made public.

The Chiu Ching-chih and Kuo Wei-chung cases were also to be handled separately. Chiu had been shot and the police were actively investigating. The autopsy on Kuo indicated he too had been murdered, but it left open the possibility of suicide and there was no clue as to who might have killed him. The cases would be split and passed on to other investigators.

"Find evidence!" the Chief had roared at his two subordinates. "And bring in Li! There's a warrant out already. You two liaise with local stations and make sure they find him."

As for the tattoos linking Chen Li-chih's death with the unconvincing suicide of Kuo Wei-chung, "A minute ago it was rogue intelligence operatives and now it's a secret society? It can't be both, and I don't want to hear either theory on the news. Don't get used. Someone's playing office politics here."

Egghead spoke first. "You heard what the man said, Wu. How do we wind this up?"

"I'm retiring. There's a big banquet tomorrow evening to see me off."

"And I'm left behind to clean up the mess? Some friend you are. Seriously, though?"

"Tell me what else you learned in Italy. And pass me that bottle of Italian wine. I'll see what I think."

Egghead stood up and performed tai chi forms as he intoned, "I must endure this humiliation to achieve results. A man in my position must not stoop to hitting a retiring colleague over the head with a bottle."

"This is pretty good. What did it cost you?"

"Fine, I'll go first. It all started when Li killed Chou. We've identified the three men at the table: Chou Hsieh-he, a military advisor to the Taiwanese government, in Rome for reasons unknown. To his left, Shen Kuan-chih, retired Taiwanese army sergeant and now arms broker, travelling on a British passport as Peter Shan. The third person isn't Russian but Ukrainian, name of Agafonov, formerly a member of parliament, now a lobbyist. The Italians confirmed that Aga-fonov has left the country; the Ukrainians say they don't know where he is. And I think the Chief is right. We need to get Li first."

"We have no idea why Li killed Chou, we don't have a gun, and we don't have a confession. I don't think we can make assumptions."

"We're not going to get anywhere until we figure out why Chou was in Rome."

"What do the Italians think?"

"They suspect he was discussing an arms deal, that Shen was setting up a purchase from whoever Agafonov was representing."

"What do the Ukrainians have to sell? AK-47s? We've got plenty of rifles."

"The answer's in the Presidential Office. There's no way they didn't know why Chou was in Rome." Egghead reclaimed the wine and poured himself a large glass. "I've got a fantastic idea, Wu, but I don't think you're going to like it."

"Let's hear it."

"Look at the people connected. Luo Fen-ying's being hidden away by the Ministry of Defence. Chiu's widow is on television criticizing the Ministry. That leave's Kuo's widow. You said she's been threatened. What if you set up a suspicious-looking meeting with her? I film it and we give the video to the media. Then whoever's been sending her threats and bundles of cash gets upset and contacts her again. We'll set up cameras and guards at her apartment. We get whoever threatens her and see where that leads. Could be the breakthrough we need."

"Using a civilian as bait? Cheap trick, Egghead. I'm out."

"Those morals won't get you anywhere, Wu. Okay, we'll be up front with her about it and set up round-the-clock protection."

"And Europe?"

"We'll identify the man in Telč within a few days. The Italians haven't failed to notice that Chou, Li, and Fat are all Taiwanese, and they're assuming this one is too. They're checking border records. And I've brought back fingerprints. It'll take time to check them, though."

Wu was thinking hard. What to say to Kuo's widow?

"And we'll need to have some people watching you when you're meeting that secret-society boss tomorrow . . ."

Wu was engrossed with his phone.

"Hey, pay attention when we're having a meeting!"

"A message from your nephew."

"Is he hacking again? Seems a bit embarrassing for us to be relying on a kid."

"He says Luo Fen-ying is an orphan too."

"What? Who's an orphan?"

"Luo Fen-ying."

"They're all orphans?"

"Time to see Huang Hua-sheng again. He wasn't being very honest with me."

23

Jinshan, Taiwan

H UANG HUA-SHENG slept with his feet sticking out of the sheets, regardless of the season. On this particular night he was woken at about nine p.m. as a draft of cold air passed over them.

"Is that you, Alex?" he called out, pulling his feet under the covers.

A black shadow leaning against the wall answered. "It is, sir."

"Good. Do you have to be this mysterious?" Huang asked, turning on the light and sitting up. "Come on then, give me a hug."

Alex moved towards him, unable to prevent a sob.

"What are you crying for, at your age? I suppose you had to turn up at this hour. The police have been here already."

Alex ceased sobbing. "I thought you wanted to motor-bike around the world when you quit, sir."

"Ah, you still remember me saying that? It's still the plan, but there's rules for people like me. Can't leave the country for three years after discharge."

"Who took over? Baby Doll?"

"Some political type got my old job. Used to be on some legislative committee, lost his seat in the election. The government gave him a job. I don't know if he's there just for the salary and the chauffeur or if they're training a civilian to take over the Ministry. He took Baby Doll on as his secretary, though."

"That explains it."

"What?"

"Baby Doll's been making phone calls."

"Not inviting you out for dinner, I assume."

"She gave me the order to kill Chou Hsieh-he."

"And you followed the order?"

"Yes."

"That's against the rules."

"How so?"

"There's only meant to be one point of contact with you, no more. He shouldn't have had her call you."

"Didn't make sense at the time. I asked where you were, but she didn't seem able to say."

"As a soldier, Alex, I've got to hand it to you. All these years and you still carry out your orders. Must have been a shock when you realized Fat had been sent to kill you."

"I didn't know until I saw him in my sights."

Ironhead nodded.

"His eyes were as weird as ever."

"Fat's been out of the Army for ages. I heard he and his girlfriend had a shop or something in Yonghe. He can't have been working for us, or I'd have known."

"Who ordered Chou killed? And who ordered Fat to kill me?"

"Must have been the same person."

"That's what I figured. And that's why I came back. If I don't track them down, they'll keep coming. I met with the arms broker Chou was with in Rome, Peter Shan. He knew Gramps."

"Shen Kuan-chih. Yes, he worked with your gramps. You probably met him when you were a kid; you'll have forgotten now, though. They were close, those two. Way back, when your gramps was a machinist, the two of them were told to evaluate the M14 the Americans were making. That's how we ended up with the Type 57."

"What do I do next?"

"Looks like it's time for Ironhead to come out of retirement. I still know people. But you're going to need to stay calm. These people are hard to track down."

"How hard? Harder than the people you used to work for?"

"The President doesn't want anyone to know why Chou was in Rome. Let's just say they're very senior and very hard to find."

"Even less reason for you to get involved."

Ironhead clapped Alex on the shoulder. "I've never been out of it, not really. Might as well make the most of that. I'd rather tackle presidents and ministers than a stubborn old soldier. Have you got somewhere to stay? Sleep here. There's shrimp for breakfast."

"Thanks, but you always said snipers have to work alone. Makes for a smaller target."

"Ha! You still remember all that nonsense?"

Ironhead rummaged through a drawer and found a very small, very old phone. "Take this. It's a kid's phone, can't do anything but make calls to a single number. So lost children and old folk can call for help."

"Or call for you?"

Ironhead laughed. "I'll call you as soon as I know anything."

Alex hung the phone's lanyard round his neck. Just like a child.

The organized-crime squad planned through the night. One team would set up at the Xinzhu High Speed Rail station and another would ride in a police helicopter, which would be following a tracker inserted into the heel of Wu's shoe.

Egghead and Wu headed for Huang's shrimp place in Jinshan, arriving at four a.m. The gate was chained tight. A wooden sign announced that the boss had headed for warmer climes and would be back in a week.

A phone call to the local police station revealed little. Huang had bought the place about six months before and had given no cause for concern.

"Do you think he's inside?" Egghead asked. "I can't see that he's got anywhere else to go."

"We'd need a search warrant. Those take time."

"We don't have time."

They walked the perimeter fence, checking for holes and cameras. Finding neither, they clambered over. A long oval pond lay in the centre of the site, surrounded on three sides by shelters to keep off the sun and rain. There were stools for the customers to sit on and dozens of slender bamboo rods in a rack, as neat as guns in an armoury.

Behind the shelters stood a two-room brick building. The front room was an office with a desk and a whiteboard with phone numbers scrawled on it. The back room was a bedroom: bed, table, laptop. The bed was neatly made, its army-green blanket so flat it looked pinned in place. Three pairs of shoes under the bed: plastic sandals, flip-flops, and sneakers. A metal cup and a washbowl containing soap, shampoo, toothbrush, and toothpaste. It was an army barracks, civilian edition. Five books on the table, all about fishing. The laptop screen was on, displaying only the desktop. Huang hadn't been gone long, and he clearly wasn't worried about his electricity bill.

"What do you think?"

"He doesn't live here. Too neat."

"Call the office. Tell them to check the property and tax records."

"We'll need the prosecutor to agree."

"You know Li at the tax office, don't you, Wu? Think outside the box. You can't let the rules hold you back all the time. You're retiring — what have you got to be scared of? And find someone to keep an eye on this place."

All of their manpower was tied up, so Wu had the local police keep watch. Their methods weren't great: an old car stopped at the junction with the main road, a camera inside filming all the vehicles that entered or left. The only road out went towards the sea and the Jinshan Highway. Or you could walk over a mountain pass to the Sun Yat-sen Highway. But even if Huang was in good shape and fancied the walk, he'd be caught by cameras once he reached the highway.

"You need to get to Xinzhu. We've cast the net. We'll just need to see what gets caught."

No other choice.

Alex didn't take the Jinshan Highway or the scenic route to the Sun Yat-sen Highway. He took a motorbike north along mountain tracks, heading for Tamsui. A new town was being constructed north of Tamsui, its towering apartment buildings still half empty. He skirted the construction sites and headed for the harbour, where he found a mostly complete building and climbed a staircase still missing its railings. On the seventh floor, battered by the wind and rain pouring through empty windows, he chose a windowsill to sit on as he inspected the building opposite through his telescopic sights.

Fifth floor and, he calculated, it would be the third window from the left. No lights on, but he went ahead, dialling a number long unused but easily recalled.

It rang until it didn't. He dialled again.

A sleepy female voice: "Hello?"

"Baby Doll?"

No answer, but a light came on and he could make out a figure behind the curtain.

"Alex?"

"Long time no see."

"Where are you?"

"How have you been?"

"You remembered my phone number?"

"You remembered mine."

They were both silent, listening to each other breathing.

"Have you seen Ironhead?"

"Yes. I'd like to see you next."

The next silence was all hers.

"Can you tell me what's going on, Baby Doll?"

The figure behind the curtain paced back and forth. She seemed to be alone. "You really want to know?"

"Yes."

"We'll need to meet."

"Can't you tell me now?"

"It's work. I can't talk about it on the phone. And I want to see you." The figure stood still.

"Okay. When?"

"You remember where we had dinner before you went to France?"

"Is it still there?"

"Yes. Tomorrow, seven p.m.?"

"Seven p.m."

Alex ended the call. The silhouette behind the curtain remained as motionless as the scope in his hand. Then more lights came on and the figure vanished.

He moved to an alleyway by the construction site. The rain continued. Tamsui: all rain and no warmth. Weather so cold it got into the people's hearts, they said.

The metal door on the underground garage opposite rolled up and a bright red Mini Cooper sped up the ramp, almost taking off as it entered the street. Alex followed the car onto the highway, his lights off, no more than a shadow amidst the wind-blown rain. A shadow formed out of five years of longing.

The red Mini ignored the speed limit and the numerous cameras. Perhaps she wasn't worried about the fines. Alex certainly wasn't, on his stolen motorbike. But then the car turned onto the elevated road by the river: no motorbikes allowed, and other drivers would be sure to alert the police. Alex desperately tried to recall the Taipei road map, then took Chengde Road and turned onto Zhongshan North to head for Minsheng East.

The red Mini was parked beside an office building. He braked and looked up to the thirteenth floor. The lights were on.

He'd been there, years ago. Him, Fat, and several of the others, including Luo Fen-ying. A party organized by Iron-head at a bar owned by a friend of his, named Chin. Fat had to carry him back to the car and Ironhead had driven them through the barrack gates at speed. The guards made a report to the brigade commander, but no more was said.

A silver Porsche emerged from behind the building and pulled up beside the Mini. Baby Doll emerged from her car, reached in the back for a bag, and then got in the Porsche. Alex didn't bother following. He had no chance of keeping up with a Porsche.

The Tamsui rain, funnelled down the river and along Minsheng East Road, caught up with him. Maybe the spark plugs were wet, or maybe the poor old bike was tired of working so hard on such a foul night. He left the motorbike by her car, an old Kawasaki to accompany her lonely Mini. Perhaps she'd be able to smell the disappointment on it when she came back.

Egghead and Wu sat in Lailai Soy Milk, one jet-lagged and exhausted from watching five movies in a row on an airplane, the other too preoccupied even to remember how long he had left until retirement. Each held a bowl of hot soy-milk porridge, and between them were dishes laden with far more calories than two men in late middle age should consume.

"Your retirement dinner's tomorrow?"

"Yeah. The Chief says he'll be there too."

"Has he said anything about you staying on?"

"Don't play innocent. You know what the butcher at my local market says? Meat comes, meat goes, but the cleaver's always there."

"What? The Chief's the meat? Careful, or I'll write to *Police Monthly*."

"You get two types of people in our line of work, Egghead. The first type is dedicated to the job, to serving the public. They think they're some kind of heroic crime-fighter, like Justice Pao in that TV show, and they'll retire proud of their clean conscience. And then they'll be sitting in some cheap restaurant having lunch and they'll run into a gangster they locked up two decades before. *Hey, if it isn't Egghead, head of the organized-crime squad! What are you doing here? Come on, I'll treat you to a steak and a nice Bordeaux.*

"The other type is half dedicated to the job and spends the rest of their time making friends. If they can go easy, they go easy; if they can turn the other cheek, it gets turned. So everyone likes them, and even before they retire an office in Taipei 101 is being decorated for them to go play at being boss. Maybe they have their American branch make sure your daughter's not short of cash while she's studying. *I'll look after her as if she was my own* — that kind of creepy bullshit."

"What are you trying to say?"

"The bureaucrats come and go. How many bureau chiefs have you seen in your time on the force? Think of that butcher's cleaver. Day after day, breaking bones, getting ground down. Chops up thousands of carcasses, but it's still a cleaver. And everyone having dinner says how good the pork is. You ever hear anyone praise a meat cleaver?"

"I get it. You want more pork dumplings."

The two sat and ate, full dishes replacing empty dishes, accompanied by the constant rain outside.

"So you're going to be a private detective?"

"Could do. Catch a few cheating husbands, find a few lost cats, knock off early and be home for dinner. Earn karma, keep the gods happy. I might get to come back as some rich kid with a nice sports car."

"All this time and I never realized what a melancholy soul you are, Wu."

"Can you blame me? It's obvious we'd crack this if the Presidential Office told us what we need to know. But their lips are sealed. They'd rather let us into their great-grandmother's underpants than tell us a precious state secret. So here we are looking for fingerprints and footprints, and they're acting all superior. Why do we have to be Justice Pao when they get to hide behind state secrecy?"

"Careful, Wu, you're getting cynical."

"What about Li, then? Living perfectly happily . . . Why'd he suddenly decide to pick up his sniper rifle and shoot a man he'd never met, and in a sleet storm? Or what about Fat? Did he get bored and decide to fly thousands of miles to kill a man who used to be his best friend? And two serving military men have died here in Taiwan. But I ask Hsiung to speak to Luo Fen-ying and you'd think I was asking out his wife."

"Have you met his wife? What's she like?"

Wu resisted the urge to crack Egghead's shiny scalp.

"Maybe you should have another porridge, Wu. My dad retired from the police when he was fifty-five and went to work behind a desk in an office so he could keep raising three sons. When I got into the academy, he sat me down. 'Son,' he said, 'don't think it's not a good job. You're a government official, even if a junior one. And there's only one rule for government jobs: don't worry about being at the top; just make sure you're not at the bottom. Don't take bribes just because you see someone else doing it. But if that person is spreading the money about, you've got to take your share. Bow to the God of War at work and get promoted, get rich. Then come home and pray for peace and quiet. Wait thirty years and you can take off the uniform, hand in your gun, and congratulate yourself on surviving.'"

"You obviously didn't listen. You're on your way to the top. Higher up than I got, at least."

"The higher you get, the sooner you're finished. I wish I could retire like you. Me, I know I'll never be bureau chief, but I can't give up this little bit of status I have. No big companies are going to take me on like my dad. I'm not senior enough to get the best jobs, and they won't risk offending me by offering anything else. Plus I've never helped make their sons' drug charges disappear or stopped the media from printing pictures of their daughters with married men. You've got to do that petty bullshit for them, Wu, or when you retire . . . I know what I'll do! I'll keep turning up at your detective agency and dragging you out for a drink."

Two simultaneous buzzes, and both men grabbed at their phones. Egghead looked at Wu, Wu looked at Egghead.

As senior officer, Egghead had the first comment. "Luo Fen-ying's father died fourteen fucking years before she was born?"

PART THREE

It takes no great learning to make egg fried rice. Good eggs, yesterday's rice, scallions, a high flame. Ham, shrimp, or barbecued pork can be added if desired. Tang Lu-sun, author of a book on traditional Chinese dishes, offers this instruction: "Add cold rice to a hot wok and fry it until the rice rattles." Here, try it. Remember — keep it hot, keep it moving.

24

I N THE FOURTEENTH CENTURY, the sultans of Ottoman Turkey began to select young slave boys from Christian households across Central Asia. The boys were forced to convert to Islam, educated, and trained as soldiers. When they were ready, they became the sultan's personal guard. They were loyal solely to the sultan, taking no wives and siring no children. Their bravery was unrivalled. Scholars believe that Christian orphans were preferred because they had no family within the Islamic Ottoman Empire and knew only the sultan, who provided for them. This made them easy to mould into killing machines.

In the first century, the Han emperor Wu selected the male children of fallen soldiers for training by the imperial guard. Known as the "Imperial Orphans," these boys became the emperor's personal bodyguards. Did this explain Alex, Fat, and Luo Fen-ying — orphans trained to fight for their adoptive masters?

Luo Fen-ying's household registration documents named her father as Luo Mei-chih. No mother was listed. A search found seventeen men named Luo Mei-chih in Taiwan. Seven were not of the right age and five were dead. That left five. It was unnecessary to contact those still living; a computer search on the identification number attached to the name on Luo Fen-ying's household registration documents soon returned a startling result: the man named as Luo Fen-ying's father had died of an illness in 1973.

So they'd taken a dead man's name and pretended he was Luo Fen-ying's father? Egghead punched his right fist into his left palm. "Imperial Orphans? I like it. Sounds like a kung-fu movie."

Wu scribbled Luo Fen-ying's address onto a slip of paper and passed it to a subordinate. "Find a couple of bodies. This is where we're going."

As usual, Wu checked the address on Google Maps before leaving. "Egghead, sir. We can't go."

"Why not? Bunions? Arthritis?" Still jet-lagged, Egghead was also red-eyed and bad-tempered after the late night and too much food.

"Forty-nine Beian Road. It's the Ministry of National Defence." Who used the Ministry of Defence as their registered place of residence?

"Now what?"

"Have we found her adoptive parents?"

Nobody responded. Egghead slapped the desk and roared, "Have we found them or not?"

That got a response. "We've found them, but there's a problem. We were going to ask them to check the results again."

"What's the problem?"

"She was adopted by someone called Huo Tan."

"Fine, send someone to find Huo Tan."

"Sir, Huo Tan is in Xinzhu."

"What, it's too far?"

"And was born in 1941."

"Nineteen forty-one?"

"Yes. He'd be seventy-five today — if he'd lived."

"Luo Fen-ying is twenty-nine. So when she was adopted, Huo Tan would have been forty-six. If he hadn't died in 1981, when he was forty."

"So her real dad died in 1973 and her adopted dad died in 1981. And she was born in 1987. Who the hell managed to give her a fake dad and then a fake adopted dad? The registration office has some explaining to do."

Wu pulled Egghead out for some fresh air before he found cause to yell at the entire police force.

Things were becoming clear. The adoptions of Luo Fen-ying, Alex, and Fat had been carefully manipulated, and that meant someone very highly placed had put pressure on social services to co-operate. That was the only way Chen Luo could have adopted Fat at the age of fifty-three, and how Pi Tsu-yin had adopted Alex at the age of fifty-eight. And how Huo Tan had adopted Luo Fen-ying when he was dead. And Chen Luo, Pi Tsu-yin, and Huo Tan were all ex-military. That was no coincidence.

They'd need to investigate those three adoptions. It shouldn't be too hard. Head to local social services and registration offices, find the original files, and the truth would emerge. The hard bit would be what to do if those original files no longer existed.

But if the files could be found and the people who signed the authorizations were still alive, then questions could be asked. If they were still alive, he'd need to congratulate them on their long life and ask if they could help with an investigation. And maybe they'd explain exactly who had asked them to bend the rules. Or maybe they wouldn't.

And what would the Bureau do if the investigation led to someone too high to touch? Luo Fen-ying obviously had friends in high places at the Ministry, or she wouldn't be registered there.

An adoption couldn't happen without the courts determining that the biological parents were dead or missing, and social services determining that the adoptive parents were suitable. If all was well, a new file would be created at the registration office. Who was so well connected that they could ensure all that happened?

"Wu, do you remember what you said when we were at Lailai Soy Milk?"

"Which bit?"

"The bit about two types of people and how I'm going to be destitute when I retire and have to beg you to take me out for dinner?"

"I do."

"So what happens if I annoy the Chief? Or some mysterious intelligence unit? Or even the Presidential Office?"

"They'll send you to the Matsu Islands. Nothing to do there, so you can wait for retirement in peace."

"There you go again with your tragic stories."

"Or you could show a bit of backbone and demand early retirement."

"Then what?"

"Stop feeling so sorry for yourself. We all know where your brother works, and we all know there'll be a job as head of bank security waiting for you."

"Oh, and that's an easy job?"

"So easy you'll die of boredom. If a bank gets robbed, the insurance company pays. If a cigarette butt starts a fire, the insurance company pays. If the paparazzi catch your brother with a mistress, you call in a favour from your police days, get a couple of gangsters to take them into a dark alley and persuade them not to sell the photos. A life of honour and riches."

"So I've got nothing to lose."

"Exactly."

Egghead clapped his palms together. "Finally I see what you're up to, Wu. You can't bear the idea of retiring without me. Unfortunately, I haven't spoken to my brother for twenty years. I'll just have to cling to my desk and see what they do about it."

The organized-crime squad was gathered around a conference table. Egghead sat at the head, issuing orders and the stench of tobacco in equal measure.

"Team One, go after adoption records for Fat and the others — and go all the way. Who signed and stamped the forms that allowed unfit folk to adopt? Find the original documents, then find the original people — whether they want to be found or not — and ask why they knowingly broke the law. Especially Huo Tan. Find his death certificate; show them there's no way they couldn't have known he was dead.

"Team Two, go after their household registration documents. An informant tells me the registration office didn't always bother scanning in earlier files when they were digitizing their records in the eighties. Find those files, find Luo Fen-ying's and Li's parents, grandparents — trace them all the way back to the Yellow Emperor if you can. Do well and there's a bonus, at my own fucking expense.

"Team Three, with Wu. See what the game is in Xinzhu.

"Team Four, look into Huang Hua-sheng. He must own something other than a shrimp shack. Find out what he actually did in the Army. Pull all the strings you've got, but be careful and keep it low-key. We don't want to scare him off."

Wu failed to sleep that night but made it onto the high-speed train at the appointed time, feeling keen and clear-headed. Two other officers, in plain clothes, sat nearby. Rather than try to nap, he consumed the flask of coffee a colleague had placed in his briefcase. Definitely not African. Nestlé 3in1.

He got off the train in Xinzhu. Which of the four exits should he take?

A young man with a military haircut approached and bowed respectfully. "Detective Wu? This way, please." Well, the Family seemed prompt and polite at least.

A Mitsubishi of some years' service was parked by Exit 3. The young man drove. There were no hulking escorts to sandwich Wu, nor was he blindfolded. And the car didn't take a circuitous route designed to disorient and nauseate. It drove directly to a farm road lined with cherry trees. The Toyota following him hung back; it was a tail, not a chase.

They arrived at what looked like old military barracks, buildings closely packed, with lichen growing across rain-splattered roofs. Oleander trees sprouted from cracks in concrete walls.

The Mitsubishi pulled up at a mottled red door; the driver opened it for Wu. "Grandfather is waiting inside."

The red door opened to a courtyard. Inside, two men of identical age and haircut were sweeping. The backs of their tracksuits marked them as belonging to the Air Force Officer Academy.

Wu was ushered through a screen door hanging slightly askew, and then a wooden door in need of repainting, into a small lounge. A calligraphy scroll hung on the wall: *Hard times expose true friends*. An ornately carved table sat in the centre of the room, and on it, incense and a memorial tablet. Wu cast a quick glance at the tablet: TO ANCESTORS. Yes, but whose?

A smiling fat man in his fifties quietly guided Wu towards an armchair that had had, to judge by its smell, a long and full life. "Please, take a seat. Think of me as Grandfather's grandson. We don't get many guests, but luckily I happen to be here while you're visiting, and Grandfather asked me to greet you."

Wu offered a gift box of tea Egghead had turned up from somewhere. "I am not sure if he drinks tea, but this is a small gift from a grateful visitor."

"You are too kind."

The man took the tea into a back room and soon re-emerged pushing a wheelchair. Wu stood up.

In the wheelchair sat a shrivelled old man. He spoke with a Zhejiang accent. "Sit, please, you must be tired after your journey. Ruo Shui sent you, I assume."

Wu was confused. Who was Ruo Shui?

The younger man whispered in Grandfather's ear, "This is Detective Wu, from the Criminal Investigation Bureau. He's come from Taipei."

"Oh, a detective. Who's in trouble? Young Lu?"

Who was young Lu?

"He's fine, Grandfather. He has a restaurant in Kaohsiung. You went there just last week and said the dumplings were very tasty. You brought some back."

"Ah, yes. Are there still some in the freezer?"

"Yes. We could give the detective some for lunch."

"Did the dean send you?"

The other man again explained. "No, not the dean. He wants to ask you for some help."

"What help, Detective? Tell me, and I'll do whatever I can."

"It's about —"

"Are there chives in the dumplings? I like chives. We should send Shun to bring some more back."

"I'll phone Lu and have him send some."

"That would be good. Express delivery!"

"I'm sorry," Grandfather's aide said to Wu. "Grandfather will be a hundred next year and he gets confused. But he is in good health, thankfully."

"Have you got my medicine? And tell Shun I'm not taking those yellow ones he bought. They make me tired."

"Grandfather, Detective Wu came especially to see you."

"He's got a temper, does Lu. Always fighting. Don't worry, Detective, I'll keep a close eye on him. If he doesn't do well at school we'll send him to the Academy. The Army will sort him out."

"The detective isn't here about Lu," the man explained again, then turned to Wu. "His memory is fine, you see, but it drifts off."

"It's about Kuo Wei-chung," Wu said.

"Young Kuo? He was always a good lad. What did he do?"

Wu was about to give up but had one more try. "He —"

"If you want to lock up Lu, go ahead. He'll only learn the hard way. Tell them to give him a beating if he needs it, and we'll pay any hospital bills."

"Come on, Grandfather, let's see if there are any of Lu's dumplings in the fridge."

"I haven't seen Shun for a while. Tell him to come and see me."

The old man was wheeled into the back room. Wu was about to leave when the younger man returned. "Grandfather would like you to stay for dumplings, Detective."

Wu gave a shallow bow of gratitude. It looked like he wasn't getting away that easily.

The two air force trainees placed condiments for the dumplings — soy sauce, vinegar, chili, ginger — and tea on a table by Wu's chair. Soon the middle-aged man returned with steaming dumplings.

"Dumplings from Lu's restaurant. Everyone makes them with cabbage now; it's hard to find them with chives. And I must apologize — Grandfather is particularly confused today. If there's anything I can help you with, I will do my best."

Wu tried a dumpling. The hot broth flowed onto his tongue as he bit into it, heavy with pork fat and chives.

"What kind of organization is the Family?"

"It's mostly the children of military parents helping each other out. For example, Lu couldn't afford to open his dumpling restaurant when he left the Army, so we lent him what we could. Three years of hard work later and he paid us back, with interest."

"Was Kuo Wei-chung a member?"

"He was. We were very sad to hear what happened."

"And did you give his widow the hundred thousand dollars?"

"A hundred thousand? No, that's not possible. Look where Grandfather lives. And we don't keep funds on hand. If one of us needs help, someone — Grandfather, before his memory started to go — asks for contributions. A few thousand here, a few thousand there. I don't remember who it was this time."

"And your name is?"

"Chang. My mother was a poor relative of Grandfather's wife. I was never in the Army, so I don't always understand how it works. I often need to ask Grandfather and he tells me what to do."

"Do you have the tattoo?"

Chang immediately rolled up his left sleeve to display a familiar tattoo on his biceps.

"Does it have any special significance?"

"Military children don't have the same childhood that others do. Their fathers are away for long periods, so they don't get the same discipline. Some end up as delinquents, some drop out of school and end up doing casual labour. We're lucky to have each other. We might not be rich, but we look after each other."

"How old were you when you got the tattoo?"

"I was in high school," Chang replied, pulling down his sleeve. "Seven of us came here to Grandfather's for ancestor worship, and then he gave us the tattoos himself. Four of us went to military school, two went overseas and got PhDs. I'm the least impressive: I joined the civil service. There will be a thirty-table banquet for Grandfather's hundredth birthday next year, at the Taipei Hero House. The entire Family will be there, no matter how far they have to come.

He helped us all when we were young." He leaned towards Wu to emphasize his point. "Those two who went to the U.S. to study? They were there for seven years. He made sure they didn't have to pay a penny, not for tuition, not for accommodation, not for food."

"Is he rich?"

Chang sat back with a sigh. "His generation was particularly close. Several of them made some money in business and helped out. But he's the only one of them left now, and his memory's going. So we all have to pull together when something needs doing."

"How did this originally start?"

"Grandfather says it goes back to the Tang Dynasty, when Zhang Xun and Xu Yuan guarded the city of Suiyang against the rebel Yan siege. Thousands were trapped for two years. The granaries were bare, they were eating tree bark to survive, but they would not surrender. In the end the defenders were reduced to a few hundred starving soldiers and the walls were breached. Zhang Xun and thirty-six of his sworn men were butchered. But other Tang generals took pity upon their orphans and contributed to their upbringing. That's how it started."

"I learned about the siege at school. I didn't know the rest."

"It's just military people looking after the children of those who've died, nothing more. Our actual written records go back a bit more than three centuries. There was constant war from the Daoguang Emperor onwards. Soldiers died for their country, but who would look after their children? Grandfather was just a master sergeant who was carrying on his ancestors' mission, with help from others."

"And what is your position in the Family?"

"I hope you won't be offended, Detective, but we don't discuss that with outsiders."

"Was your father in the Army?"

"He was. He died young. My mother raised me and my brother with Grandfather's help."

"How many of you are there?"

"There are four or five generations of us in Taiwan now, but I'm not sure how many. Shun might know."

"Who is Shun?"

"Another of Grandfather's adoptees, his favourite. But he's been away, so I was called in to help."

"Did his parents also pass away?"

"Grandfather got him out of juvenile detention when he was fifteen. I'm not sure about his parents."

"It's a moving story. The two air force trainees outside?"

"They visit Grandfather when they're on leave. Their fathers are Family and they get sent here to help out. Sweeping the courtyard, cleaning the windows, that kind of thing."

"Wouldn't it be easier if Grandfather had a nurse?"

"That, Detective, shows you haven't understood who we are or how many people he has helped. How many people died in the wars of the 1950s? Grandfather did everything he could for the orphans of Family members, and they all remembered that when they grew up. There's no need for a nurse when there are so many people like me willing to help."

A woman carrying a basket of vegetables came through the door as he was speaking. "It's freezing outside, Mr. Chang," she said to him. "Did you eat already? You should have waited. I was buying food."

"This is Detective Wu, from Taipei. Grandfather wanted him to try Lu's dumplings."

"Who gives a guest frozen dumplings? And how is he this morning? I'll take him out for a walk later if the weather gets better." The woman walked through to the back room.

"The wife of one of our members. Members who live nearby take turns helping out."

Wu bent over the dumplings and ate until none were left. He was on the point of leaving when he realized he had almost forgotten an important question. "One more thing — what is Grandfather's name?"

Chang grinned. "Huo Po-yu."

Related to the Huo Tan who had adopted Luo Fen-ying, perhaps. As Egghead would say, the investigation was developing to their advantage. "Any relation to Huo Tan?"

"Huo Tan? Could be one of the children Grandfather looked after. I'm afraid I'm not senior enough to know much. I've just heard bits and pieces."

"How many orphans has he looked after?"

"That's even harder to say. Some of them are in their teens. They come to pay their respects and then head off to study or work, and we help them out financially. The younger ones are given to other members to raise. He's very generous. Social services, military services — they've given him dozens of children to look after when they haven't been able to cope. This place might look rundown now, but it used to be full of laughter. The upstairs was all bunk beds, with about a dozen boys. The girls slept downstairs, with Grandmother. That's Grandfather's wife."

"And where is she now?"

"No longer with us. She managed the accounts. Grandfather never knew how much was in the bank; she looked after that side of things. I think he'd be in better health if she was still here."

Wu and his police tail left as they had arrived, his associates quietly and unseen. On the train back, one of the plainclothes officers returned his phone. The headline news was a press conference at the Bureau, the Chief confirming that Kuo Wei-chung had killed himself and revealing a suicide note found on his laptop. Perhaps he'd meant to write at length to his family and friends, but in the end he left only a few words: "I didn't betray anyone." The Chief commented that perhaps Kuo had been suspected of having an affair, had been questioned by senior officers, and, unable to clear his name, had killed himself because of the stress.

There was also an update on the Chou Hsieh-he case. In-depth investigations had revealed that he enjoyed a luxurious lifestyle and owed money to loan sharks, and so had been shot. Alexander Li, the suspected murderer, was on the run, possibly in Taiwan. And the Chiu Ching-chih case was believed to be unrelated. The police were continuing to investigate with help from the Ministry of National Defence.

The journalists had many questions. The Chief rebuffed the onslaught by repeating that investigations were ongoing and details could not be discussed. Egghead and the other section heads were lined up behind the Chief. Wu could not read Egghead's expression.

He had plenty of emails and texts to get through as well. He checked Egghead's first: *I'm approximately a million times more stressed than Kuo and I'm not killing myself. But if I do, here are my final words: "Everyone betrayed me."*

Wu laughed and replied. *Do we know anything about Huo Tan yet? See if there's any link to a Huo Po-yu. Could be the adoptive father.*

The next message was less amusing. It was from Kuo's widow. *Detective, what's going on? That message he left wasn't for me, so who was it for? Can't you find out?* He looked out at scenery distorted by a rain-streaked window.

In Taipei he sent the others back to the Bureau and took the subway to see Mrs. Kuo. She was sitting on the bench outside the convenience store again, staring blankly at the ground. He accepted a peppermint cigarette from the box she offered. They sat in silence, blowing smoke into the wind and rain.

"Have you given up on the case?"

"We can't find any solid evidence that he was murdered."

"You promised me, Detective."

"I know. I remember."

"What about the boys? What about me?"

There was nothing Wu could say.

"I could sell the apartment and move out of the centre. The money will last two or three years if I'm careful. After that . . ."

There was still nothing Wu could say.

"That message he left on his computer. He wasn't talking about betraying me or his children. He was saying he hadn't betrayed whoever drove him to suicide. Who was it?"

Wu nodded. He had to ask her. "I do have one idea, but I'm not sure you'll like it."

"Go on."

"Whoever it is, they sent you that money to stop you talking to the police. They're obviously concerned about what you say and do. Can I ask, is there anything you're hiding?"

"Oh, you can't find the murderer so you're coming after me?"

"No, *they* think you know something, but they're not sure if you've told the police or not. In particular, who that message was meant for."

"We never looked at each other's phones or computers."

"Think. Anything, no matter how small."

The woman lit a fresh cigarette from the butt of the last. "There's nothing."

"Okay, tell me how you met."

"I was eighteen. We were at school together. He never had a lunch with him. Everyone else would be eating their lunches and he'd shoot hoops. Later his friends started sharing their lunches with him. You know how hard times were back then. Nobody else missed the food they shared, but it added up to a full meal for him."

"Didn't his parents give him anything?"

"He was an orphan."

"An orphan?"

"From Burma."

"The Lost Army kids?"

Wu remembered that, while the bulk of the nationalist army had fled from China to Taiwan in 1949, some had ended up in northern Burma growing opium. The Burmese drug lord Khun Sa was among them. International pressure forced the army to disband. Some had left for Taiwan and some moved to Thailand, where the government was offering assistance. Most of those who stayed sent their kids to

Taiwan for schooling, with the Overseas Community Affairs Council helping financially.

"So he was born in Burma and his parents stayed there?"

"Yes. They died there."

So Kuo had parents but would have been as good as an orphan in Taiwan. Another one. There had to be a connection with the Family. Kuo must have known something that got him killed. Wu's hands started to tremble with excitement. Things were falling into place.

"Did you visit him when he was training in Germany?"

"Once."

"Did anything seem unusual?"

"Was he playing around, you mean? Wei-chung wasn't that kind of man. No. He'd made friends with an old Chinese man who lived nearby. He seemed perfectly happy."

"A relative?"

"No, just a friend. Uncle Shan, he called him."

"Shan what?"

"I can't remember, or I never knew. I just called him Uncle Shan too."

Wu resisted the urge to call Egghead. "Mrs. Kuo, I think some friend of your husband asked him for a favour. What favour, I don't know. But it was something they wanted kept quiet, and that's why you were threatened. I hope you can continue to trust us, but . . . Listen, if you pretend to be in regular contact with us, they'll try to stop you. And that gives us a chance — our only chance — to catch them."

"It sounds dangerous."

"We need your help if we're going to finish this."

"And you want me to play along."

"The Bureau will make sure you and your children are safe."

"How? Will my children be in danger?"

"You'll have round-the-clock protection."

Wu lit another cigarette for her. She sent a cloud of smoke into the rain. "I thought I might take the Chiu woman's lead. Make a banner and go on a hunger strike in front of the Ministry. Not my style, though . . . Tell me what to do and I'll do it."

"We'll send someone to install cameras tomorrow. Then you send me a few text messages. That'll get them nervous and they'll come find you."

"I don't have much of a choice, do I. I'll leave the boys with my parents."

Wu stubbed out his cigarette and stood up.

"You're retiring next week, I hear. Your office told me. I phoned when I couldn't get a reply from you."

"Still got" — Wu looked at his watch — "a few days."

"And what happens to Wei-chung's case then?"

"Don't worry. Someone else will take over." Wu couldn't meet her gaze as he told the lie.

"It's not just about the money. I want to know the truth. I was eighteen when we met, and there's never been anyone else. We started dating in the last term of high school. I made him lunches every day. You've got to understand how dedicated he was to our family. Once the kids were born, he never left the house except for work. He loved us."

Wu nodded. But Kuo Wei-chung was a member of two families, and one had destroyed the other.

He walked Kuo's widow home and watched her slender frame as she opened the door. She turned to seize his arm, her fingers pressing through his jacket. They held each other's gaze for what seemed a long time before her hand fell away and the door closed behind her.

Wu walked into the rain and shivered in the wind, unsure of where he was going.

Alex pulled his cap lower and left the supermarket, heading for a cluster of apartment buildings. The development had been built on army land, a joint venture between the military and the property developers. Most of the apartments had been bought by serving members of the military, with one building retained by the Army to use as temporary accommodation when needed. The entrance to that building was protected by cameras and a security guard.

But the door he headed for was guarded only by an old man engrossed in a mah-jong game on his computer. He waved the identification card on the lanyard around his neck in the man's direction. One glance, then back to the game.

He took the stairs to the basement and followed the cables on the wall until some of them disappeared through a hole. He forced open a rusted metal hatch nearby and wriggled through the opening to reach the basement of the adjacent building. Then he brushed the dust from his Taipei Power uniform and took the elevator to the twelfth floor.

He rang a doorbell. A woman's voice asked who it was.

"Taipei Power, checking your supply."

A woman wearing a facial mask opened the door. He pushed her back into the apartment and placed a large adhesive bandage over her mouth before she could scream, then wrestled her hands — both in moisturizing gloves — into handcuffs. Luckily, she was alone, the children on holiday with their grandparents.

It was a large apartment: three bedrooms, two living areas, and two bathrooms. He pushed the woman into a bathroom off the main living room and sat her on the toilet. That'd keep the floor safe if she wet herself.

She struggled through all of it. Once he had her sitting down, he motioned for quiet and used a second pair of handcuffs to secure her feet. Her toenails were freshly painted, with cotton wool still between the toes. Was that dark green colour the fashion now?

He took her phone, found her partner's number, and sent a message: *Come back if you can. My mother's here and she's taking the train back at eight.*

The kitchen was a mess. Alex cleaned up and chopped what ingredients he could find to make a chicken broth. When had he last had a proper meal? He checked the fridge: eggs and leftover rice. He knocked up a plate of egg fried rice and then sat on a stool at the counter to eat and check the woman's phone. There was a reply.

He checked the pot of broth and gave it a stir. Chicken broth would be just what they'd need after their ordeal.

He heard kicking at the bathroom door and went back in to tape the woman's feet to the pedestal of the toilet. Three times around should be enough. He made a shushing gesture again as the woman glared at him through her mask.

A key in the door. It opened. A man in a dark grey overcoat entered and bent to put down his briefcase and remove his shoes. As he straightened up, a sleeping bag was pulled over his head and down to his feet, leaving nothing but checked socks visible. Alex pulled the bag's zipper closed and fastened it around the middle with tape. The man yelled and fought. Alex swung a punch at the middle of the sleeping bag. The man inside yelled and then fought no more.

He threw the man over his shoulder and carried him to the sofa. He couldn't be bothered with handcuffs again but secured the man's feet with the remainder of the tape. He pulled a folding knife from his belt and slit open the bag at the man's neck, then held the blade to the sagging skin of his throat firmly enough to draw a drop of blood.

He fetched a bottle of Hennessey XO from the liquor cabinet. Bureaucrats always had the good stuff. He'd intended to give the man a drink, but why bother? He poured himself a glass instead.

"Forgive me for turning up unannounced, Deputy Minister, but I need you to answer a few questions. And please don't worry about your lady wife; she is unharmed and safe in the bathroom. I made some chicken broth for you to have once I've gone. I hope you like it. So, answer my questions and very shortly you can be eating dinner as if this never happened.

The man stopped struggling.

"I understand you skipped national service."

"I failed the physical."

"But you read up on the military and turned yourself into a bit of an expert."

"No."

"How long have you been at the Ministry, Deputy Minister?"

"Seven months."

"Got the hang of it?"

"More or less."

"Did you know Chou Hsieh-he?"

No response.

The knife ran lightly back and forth across the throat.

"I knew him, but not well."

"What does that mean?"

"He was an advisor. We were in meetings together, but I never spoke to him outside of work."

"What was he doing in Rome?"

No response.

"Who is Shen Kuan-chih?"

No response apart from a flinch.

Alex pulled off one of the man's socks. Clearly not a foot used to exercise. And flat-footed — no wonder he'd failed the physical. Alex poked at the instep with his knife.

"I can't tell you. It's a state secret."

Alex had learnt this trick in Iraq. Place a blade in the instep and steadily increase the pressure so it slips deeper. The screaming started when the knife hit bone. Alex pressed harder. The screaming stopped, replaced by frantic gasps.

"He's an arms broker. Works for two American firms."

And harder again.

"I can't tell you about Chou. He's the President's man."

What would it feel like if the knife went all the way through? Alex wondered. More painful? Or would that let a cooling breeze into the wound?

"You really can't say?" He removed the knife. Blood dripped to the floor as he removed the other sock.

The man twisted his feet upwards, as if they could retract into his legs. "Chou was working on an arms deal."

The tip of the blade brushed the soft skin of the man's other instep.

"He'd worked in Russia before and met some Ukrainians there."

Just a little stab.

"And Ukraine said it'd sell us missiles and submarines."

A little more.

"He said we could get the designs for the Kilo-class subs and sub-launched anti-ship missiles."

There's the bone again.

"He was sure he could get the subs." The screams became sobs.

"I thought we were trying to buy American submarines," Alex said. "Why would we buy Ukrainian subs?"

The poor man. A deputy minister reduced to weeping and sniffling like a child. He'd suffocate himself if he wasn't careful. The worst thing, though, was the urine seeping through the sleeping bag.

"They're cheaper."

"That's all?"

"And they'd give us the designs and engineers so we could build our own."

Alex removed the knife and wiped it clean on the Deputy Minister's trousers.

He'd forgotten the most important question. "I forgot to introduce myself. I'm Alexander Li. Have you heard of me?"

No response.

"I'll ask again. Alexander Li. Have you heard of me?"

"I don't remember."

"Careful, I might get offended."

"Wait! You were on the news. You killed Chou Hsieh-he."

"Had you heard of me before that?"

"No, never. Just from the news, and police press conferences."

"Have you ever given orders to intelligence agents in Europe?"

"In Europe? Do we have anyone in Europe?"

"Okay, relax. It's just a couple of holes in your feet. A bit of antiseptic and a Band-Aid and you'll be fine. Tell people you dropped a knife — twice. And remember, your wife's in the bathroom. Don't move for five minutes, then let her out. I'll put the key to the handcuffs by your feet. The chicken broth needs another twenty minutes. There's some of my egg fried rice left as well; it'll go perfectly with the broth and some XO. And forget this ever happened."

Alex cut the tape securing the sleeping bag at the man's waist, stowed the knife back in his belt, and left, retracing his route through the basements and nodding to the old man playing mah-jong at the exit. He was in no rush to get away. The man had spent his entire life pursuing his political ambitions, with some success. He had a plush government apartment, a huge car, and a personal driver. There was no chance he'd report Alex's visit. He'd rather admit to having dropped a knife on his foot — twice — than risk losing his job.

That was something else Ironhead had taught him. A successful man's biggest weakness is his fear of being ordinary again.

Alex slipped out of the Taiwan Power overalls and hailed a cab to the restaurant. It was too early for dinner, but he handed the girl at the front desk a thousand-dollar note and a white rose. The rose was for Baby Doll. Hopefully she would forgive him for standing her up.

At the office, Wu was met with raised thumbs and backslaps. His desk was piled with brightly wrapped gifts, although the biggest was covered with a thick blanket of brown paper and packing tape. From Egghead, of course. A stone borrowed from the Colosseum?

"Open them, Wu. I'll take notes. Anyone suspected of regifting or giving you stale tea will be passed over for promotion."

He opened Egghead's first, bemoaning the waste of paper as he removed layer after layer. A magnum of Italian Chianti. A week's worth, under his wife's strict rationing.

"A good gift, eh? Just think, the day you retire you can sit back and watch the sunset with a glass of wine and think of all the girls you've loved."

Wu stared at the bottle. The grief and fear of Kuo's widow had not left him in a mood for celebration.

"It's all arranged," Egghead told him, getting back to business. "We're installing the cameras at Kuo's this evening. There'll be four of us nearby in plain clothes and two response cars on standby."

"The Chief said —"

"He just wants a promotion. Me, I'm thinking retirement might not be so bad. We can be private detectives together."

"Have we got anything on Huo Tan?"

"What will I do without you, Wu? Huo Tan's parentage is unknown. He was adopted."

"Adopted?"

"By a man named Huo Po-yu."

"Grandfather!" Wu had anticipated that, but he still had to sit down in shock.

"Don't get excited. It's progress, but it's not much progress. Huo Tan's generation adopted three kids, and they all joined the military. Two are involved in this case: one murdered, the other running around trying to find out who wants him dead."

"Not just three. There's a fourth orphan of sorts. Kuo Wei-chung was born in Burma and came here alone as a child."

Egghead whistled. "They've got their own orphanage. Five deaths, and four orphans linking them. If they're all Family members, then this is Family business. All we need to do now is find whoever's giving the orders."

"I don't think it's Grandfather. He's almost a hundred and barely knows what's going on."

"I heard the recordings from your shoes. We got hold of his medical records. There's a lot there, but Parkinson's is the big one. We've got people looking into how he adopted Huo Tan, but it doesn't make sense. If Huo Tan was already dead, how'd he adopt Luo Fen-ying? It'll take a while to figure out, but the files aren't going anywhere."

"So what's next?"

"Next is your retirement dinner, more presents, case handover, and a three-car escort — with sirens — to take you home. Proudest day of your life, but don't tell your wife."

"And the case?"

"See, you can't stop thinking about work! Like hell you're retiring. Tell them you've decided to stay. We'll have the dinner anyway and you can take us out next month to make it even."

"I couldn't do that."

"I'm kidding. Anyway, the dinner's booked, so let's just try not to get too drunk. The Chief and his deputy, plus the other brass, are all too busy to make it, so it's just the squad. You'll get through it."

"I'll get through it? Is that the best you can say about my retirement dinner?"

But that was all anyone could ever do. He watched as mobiles rang and unexpected jobs cropped up and guests excused themselves.

It was almost Chinese New Year and the forecast called for temperatures below zero. It was snowing on Taiwan's highest mountains, which was nothing unusual, but even Taipei's nearest mountain, Yangmingshan, saw a five-minute snowfall — no small event for a mountain only 1,200 metres high on a subtropical island. The cold snap was being blamed for killing 104 people over the past two weeks, mostly old folk. Perhaps they would have died anyway, but the weather could not escape all blame.

He managed to get in plenty of drinking between the dinner's start at seven-thirty and when the last guest left two hours later. Everyone who came to pay their respects seemed to be working from the same script: "We'll have to stay in touch."

Was that it? Wu started to think he'd have been better off going to military school. Maybe he could have got one of those tattoos.

A message arrived from the officer who'd been tasked with going through the household registration files. Egghead peered over Wu's shoulder as he read it: *I'm figuring it out. Pi Tsu-yin adopted Alexander Li; Chen Luo adopted Chen Li-chih; Huo Tan adopted Luo Fen-ying. But Pi and the others were all adopted by Huo Po-yu. Details below. I'm seeing what else I can find.*

Huo Po-yu, a.k.a. Grandfather, born 1917. Known so far to have adopted five children:

Pi Tsu-yin, born 1929. Adopted Alexander Li in 1988.

Chen Luo, born 1940. Adopted Chen Li-chih, a.k.a. Fat, in 1994.

Huo Tan, born 1941, died 1981. Adopted Luo Fen-ying posthumously.

Shen Kuan-chih, a.k.a Peter Shan, born 1945.

Liang Tsai-han, born 1947. Former army lieutenant general, now in the United States.

This was something. Huo Po-yu had adopted five children, and three of them had adopted Li and the other two.

"Shen Kuan-chih's one of them as well?"

"I'd thought he might be," said Egghead, his expression serious for once. "So, a lot of people couldn't make it to Taiwan in 1949, but they managed to get their children here through friends or family. And those kids got registered as belonging to whoever was looking after them. But you can tell this isn't right. Pi's only twelve years younger than Huo Po-yu and they don't share a surname. Someone obviously pulled strings."

"I know a lot of people didn't escape, but did they all give Grandfather their kids?"

"Wu, think about why they couldn't get out but somehow their kids could."

"It's odd."

"It's not. The ones left behind on the mainland were spies. The government got their kids out and made sure the Army provided for them. Or they were keeping them as hostages, in case anyone fancied changing sides."

"But Grandfather adopted five of them? Liang Tsai-han would have been only two."

"Wu, Grandfather must be ex-Intelligence."

"How can he be ex-Intelligence and the head of the Family?"

"Who knows? Maybe they're all spies and that's why they keep such a low profile. What we need to remember is that they'll know we're getting close."

"We're police. That's our job."

"And who will win if the Bureau has to go head-to-head with Military Intelligence?"

The idea of tangling with military intelligence got Wu's alcohol intake oozing from his pores in cold, boozy sweat. He jumped in a taxi to check on Mrs. Kuo.

The watchers were all in place. The command vehicle had screens showing eight views of nearby junctions, as well as the apartment's doors and windows. Wu rang the bell. She answered, saying she was just on her way down for a smoke.

"Everything's in place," he told her when she emerged. "Are the children with their grandparents?"

"Have you been drinking, Detective? You're covered in sweat. Would you like to come up for tea?"

"No need, I'm just passing. Is everything okay?"

She withdrew the hand intended to guide him through the door. "Yes."

As she spoke, an aluminum baseball bat cracked across Wu's spine. Mrs. Kuo caught him as he fell, and another baseball bat struck at his calf. She screamed. A third baseball bat was falling when a plainclothes officer rounded the corner, gun drawn. A crack rang out from the trees and the policeman fell, shot.

Wu pulled Mrs. Kuo to the ground and lay over her, reaching into his jacket to draw his own weapon. Another shot slammed into the door frame, and Wu recalled that he hadn't taken his gun to dinner.

Three more plainclothes officers rushed towards them. Three more shots came from the park and sent them scattering for cover. How many of them were there?

More shots.

"Inside! Get inside!" Mrs. Kuo screamed.

It wasn't safe to stand up. The streetlight had been shot out, and two masked men were rushing forward with base-ball bats. Wu was years out of practice, but his karate came back to him. One kick found the first man's shin and sent his bat past Wu's ear; a second swept the other man's feet from under him and he sprawled forwards into Wu.

The second man's bat connected with his left shoulder as they fell, and Wu felt his arm go numb. He warded off the man with desperate kicks, but his assailant used the space to draw a gun — it looked like a converted blank-firer. The barrel swung to point at Wu's face. As Mrs. Kuo clung to him from behind, he spread his limbs to provide more cover.

He heard, with great clarity, the sound of a bullet enter-ing flesh. The gun pointed at his face fell to the floor; the man holding it slumped at his feet. The same sound again. This time a man running from the trees, gun in hand, fell.

Somewhere, someone yelled "Split!" The three plain-clothes officers emerged from cover and jumped on the three attackers around him. Police cars arrived as they struggled.

It's all gone to shit, Wu thought. They had three detained at the scene. Several others were fleeing, with more police in pursuit. And everywhere, members of the public had been filming on their phones. Weren't they scared of ricochets?

He stood, taking a moment on the way up to rest with one hand on the floor, then helped Mrs. Kuo inside. He turned to look at the tall buildings opposite as he closed the door. A shadow on a rooftop, carrying a rifle in one hand and waving to him with the other.

Alex removed the sights from the M1 and placed it, in two pieces, in a toolbox. He had come to speak to Kuo's widow but had noticed a surprising number of concealed weapons in the vicinity. So he'd found a good viewpoint and was ready when the guns came out. He'd had no choice but to save Wu. Wu couldn't die yet — he still had work to do.

Alex leapt the narrow alley to the adjacent building and took the fire escape down to merge with a crowd of shoppers. The attackers didn't look professional, he thought, with their baseball bats and converted guns. They looked like cheap hired thugs.

But he couldn't hang around to confirm. He boarded a metro train and sat down. Checking his phone, he saw two missed calls.

He'd need to ask about Kuo Wei-chung another time. If Kuo had known who was behind it all, maybe his widow did too. And perhaps she was telling Wu right now. Why else would they be so keen to kill him?

Wu had suffered two strikes from baseball bats but no bullet wounds. He'd be taken to hospital to be checked over and debriefed, and Alex knew he couldn't get near him there. The men the police had caught would be taken back to the Bureau, and the guard on the Kuo woman would be stepped up, so he couldn't speak to her either.

He spent some time reviewing the latest news coverage of the Kuo and Chiu cases. That just left him with more questions. Chiu was in charge of army procurement and Peter Shan was an arms broker. Kuo had been in Germany for training — was he also involved in the arms trade?

As for Wu, he was getting close enough to be a threat to whoever was pulling the strings. But he couldn't get near Wu, and he didn't have much time. He had to take the risk and dial his number. A text message would not do; he had to ask this question personally.

Public telephones had become hard to find in Taipei, but he tracked one down outside a telecom office. And it still took coins. He took a deep breath and dialled Wu's number.

No answer.

He called Ironhead next.

"I've got something. There's a military procurement connection," Ironhead told him, his voice steady and sure.

"Me too. Kilo."

"Kilo? What the hell's that?"

"Russian-made sub. Ever heard of it?"

"I'll look into it. Where are you? Stay close, wait for my call." Never a man to waste words.

Alex called Wu's mobile again. It was answered, but not by Wu.

"I'm looking for Detective Wu."

"He can't talk right now."

"I have to speak with him."

"Who is this?"

"His nephew."

"And since when does Wu have a nephew? Wu, can you talk? He says he's your nephew."

Wu's voice: "Hello, nephew."

"Detective, it's me."

The line was silent for a few moments. "Go on."

"Can you talk?"

"Quickly. I'm on a drip."

"Those men this evening were trying to kill you. They think you know too much."

"I know that."

"Was Kuo linked to Fat and Chiu?"

"Yes. Do you want to come and see me tomorrow to get the money?"

"What was the connection?"

"I told you, you'll need to come and see me tomorrow. I'm in the hospital just now, remember?"

The line went dead.

Go to Wu's house? Was he setting a trap?

His mobile rang. Ironhead.

"I've read up about Kilo. Russian-made sub but some of the designers were Ukrainian. Capable of launching anti-ship missiles while submerged. So Chou was in Rome to meet with a Ukrainian intermediary. We should meet, go over the details."

"The shrimp farm?" Alex had resisted the temptation to suggest Chin's bar.

"No, the cops are all over it. Remember where I used to take you for a drink and a pie?"

"I remember."

"See you at one. And watch your tail."

Wu would have to wait. Alex stowed the toolbox and started the motorbike.

Wu hadn't heard from Alex again by the time he got home. His wife was waiting for him, furious. "What do you think you're doing, getting beaten up just before you retire?"

There was not much to be said to that.

She softened after venting her anger and went to the kitchen to make a bowl of wonton noodle soup. His son emerged, surprisingly, and also demanded a bowl. Wu reached out for a drink, but his wife slapped away his hand.

"Go on, Mum, let him have a small one."

His wife went to bed in a huff, annoyed by her son's betrayal. "You're both the same, ignoring me. Fine. He's got your surname, you look after him. I'm done!"

His son poured him a drink — only a small one, whisky in a tiny glass. Fine, then, a small one. Anything to keep everyone happy.

His son had not come out for the wonton noodle soup. He whispered to Wu, "I've confirmed it, Dad. We really were hacked."

"Who's going to hack a retired policeman?"

"Yeah, it's weird." His son was clearly hoping for an explanation. "What else have you found?" he asked.

Wu knew he shouldn't say anything, but he couldn't help but share his excitement with his son.

His son stared at the screen. "That's incredible! Huo Po-yu adopted five kids and they adopted the others. It's crazy."

"You can't tell anyone. And stop all the hacking, you hear?"

"I hear."

His phone rang. A woman's voice. "Detective Wu, I hear you've been trying to get in touch. This is Luo Fen-ying."

Wu leapt to his feet, grimacing as bruised muscles complained.

"I've been away. Is it urgent?" she asked.

"Where do you live? I just need an hour."

"About Alex and Fat? I haven't spoken to either of them for ages. I'm not sure there's much I can tell you."

"Are you in Taiwan? Just an hour."

"Okay, but later? Midnight?"

"That's fine." Wu made a note of her address. "Where is this?"

Luo laughed. "A friend's studio. She's an artist. A few of us girls are having a drink."

"Are you sure it's convenient?"

"Detective, a moment ago you were desperate to see me, and now you're worried if it's inconvenient."

"Okay. I won't be late." Wu pulled on his soaking wet jacket.

"Dad, if you go out now Mum's going to be worried sick."

Wu smiled. "I've got to solve this case before I retire. You might not see it, son, but you take after me. One day, someday, some year, you'll realize that. And when you do, you turn up here with a bottle of something nice and admit it."

His son laughed.

His wife shouted from their bedroom, "You're ganging up on me now! All the years I've wasted on you both!"

Wu clasped a hand over his son's mouth. "I'll go apologize before I go out, or she won't sleep and we'll both suffer for it tomorrow. She's your mother and my wife, and the happier she is, the happier we'll be."

25

ALEX DREW HIS KNIFE and levered the soles from his boots. He preferred a military boot, and this pair had accompanied him for three years, from the rolling dust of the Iraqi desert to the sucking salt marshes of Ivory Coast. He worked quickly, if regretfully, removing the tough outer sole before replacing the boots on his feet and taking a couple of exploratory steps in a puddle.

Soundless. And no boot prints, just the featureless impression of the midsole. The French Army treads would have been easy to identify, and he wasn't sure if there was a single other pair in all of Taiwan.

He checked his rifle and ammunition. Nine rounds. Hopefully unneeded.

And go.

The motorbike was parked on Gongguan Road. It was almost eleven p.m., and the crowds usually drawn by the movie theatre and Shuiyuan Market had been driven off by the chill wind. The shops had closed their shutters, the roads were empty.

He turned right onto a path skirting a hillside park, his solitary shadow stretched long by the streetlights. The path ran below the elevated expressway. At a dark spot he checked that no traffic was approaching and clambered up the concrete retaining wall, hands and feet carrying him swiftly up the 300-metre slope.

The hillside above the wall was scattered with buildings that had never been formally approved: one storey, two storeys, two storeys with an extra added. The passageways between the buildings were narrow and twisting, wide enough for only two to pass. Few lights on: most units seemed uninhabited.

Then he saw it: a light in a window, and heard a female voice, the thick accent from some mainland province. Ironhead had once had a friend who lived there, a man said to make Taiwan's best pies. The crust was slightly scorched and bready in texture, with enough fennel flavouring the lamb to give pause at first bite and cause addiction with the second. Ironhead liked to have a drink with his pie. He'd order two pies ahead of time rather than risk cold pie. Fat had once eaten sixteen in a single sitting.

He rounded a corner. The pie shop was now a café, its iron door chained shut. Alex slipped off his waterlogged boots and socks and climbed up the side of a dark building nearby.

The drizzle kept coming, and every streetlight in sight had failed.

Wu's taxi turned into Tingzhou Road and passed Shuiyuan Market and the movie theatre, stopping at the junction with the hillside road. He was early; he'd walk. It wasn't far, but there was barely a single light on Treasure Hill. Why had she wanted to meet there?

Nobody had lived on Treasure Hill originally. In the 1970s, migrants from Fujian had built a temple to the Goddess of Mercy and the Buddha there. Then poor immigrants and old soldiers moved in on the slopes above the temple, building boltholes of brick and wood, creating one of Taiwan's most notorious shantytowns. The city government had tried to clear the site several times, but old soldiers knew how to fight and the cultural community didn't want to lose one of the few places where artists could afford to live and work. So Treasure Hill was designated a part of the city's history, worthy of preservation. The government reclaimed buildings as they became empty and rented them to artists. In the decade since, a substantial artists' colony had formed.

Was Baby Doll's friend an artist? He'd thought about telling Egghead where he was going, but what was the point when he didn't know if she'd say anything useful? He'd call Egghead if he had anything to tell him.

One block into Treasure Hill and Taipei disappeared. All was dark, all was still. And the rain was still coming. Typically the period before Chinese New Year was dry, but not this year. Plenty of rain for the farmers.

Wu turned to pray as he passed a pavilion dedicated to the Goddess of Mercy — for peace, as always when he passed such a place, never for money or status. He patted the gun at his hip to ensure it was still there. As Alex had said, they were after him.

He walked on, rain penetrating to his skin. One day to retirement.

⊕

In pitch darkness Alex crept along the ridge of a rooftop until he reached the edge. With a practised roll he slipped to one side, his head emerging only as far as required to survey the battlefield through night-vision goggles.

His pocket vibrated. He pulled out the toy-like phone. Ironhead: "Not coming out to say hello?"

"Have you found out what Chou was doing in Rome?"

"Yeah. The Ministry of Defence had decided the Kilo subs were the preferred option. Chou was there to discuss the deal. If we got the blueprints and the engineers, we could build our own. Quite the feather in his cap. Come down to the square and find me."

"Wouldn't the Americans object if we spent our money with the Ukrainians?"

"The government wanted the subs and didn't care what the Yanks would say. The Ukrainian economy's shit, but they've got plenty of researchers and engineers to sell. Chou put the deal together. Apparently the Ukrainians originally wanted to sell us tanks, at a tenth of the cost of the U.S. ones, but what were we going to do with tanks? Have a parade? Subs could be useful, though. And Chou was the President's own advisor, with access at the very highest levels. Nobody was going to tell him no."

"If it was such a good deal, why'd they tell me to kill him?"

"Alex, what do I know about politics?" Ironhead was getting impatient. "I'll see you at the square. Or do you not trust me now as well? I'm a shrimp farmer, and happy as I am. I'm not about to hand you in for the reward."

"I hear that the standard commission on an arms deal is three-thousandths. The U.S. M1A2 tanks cost thirty billion, so three-thousandths is ninety million. If Chou had pulled off the sub deal with the Ukrainians, what would we have paid for the blueprints and engineers?"

"I'm an old soldier, son, and I was never good at math."

"What I'm saying is, the tanks were Shen Kuan-chih's deal. He wouldn't have made anything if Chou bought the Ukrainian blueprints and engineers."

"You're confusing me."

"And there's something else I haven't been able to make sense of."

"Let's hear it."

"Baby Doll gave me the order to kill Chou. I assumed she did so on your instructions, but you'd already quit. But then Fat was sent to kill me, and you're the only person he'd work for. Plus, Fat knew where I lived, and the safe house in Budapest. How?"

Alex had continued watching for any movement as he spoke. He spotted a figure moving on a rooftop about 120 metres away. Ironhead?

"You'd need to ask her that. She'll be taking orders from within the Ministry — that's her job. Alex, you never worked for me; you worked for the country. When I quit, obviously whoever took over would be giving you orders."

Alex briefly pocketed the phone, pulled an inflatable dolphin from his backpack, and blew it up. He weighed it down with his jacket and then rolled down the roof to the parapet.

"Are you still there?"

"Sorry, sir. Bad signal."

"You think I set you up?"

"No. I just can't figure it out. The instructions for Chou were so precise. How could anyone know his movements that well? Was it someone on the scene? Who is Baby Doll's superior now?"

"One of the deputy ministers. A civilian."

"Does he know about me?"

"I never covered it in the handover, but you're in the files. For fuck's sake, Alex, I wasn't in touch with you for five years. What do you think happened? I retired, got bored, and decided to get you to shoot one of the President's top advisers? Too many loud bangs next to your skull, that's your problem."

Alex heard footsteps. He used the cover of a heavier gust of rain to slip over the parapet and onto the roof of the adjacent building. The metal panels clanged as he landed — so much for staying concealed. He hurried along the sloping roof to the downspout, pushed his night-vision goggles to his forehead, lifted his rifle, pressed his cheek to the stock, and looked at the roof opposite. Too much rain to see anything.

The figure responsible for the footsteps stopped by the flagpole in the small square, a space enclosed on three sides by buildings. A sudden light, and in the glare of a mobile phone screen he saw Wu. What was he doing there? Wu had no umbrella and the raindrops clinging to his grey hair glistened in the light of his screen. An easy target.

There was no other noise except the rain. Alex could make out Wu's words: "I told you to get on with your studying and not worry about — What news? They found what? The identity of the third sniper? I remember, the one found in the Czech —"

The rain grew heavier. Alex edged forward two paces. The figure on the roof opposite continued to move.

"— Chang Nan-sheng, retired army officer? What did the Ministry say at the press conference?"

Alex's gaze snapped back to Wu. He knew that name!

"The shrimp guy is Huang Hua-sheng, not Chang Nan-sheng. What? Speak up! Chang was Huang's trainee? The year after Li? Have you been hacking again?"

Another shadowy form moved, this time to his right. Ironhead was not alone.

"We'll talk when I get back. Print it out for me."

Wu had put his phone away and was looking around when it rang again. He lowered his head to look.

Shit. A laser dot on the flagpole behind Wu's lowered head! No time to think.

"Down, Wu! Down!" Alex twisted as he yelled, bringing his rifle to bear on the second figure and firing. The bullet spiralled through the rain and the red dot disappeared.

Wu dropped to one knee and a single bullet cracked into the flagpole above his head.

Wu's injured back had prevented him from dropping to the ground as quickly as he'd like, but he managed to kneel. He swapped the mobile for his gun, then heard a bullet hit the flagpole above his head. He was at risk of getting used to that sound. He raised his gun and scoured the uneven rooftops of the buildings around him.

The latest news from his son had confirmed his suspicions: a litter of orphans manipulated into acting as a private army. And while Grandfather should have been in charge, he didn't have much of a grip on his faculties anymore. So someone else had taken advantage and acquired their very own private military force.

Alex was off the rooftops, pressed up against a wall and peering around a corner in search of targets.

Ironhead's voice came from his mobile, which was jammed between his ear and his motorbike helmet. "Are you going to believe the police over me, Alex? I'll tell you whatever you want to know, but let's find somewhere with fewer cops."

Wu's shout came before he could respond. "This is the police! Throw down your weapons and come out!"

Alex had kept his eyes fixed on the spot where the red dot had emanated from, even as he jumped down from the roof. Middle window of a building ahead and to the right. The shooter was clearly after Wu, not him. And it wasn't Ironhead. Ironhead would never have chosen such a poor spot.

That made two: Ironhead and the shooter.

Alex watched the window through his sights. He could just make out a rifle barrel and silencer.

Wu was a big target, even crouched. And why was he still on the phone?

And then Alex heard a mobile ring at that window.

"This is Wu. Where are you?"

Alex saw the light of a mobile phone screen behind the rifle barrel. He saw a figure in the light. He held his breath as he took aim. But how could it be . . . ?

Baby Doll's rifle shifted to point at Alex.

Less than a hundred metres away — no need for him to worry about accounting for wind and rain. Instinct would be enough. He pulled the trigger, crying out her name to himself as he did so.

Baby Doll screamed. Her rifle cracked as it fell, sending a bullet towards Alex, through the rain, through the dark, to slam into his helmet and career off into the night. The helmet fell open in two halves and his mobile landed in the mud. Alex grabbed it as he rolled, then zigzagged across the square to reach Wu.

"Get down!"

"Alex? Did you kill her?"

A bullet pierced Alex's upper leg. This time it was not content with just a flesh wound. He felt his femur break and steeled himself against the pain as he grabbed Wu and hauled him, rolling, into the cover of an alleyway.

The screen of his mobile flashed. "Good work, Alex. You remembered what I taught you about bait. An inflatable doll would have been better than a dolphin, though."

And Baby Doll had been Ironhead's bait, Alex realized. Baby Doll.

"Huang Hua-sheng?" Wu asked, nodding at Alex's mobile. He pushed himself clear of Alex and ran out of the alley, shooting at the surrounding rooftops. Shots hit brick walls and metal roofs, silencing for a moment the wind and rain.

"Huang Hua-sheng, this is the Criminal Investigation Bureau. Put down your weapon and come out!"

Alex didn't try to stop the man. He knew Wu was providing him with the distraction he needed. He eased the barrel of his rifle out of the alleyway entrance and took aim at the rooftops. The raindrops bounced from the roofs with a crisp rattle. Alex listened for any change that might indicate someone on the move.

He saw a telescopic sight emerge from the rain. Pointed not at him, but at Wu.

A quick flame and Wu clutched at his right side, falling to land in a puddle of rainwater. His gun slipped from his hand and landed several paces off.

Alex immediately realized his error and why Wu had not been safe. Capture by Wu would mean the death penalty for Ironhead. But he couldn't kill his former teacher, and the testimony of an assassin guilty of murdering a government official wouldn't be worth much. He now saw that the Deputy Minister had not been lying when he said he had never heard Alex's name. It had been Ironhead all along, giving him the order to kill Chou via Baby Doll.

Wu lay prone in the rain. His plan to act as bait so Alex could take a shot at Huang hadn't worked, and now he was a sitting duck. A new pain tore through his left shoulder and blood splattered his face.

He tried to focus. Alex had killed Luo Fen-ying. Huang wanted him, Wu, dead. Huang had been giving Luo orders. Huang, like Luo, was registered as living at the Ministry of National Defence. If there was some mysterious unit at work, Luo and Huang were it.

Wu was immobilized, unable even to shift his nose away from the rapidly encroaching rainwater. Twenty-four hours to retirement.

He reached for his gun. Too far, but his fingers found his mobile. The screen lit up. Who was phoning him now?

Unable to think of any other way to help Alex, Wu drew a deep breath, winced, and started yelling. "Huang Hua-sheng, the police know everything! You used your

Intelligence connections to change the files, but you and Shen Kuan-chih are brothers. He didn't want Chou messing up his arms deal with the Yanks, so you had Luo Fen-ying tell Alex to kill him. And then you sent Fat and Chang Nan-sheng to keep him quiet. It was all you! Now give yourself up!"

A laugh rang out, accompanied by a bullet. It ricocheted from the ground near Wu, sending water flying instead of sparks.

"Don't listen to the cop, Alex! That's what I was going to explain to you tonight. We're a family, and that means loyalty, responsibility. Chou was obsessed with buying subs from the Ukrainians, Alex. But arms are how the Family makes its money, through Shen Kuan-chih. He could have got submarines if he wanted.

"Fuck, Chou was talking about how he'd get our pilots trained on MiGs and Su-35s. Met a few Ukrainians and thought he could have a monopoly on all the arms deals. And Chiu fell for it, even went there for a demonstration of anti-tank missiles. Nothing but a desk soldier. When you killed Chou, that put an end to the government's plans to buy the shitty Soviet subs and put Shen's deal with the Yanks back in play.

"It was what I had to do, as a part of the Family. As for sending Fat after you . . . I'm sorry, Alex. I had to look at the bigger picture. I hope you can forgive me for that."

Alex fired a short volley at the rooftops. If Ironhead saw a chance to raise his head, Wu was dead.

But there was the problem with the M1: it was a semi-automatic, and he only had nine rounds. One round now.

Ironhead shouted down to him again. "Your Gramps's M1, Alex? The dozen or so bullets he left you must be about finished by now."

It was Wu who answered him. "Huang, you were Grandfather's sixth adopted son. We know it all. Throw down your weapon and come out. You can't get away."

"Ha! You think because you met Grandfather that means something? Did he tell you he adopted me? Have you got any witnesses you can put on the stand? Your only witness is Alex, and a murderer's word isn't going to help your case."

Alex pulled back the bolt of the M1 and fished out the final round, then placed it back in the chamber. Ironhead had to hear that he wasn't done yet, to keep him wary and to keep Wu safe.

And he had to keep Ironhead's attention. "Forgot to tell you, Ironhead, I went to visit Baby Doll's boss. The flat-footed deputy minister. He'd never heard my name until he read about me in the papers. It was you. I knew it was you, telling her to pass on orders to kill Chou, telling Fat to come after me."

"Alex, we're family."

"We *were* family."

"Remember the tattoo I showed you on my shoulder? It's the same one you've got on your left shoulder, put there by your Gramps when you were fifteen. What did he tell you? Bear the pain and remember what the tattoo means: you're Family."

"So what?"

"You're a part of our family. You always will be."

"Then why did you send Fat to kill me?"

"We should have explained what we do earlier, but your Gramps wouldn't have it. He got fearful in his old age. I got you into Military Intelligence and set it up so you could spend time in the French Foreign Legion, become the kind of person we need. You're one of us, Alex."

"Nobody ever told me anything about that tattoo."

"He was a pot that never boiled, your Gramps. Never spoke up when he should. But you weren't like Fat and Baby Doll, Alex. I had high hopes for you."

Wu risked an interruption, "Kuo Wei-chung was Shen Kuan-chih's man. Shen told him to kill Chiu, but Kuo refused. So then you killed Kuo, right, Huang? Kuo was Family, so you arranged to meet him at the hotel. He turned up with beer and food to show respect to his senior, and he just sat there while you pulled a gun on him. Where do you rank in the Family, Huang? Have you taken over now that Grandfather's not well?"

Alex wiped the rain from his eyes, still searching for a target.

Sirens approached, then the sound of boots and Egghead yelling through a megaphone.

Wu had been making up a story from the fragments he knew, hoping to distract Huang. But now he realized it all made sense. He resolved to live. Nobody would believe Alex otherwise and the case would go unsolved.

Had his son sent Egghead? No, his son didn't know where he was.

Wu flexed his right hand. Not working. He tried his left hand. Working. He stretched forward to a crack in the paving stones and tried to pull himself forward, but then he stopped as he felt the wound in his side tear wider. *A carcass on a butcher's table*, he thought, *waiting for the cleaver*.

Another bullet, this time in the left leg. Wu cried out, then went limp.

⊕

Two more shots landed near Alex. He didn't move. This was the only position he could watch Wu from, and with the police almost on the scene, Ironhead would be desperate to ensure that the detective never spoke again.

"I'll make a deal with you, Alex," Ironhead said. "We'll talk about this another day. Meeting the cops isn't going to do either of us any good right now."

Alex kept his mouth shut tight. A sniper needed preternatural patience. In Iraq he had once lain motionless in scrub for a day and a night, not urinating, not eating, not closing his eyes, waiting for the opportunity to strike. He held his rifle steady in the arms Ironhead had forged into steel, pressed close to the eyes Ironhead had trained to remain untiringly open.

The footsteps of the approaching police were rounding the former pie shop. Lots of them, gear rattling. He could hear rounds being chambered.

Alex stayed put. If Ironhead wanted to kill him, he'd have to show his face. If Ironhead wanted to make sure Wu was dead, he'd have to show his face. If Ironhead wanted to escape . . . Well, he'd have to show his face.

Ironhead jumped from the roof. Alex aimed at Ironhead, Ironhead aimed at Wu. Alex shot first. A puff of smoke bloomed, a white flower at the end of his barrel. His bullet hit Ironhead's shoulder. Ironhead spun, his bullet going high, a firework.

Ironhead couldn't gamble that Alex was out of ammo. He leapt through a ground-floor window.

Wu had stretched far enough to get a fingertip on his gun. The sound of police boots in rainwater was coming closer. He strained to lift his head and managed to make out Alex's rifle and the window it was targeting.

If Ironhead went out the back, he would find himself amidst a column of heavily armed policemen. If he went out the side, he'd hit a dead end.

Wu recalled Professor Wang's words: *a pig under a roof.*

Alex remained patient, but it was starting to feel like a win. He'd seen Ironhead's rifle — a U.S. McMillan TAC-50, with bipod. The gun used by a Canadian Special Operations sniper in Iraq in 2017 when he killed an Islamic State insurgent at a distance of 3,450 metres — the longest sniper shot in history. But hadn't Ironhead always said hit rate was more important than distance? Perhaps he'd seen the gun used in *American Sniper* and just thought it looked cool.

The two men were twenty metres apart. Alex was holding a vintage M1, deactivated and put back together again. Ironhead was holding a TAC-50. Alex had no bullets and was almost out of patience. Ironhead should have been holding all the cards, but he'd got himself trapped on dead ground.

He watched as Ironhead risked raising his rifle over the windowsill and running the sights over the square until they fell on him. Alex did not run. He put down his M1 and watched as Ironhead grinned.

"How did you know about the commission?"

"Found it online."

"I always put off telling you about the Family, Alex. You're too clever. The smart ones don't take orders well."

Ironhead's grin faded, and as soon as it did, Alex yelled, "Shoot!"

Two shots rang out in unison and a blade sliced across Alex's cheek. He stood still, watching. Ironhead lurched backwards as the TAC-50 dropped from the window. Smoke emerged from the barrel of a police-issue Smith & Wesson semi-automatic.

Alex gave Wu a thumbs-up. "Good shot."

"You take care, Alex."

"And you hold in there. You'll be fine." He disappeared back into the alleyway.

Wu let the gun fall from his hand as he watched Alex go. It was definitely time to retire: he'd obviously forgotten how to be a cop. He wasn't feeling even the tiniest regret that the suspect in the killing of Chou Hsieh-he was escaping. But he'd made the shot and saved both their lives. Not a bad end to his career, overall.

"Wu! Wu! Are you okay?"

Armed policemen swarmed into the square. Egghead scurried to Wu's side, keeping low behind a bulletproof riot shield.

Flashlights and searchlights cast out the dark of Treasure Hill. Four assault rifles stormed the building in front. One voice called out: "One man, dead. Single shot to the forehead."

Wu tried to laugh but no sound emerged. Perhaps his wound was letting all the air out, he thought. And never mind what anyone else thought, he'd solved all five murders to his own satisfaction on his last day. A job well done.

Egghead helped him onto the stretcher, questioning him as he did so. "Where's Alex?"

Wu changed the subject. "How did you get here?"

"I thought you agreed to meet Luo Fen-ying at midnight."

"Trick I learned recently. Snipers always arrive early to make sure the battleground is set up properly."

"Aren't you too old to be learning new things?"

"You've been tapping my phone and hacking into my computer, haven't you. Were you scared I'd steal your glory? I only had one more day."

"Well, you never told me you'd met with Alex. So I checked your emails. Hell, were you trying to earn all your karma at the last minute?"

"My job's to crack cases. Alex was a lead."

"He's a killer, and he's gotten away. How do I explain that to the Chief? The press will be all over this; the government will be issuing statements. This is not how you crack cases."

The stretcher was raised and Wu went with it. A helicopter rotor whirled above, almost drowning out Egghead's last cry: "Fucking hell, Wu, you get to retire! I don't. You know I —"

Wu finished for him. "— love to be the boss."

26

A SHOT TO THE GUt is the most painful way to die. It won't stop your heart, but the wound never stops bleeding. Eventually you bleed out, the heart has nothing left to pump, and consciousness fades away. A shot to the lungs or another major organ will make things faster. But Ironhead had hit him just right: through one side of his belly, tearing open large and small intestines and starting a slower bleed that gave him half an hour before death's approach. He'd held on for twenty-five minutes before they got him onto the stretcher. Should he consider himself lucky?

The Bureau announced that the Chou case, with its six associated deaths, had been solved. No mention was made of the Family — what good would it do? Military procurement and intelligence agencies in the hands of a centuries-old secret society? How many Family members remained in high-ranking military and government posts? Compared to them, the bureau chief was but a lowly subordinate.

The Chief faced a dozen cameras and a hundred reporters and explained it all. It was an explanation that wandered here and there yet somehow sounded plausible. He did not mention that Kuo Wei-chung was Shen Kuan-chih's man, or that Kuo had refused to kill Chiu Ching-chih. But he did blame Huang Hua-sheng for Kuo's death. Kuo, he said, had learned too much and was about to inform his superiors.

And that seemed a happy ending of sorts. Kuo would be classified as having died in the line of duty; Wu had made it clear he would go public otherwise, and nobody would come out of that looking good. Kuo's widow had won justice for her dead husband, and her children would receive his pension and life insurance. She would never know the full truth, though, and she'd be left raising her children alone.

It turned out that Huang Hua-sheng had been Luo Fen-ying's adoptive father. Wu could imagine how he had manipulated her, Fat, and Chang Nan-sheng: *for home and country* — just like the emperor's Imperial Orphans. They had their truth and they believed it completely. Perhaps they were happier for it.

Wu remembered Grandfather sitting in his wheelchair in that rundown building and dreaming of the chive dumplings in the freezer. He had spent his life helping orphaned children. Did he understand that one of them, Huang Hua-sheng, had usurped his role and issued orders in his name?

What if he stayed on at the Bureau? Wu thought. Perhaps if he hadn't solved the case. As it was, the Chief was not inclined to keep a detective with a disregard for orders and a tendency to show off. Egghead's father had it right: Don't be at the top, don't be at the bottom. Serve your time, and if luck sends promotions your way, take them. But if it doesn't, watch others get promoted. At the end of the day, the pensions aren't that different.

It was two months before Wu was mobile again. He had a bullet scar the size of a silver dollar on the right side of his belly, though he didn't think of it as a scar. He thought of it as a medal, presented to him on the occasion of his retirement.

He steered his walker towards the kitchen. His son was trying his hand at egg fried rice, a recipe Wu had received by text message from an unknown number. His son had decided to give it a shot, and why not?

"Hey, Dad, did you know that God once asked Dante what the tastiest food was? And Dante said eggs. Then God asked what kind of eggs. Dante said salted eggs."

Salt with eggs, sugar with steamed buns.

Wu patted his son on his back. "Learn to make egg fried rice and we'll make a man of you yet."

He knew his own dad would arrive soon with his trolley full of ingredients. Would he be unhappy to see the kitchen occupied? Perhaps it was time for Wu to tell him to stop cooking for them. *Look*, he could say, *your grandson can do it now.*

They should go over to his place once a week. That would be better than his coming to them every day. It was difficult for his wife, dealing with both husband and father-in-law. And no easier for him, an oldish son and husband, dealing with father and wife.

He shuffled onto the balcony and patted his pockets in search of cigarettes. Had his wife confiscated them? How many packs was that now, a hundred? Fifty at least. His chain smoking seemed a foolish habit when his wife begged him to stop, but it was one he'd enjoyed for decades and clung to.

He wanted to go to Julie's for a cup of coffee — African, Brazilian, whatever. A nice long sit in the sun with Julie's dad while he explained that the Family was no ordinary organized-crime gang, and that even the biggest of bosses needs to retire, or there'll be no time for anything between the throne and the wheelchair.

His wounds were healing well and the doctors said he could start work at the detective agency in a month. A new start. Every day a new start. Tomorrow would be the dinner for Egghead's departure from the Bureau. Wu hoped his promotion would treat him well and that his liver could keep up with the drinking.

His mobile rang. "Hello?"

"You're looking better, Detective."

"Better than I was two months ago. Yourself?"

"Recovering as well."

"Where are you?"

"Look at the pavilion in the park, to your left. Look very closely."

"I'm looking very closely."

"See those flowers beside it?"

"I do."

"That means it's spring."

"Fascinating."

"Look at the pedestrian bridge below you. Look very closely."

"I see it. There's a dog."

"It's just done a shit. The owner's pretending she didn't notice."

"I'll have her fined."

"Look at the bench in the middle of the park. Look —"

"— very closely."

Wu looked very closely at Alex, who was standing by the park bench as he spoke into his phone.

Alex removed his hat and dark glasses and bowed deeply in Wu's direction. "Now look at the plane that just took off from the airport. Look very closely."

Wu watched the plane for a minute. Then a second minute. Until his wife summoned him inside.

"Lunchtime! Your son's having some kind of episode and has decided to cook. There's rice and water everywhere. I don't know what I'm meant to do with the pair of you!"

"How'd you get on, son?"

"Not bad. Egg fried rice. I added some shrimp."

His son proudly placed a bowl of fried rice in front of him. Pink shrimp, yellow egg, green scallions. Wu looked very closely.

Acknowledgements

My love of firearms began in high school, when I was selected for the Taipei Fuxing Senior High shooting team. Our coach was Yu Kuang-hsiu, an expert army sniper. Twice a week we followed him, M1 rifles slung over our shoulders and ammo boxes in our hands, up to the shooting range hidden in the hills of Datunshan, and I learned how to use physical exercise to help ease the asthma I had suffered since childhood.

I was dropped from the team the night before a competition, due to my poor scores. I was most disappointed. But on those marches up to the shooting range, I met Zhang Xue-liang, a former warlord and Republican general who spent decades under house arrest for his instigation of the Xi'an incident. That meeting led, many years later, to my novel *An Unlikely Banquet*, in which the great artist Chang Dai-chien cooks for the one-time warlord.

There is gain and loss in all that we do. It is the process that matters, not birth or death.

During national service I served in the army's 206th Infantry Brigade, 616th Regiment, 2nd Battalion. The 6th Army Command chose our regiment to participate in a military exercise. Twice a day every officer in the regiment formed a platoon and ran five kilometers, M14 rifles weighing heavy in our arms. Several times I thought a bone had snapped under that weight; three months later I had developed a love of running that has stayed with me to this day.

Our performance on the day of the exercise was passable at best. Fortunately, a reserve platoon leader, also surnamed Chang, succeed in launching a rifle grenade into the mouth of a machine gun nest we were assaulting, turning the tide of battle. I remember the wide arc of the grenade, the narrow mouth of the machine gun nest — a miraculous shot. I recall the kneeling position he adopted for stability, how he pressed the butt of his M14 into the soft mud, and how he ignored the hail of enemy bullets. He took a rifle grenade in his left hand, placed it in the launcher, took sight, and with a sigh pulled the trigger.

I watched the grenade fly. It flew over muddy ground, over the heads of reserve officers soon to leave service, over trenches and fortifications. It flew so far into that blue sky I thought it would never fall to earth.

The judge raised a red flag. The grenade flew into the machine gun nest, and victory was ours.

Why had he sighed? He was, he said later, simply happy to be able to stop after the frantic half-kilometer assault.

Thanks to that shot we were granted three days of leave, to return to Taipei and see our girls.

Thanks to Hou Er-ge, formerly naval special forces officer and firearms expert, who inspired me to tell a sniper's story.

Thanks to two Taiwanese writers, Sean Hsu and Wolf Hsu, for discussions of plot and publishing. Writing is a lonesome trade, and having companionship brings me great warmth.

Thanks to Gray Tan, whose faith in me spurred me to keep writing.

And thanks to the M14 rifle. It is old, it is heavy, and it is hard to clean. But when I press my cheek against the wood of its stock and see the familiar crown of its front sight through the rear aperture, my restless soul is calmed.

CHANG KUO-LI, April 2020

Chang Kuo-Li is an award-winning novelist, historian, poet, and playwright. He has published more than thirty books over the course of his career, many of which have been adapted for film and television. He lives in Taiwan.

Roddy Flagg is a freelance translator who resides in Edinburgh, Scotland. He has translated short stories by Diao Dou and Chen Chongzheng, among others. *The Sniper* is his first full-length translation.